CONTAMINANT of CONCERN

A "LUKE GRAHAM" SERIES

CONTAMINANT of CONCERN

JOEL S. JOHNSON

Bay Meadows
— PRESS —

Published by:

Bay Meadows Press

Littleton, Colorado

www.JoelSJohnson.com

Book design by Journey Bound Publishing

Paperback ISBN: 979-8-9955892-0-4
Ebook ISBN: 979-8-9955892-1-1
LCCN #: 2026908894

First Edition
10 9 8 7 6 5 4 3 2 1

AUTHOR'S NOTE & ACKNOWLEDGMENTS

The main inspiration for *Contaminant of Concern* arose from my decade-long career as an environmental engineering consultant, working on Superfund sites and other soil and groundwater remediation projects. Throughout these experiences, I was struck by the many opposing viewpoints among stakeholders—regulators, attorneys, scientists, impacted neighbors, and environmental advocates—each seeing problems and solutions differently. I also noted that with more than twenty million known organic compounds, and DDT as only one example, toxicology remains an inexact science: Determining the precise health risk from DDT, whether alone or in combination with other organic compounds, is unlikely now or in the foreseeable future. This scientific uncertainty further heightens the conflicting perspectives among those involved.

I concluded that many of my environmental consulting experiences are best shared through an entertaining mystery based on real and fictionalized events.

Thanks to my writing partners, Ellen Kingman Fisher, Sherry Kenney, and Eva Fox Mate, for meeting me virtually three mornings a week over several years as I worked my day job and wrote *Contaminant of Concern*. Their inspiration and knowledge truly helped. My wife, Peg, was the first reader and gave great feedback, along with my daughter, Rachel, and son, Mitch. My editor, Eva Fox Mate, made the manuscript more enjoyable and easier to read. Special thanks to David Mohrbacher, PE, for his assistance with organic chemistry over the years.

I also appreciate the valuable feedback I received from others in writing classes I took at Gemini Writer's Studio and Writer's Digest University.

I thank Veronica Yager and Valentina Vasquez of Journey Bound Publishing for completing my effort and bringing it all together into a physical book. Thanks also to Kayla LeFevre for proof-reading and Megan Epperson for the eye-catching cover design.

DEDICATION

To the real-world people who strive every day to pragmatically improve our environment.

PROLOGUE

Earl Kemp opened the hatch on the bottom of the distillation tower. The smell of the organic solvents burned his nostrils and forced him to step back, gasping for fresh air. It was his third day on the job at the DDT manufacturing plant in Torrance, California, and this was his indoctrination into the workforce as the low man on the corporate totem pole. He took a deep breath before he stuck his shovel into the six-foot diameter steel tower and scooped up a shovel full of white sludge. He carefully turned and splashed it on the ground next to the tower. It took him fifteen more scoops before he had the tower cleaned out and considered the job complete. *Only four more towers to go before a break.*

He stood up after cleaning the last tower, a bit light-headed. He walked to the employee break room on the maze of elevated wooden planks that allowed workers to avoid walking in the mud around the plant. Some of the sludge had splashed on his pants and shirt, but it evaporated quickly, leaving a white residue that he knew was DDT, known to organic chemists like him as dichloro-diphenyl-trichloroethane. Most people knew it as the best pesticide on earth.

He graduated from Long Beach State College in the spring of 1963 as a chemical engineer and was excited to start his new career at an actual manufacturing plant. Many of his classmates had gone into the oil business in the Los Angeles basin to seek their fortunes. He wanted to help wipe out malaria worldwide and save millions of lives by manufacturing DDT, at that time the most effective pesticide in the world, against the disease-carrying mosquito.

He was used to hard work, having grown up working on the farms in Orange County when not in school. The physical work had helped him maintain a lean, tough physique. At slightly over six feet in high school, he'd been a star athlete on the football and basketball teams and played linebacker in college.

His mother, Betty, and father, Hank, were considered Okies by the Californians, having fled Oklahoma in 1936, along with thousands of other Oklahomans, during the height of the Dust Bowl. They were simple farmers who understood how to care for the land and make a living. However, they were determined to see Earl and his younger brother, Nolan, educated, in the hopes that their sons would rise from the poverty and prejudice they had endured. Earl was grateful, every day, for their sacrifices.

Several plant operators had gathered in the break room when Earl walked in to wash his hands and face. He paused to admire the Ridgid Tool calendar on the wall above the sink. It sported a busty young blonde in a swimsuit while advertising pipe cutters. With a spark of embarrassment, Earl wondered if the secretaries ever made it this far back in the plant. His mother would disapprove of the calendar, but he had to take a second look.

His sack lunch and a few soft drinks were in the refrigerator, along with various forgotten items with their unique smells. Hard hats and dirty gloves were scattered on the vinyl table tops as the operators kicked back and ate the donuts supplied by Luis, who'd lost the baseball pool that week. Luis worked in the Dry Product Handling Department, where he packaged DDT in forty-pound bags for shipment. He was a solid man of Mexican descent who always had to wear a mask over his nose and mouth. Whenever Luis removed his mask, the white DDT dust made his black hair appear to have a tinge of gray, though he was in his early twenties. Even the gold chain and cross he wore around his neck became dull with a coating of dust.

Earl put a dime in the coffee jar and poured himself a thick, black Folgers coffee. He pulled up a chair and sat down with Luis. "My name is Earl; I'm the new guy here. Thanks for the donuts."

Luis leaned back in his chair and took a long drag from his cigarette. He stared at Earl, wondering, perhaps, whether Earl had just made fun of him, or if Earl was genuinely appreciative of Luis' gift. "Yeah, yeah. I should have never bet against Sandy Koufax and the Dodgers. I hope you know your baseball. Otherwise, make sure you remember when you buy the donuts next time that I like the chocolate-covered ones with little sprinkles, and John likes the ones with jelly in the middle."

Earl was a football guy who paid little attention to baseball, but he knew the Dodgers had come from Brooklyn and won the World Series a few years ago. Earl was paid more than most operators as a chemical engineer, even those who had worked at the plant for many years. Maybe he should intentionally lose the pool next week and buy the donuts to ingratiate himself with the operators. He pondered it a moment before his competitive nature got the best of him, and he became determined to study baseball instead.

The gruff and commanding Senior Plant Operator, John McGraw, pulled up a chair and stuck out his hand. Earl shook it with a firm grip. John's company shirt looked like it hadn't been changed in a few days. His safety glasses were permanently fogged from chemical exposure, though he tried unsuccessfully to clean them on his polyester shirt. Earl wondered how he could see through them.

"Earl, nice to meet you. I heard you was a farm boy growing up. You ever use any DDT on the farm?"

"Yeah, we use DDT when the bugs get bad. It's really helped our production. That's how I first heard about this place. I was always fascinated DDT worked so well. Once you spray it on the plants, it never seems to leave them. In fact, DDT is probably part of why I like chemistry so much," Earl said, laughing at his own joke.

John nodded. "That's good, Earl; you should fit right in. We're always trying to improve things around here and are damn proud of what we do. So, do you have a wife and kids?"

"I got married last year. Patty and I met in high school. We're expecting our first in about three months and I can hardly wait. Patty's a bank teller in Anaheim. Things will change when the baby comes, of course. We'll have to get on a tighter budget, I suppose."

"Look out. You got a mosquito on you!" Luis said.

Earl grabbed his arm and searched for the mosquito that wasn't there. The others in the room laughed as Earl felt his cheeks burn. It was a pretty good joke—another part of the new guy's initiation.

"There ain't a mosquito stupid enough to get within a mile of this place," said one of the other men at the table. "The DDT will kill them in mid-air, as soon as they fly over the fence. I ain't seen a roach in the past two years, either. This is the best place in the world to work if you don't like bugs. You know, Earl, you can take a bag home if you want and use it in your backyard. I put it on my tomatoes and have the best ones in the neighborhood. I only have to apply it once or twice during the season. I gotta say, though, it's hard to get it off the tomatoes unless you use some soap or vinegar."

The conversation halted when Earl's new boss, Clarence Wright, walked across the room and put his hand on Earl's shoulder. "I see you've made some new friends, Earl. You're working with a great group of guys. They know their stuff, and you can learn lots from them." Mr. Wright eyed the half-eaten box of donuts on the table. "Who the hell bet against the Dodgers this week?"

Luis moaned. "That would be me, Mister Wright. But I got a feeling that Earl's gonna be buying real soon."

***

Earl followed his new boss down a gray hallway to the corner office. The office was small, with a large oak desk and a few stacks of neatly organized papers. Like the hallway, the floor was covered with squares of dirty linoleum. He sat down on the edge of the lone metal guest chair. It was as grungy as the floor, and padding bulged from the cracked leather seat. He was glad he had long sleeves and didn't have to put his bare skin on the armrests.

Earl looked around the room while Wright got settled behind his desk. The paneled walls were filled with crooked photographs of Wright smiling and shaking hands with numerous other men. An award from the local Rotary club, announcing Wright as the club president, hung on the wall next to several pictures of an Army platoon.

Wright lit up a Lucky Strike cigarette and offered one to Earl.

"Thanks, Mr. Wright, but I never took to smoking."

"I started in the war. It helped calm my nerves, and we didn't have much else to do when we weren't getting shot at."

Wright must have noticed Earl looking at the memorabilia on the wall. "That's the last picture of my platoon, in Anzio, Italy, back in '44," he said, nodding toward the photos. "We took the beach as part of Operation Shingle. I was just a kid from North Dakota in the 3rd Infantry Division. We took the beach and moved inland. The Germans had been there for a while, and they'd drained the swamps to get rid of mosquitoes and malaria. Once we arrived, though, the bastards shut off the pumps and re-flooded the area, hoping we would get malaria. It was my first exposure to the Anopheles mosquito. I still can't believe that after everything we'd been through, from Tunisia to Sicily to Anzio, some of my buddies died from a goddamn mosquito bite."

"Did you ever get malaria, sir?" Earl asked.

The desk chair screeched as the big man leaned back. "No. I lucked out. Maybe the mosquitoes didn't like me. Italy was in shambles after the Germans left, and people were sick everywhere. That's when pesticides like DDT were brought in and sprayed on everything and everyone. It made an enormous difference in saving lives in '44 and '45. That's enough about me, though. I want to welcome you aboard. I've been trying to get a chemical engineer around here for a long time, but Corporate never seemed to have the budget. You can make this place operate better and more efficiently. It's been run by salesmen and operators for a long time, meaning it's a hodgepodge of things that don't work as well as they could. The vendors want to sell their stuff, even if it's not a good fit, and the operators aren't technical enough to know what they should buy."

"I'm excited about the opportunity to work here, sir. I know I can make a difference."

Wright chuckled. "No need to sell me anymore. You already have the job. Now, it's about results. We have to figure out a way to cut our chemical costs. We're using too much chloro-benzene solvent to make the DDT. That stuff's expensive, and we lose a lot when we throw the tower bottoms on the ground during cleaning, like you did this morning."

"Isn't there a way to distill it and use it again?" Earl asked.

"That's what I want you to figure out. If we reduce the amount of sediment, we could send it down the sewer, as we do with the rest of our waste. But we would clog up the line if we did that now. We need more options."

"Let me think about it. I have some ideas. We analyzed similar reactions in our organic chemistry lab class."

"That's great. You're exactly what we need around here. Someone with new ideas."

"How long have you been working here, sir?"

"I hired on after the war, in '45. That's when we built the plant. The military wanted lots of DDT to kill insects, par-ticularly those damn mosquitoes. Like I said, in the South Pacific, so many of our boys never even got a chance to fight the Japs. They died in the training camps. That's a soldier's worst nightmare—dying before he even gets a chance to fight." Wright pushed a stack of papers aside and leaned forward, setting his thick forearms on the scarred desktop.

"You may not know this, but DDT was invented in the late 1800s by a Swiss chemist named Paul Müller, who figured out how to turn it into a pesticide shortly before the war. He even won the Nobel Prize in '48. Can you believe it? The Nobel Peace Prize. Think of the thousands, probably millions of lives he's saved worldwide, both during and after the war. Müller is a hero in my mind. If I ever get a chance to meet him, I'll gladly shake his hand. This kind of thing makes chemistry great. It's why people like you and me chose to get into the profession. You should be proud of what you're doing."

Earl nodded. The older man was right. A desire to make life better through chemistry had drawn him to his profession. "I read the poster in the lobby that talks about Müller and the invention of synthetic pesticides. I never knew farmers used natural pesticides, like nicotine and pyrethrum, before DDT. I guess they were better than nothing, but they sure didn't last long."

"That's why you never see insects eating cigarettes. The nicotine kills them. Nature has quite a few pesticides, but none are as good as synthetic DDT. On another subject, I know the entry-level pay isn't that great, but you'll make a lot more in a few years if you put your head down, work hard, and learn everything you can."

"The pay works for now. It's a lot more than I was making in school," Earl said, with a chuckle, wondering if it was the right time to broach what might be a sore subject. "I do have one question though, sir," he added, after another long beat had passed.

"Sure. Shoot."

"Some of my friends tell me that DDT is bad for the environment and causes cancer. I've never heard anything like that, but I thought I should ask someone that knows if that is true."

Wright made a face. "Yeah, I heard rumblings from our corporate guys last month. Some of these 'naturalists' get things wrong because they don't know shit from Shinola. They've never been on a farm and can't even spell 'malaria.' There might be a few side effects from synthetics, but the pros outweigh the cons."

Wright rose to his feet. "Feel free to stop by if you have any more questions, Earl. Glad to have you on board."

Earl walked back to his cubicle and admired the picture of his beautiful, brunette wife on his desk. Patty was even more excited about his new job than he was, not just because they had a baby on the way. She was proud of him and announced to anyone who would listen that he was involved in manufacturing a product that saved millions of lives each year.

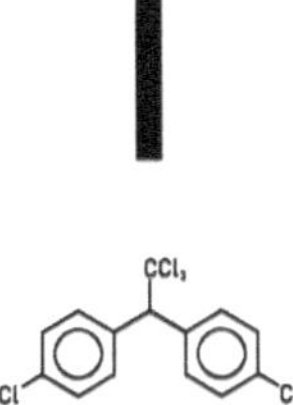

uke Graham turned his 1985 blue Honda Civic into the covenant-controlled neighborhood and immediately noticed the street crowded with several parked cars. He maneuvered around a car that partially blocked his driveway and entered his garage. His stomach knotted as his wife, Kara, met him at the door with puffy eyes. Even Columbo, their six-month-old Havanese puppy, appeared somber. A half-made salad and a glass of chardonnay were on the kitchen island.

"They brought in a hospice nurse today to take care of Angela," she said. "The doctor gives her a few days, at most."

"Wow." Luke's heart sank. "I can't believe it. She went downhill so fast. I guess it's been three years, but still. They said she was cancer-free last year. Have you seen her today?"

"I haven't yet. There's a lot of people over there right now. I'll go in the morning when the sun is out and I feel better about it."

"I'll go with you. I don't have any meetings until 11:30," Luke said, mentally reviewing his calendar. "I haven't seen her in a week. It sounds like it could be the last time, huh?"

He held back tears as he spoke. Ever since he and Kara bought their house five years ago, in 1995, Angela and Bill had been their next-door neighbors. Angela had brought a housewarming gift over the day they moved in. They'd built on that initial act of kindness, and became good friends. Only forty-six, Angela had taught high school history, until she became too ill.

He let out a long sigh. "I guess there's not much we can do right now. I'm starving, and the kids probably are too. Plus, I have to finish reviewing a report tonight."

"Yeah, I've got some work too. It's been hard to focus; maybe it will help to think about something else for a while. I'll make some spaghetti."

"What do you think, Columbo?" Luke said, giving the dog a pat. "Your puppy brain hasn't been exposed to terminal cancer and what it's like to miss someone you really love. I wonder if dogs know how to grieve?"

"Even if they do, it's not for long. Animals seem to forget everything a day later. That's one of the reasons I like having pets," Kara said.

"Do you think they know when they are sick and will soon die?"

"Probably not," Kara said. "But their owners do. Dogs live their lives to the fullest every day, until they don't have another day."

***

The next morning, Luke let Columbo into their small, fenced backyard. It was a beautiful fall morning, and he stood for a moment, breathing in the crisp air. The leaves on the neighborhood's ash and birch trees had changed to a brilliant red and were beginning to fall. Autumn was Kara's favorite time of the year, and he understood why. As a long-distance runner, it was easier for her to train when the Denver temperatures dropped into more civilized numbers. She was out for her daily run now, while he fed the kids and prepared them for school. As he walked back into the house, he realized the old adage was true. Children grew up fast. Nathan was seven and starting second grade, while Kaylie was five and in kindergarten.

Breakfast today consisted of cornflakes, microwaved bacon, and apple juice. The kids weren't picky, which was a relief, given Luke's limited cooking skills. Kara returned home in time to devour the remaining bacon, even though she was a self-proclaimed pescatarian. They'd decided not to tell the kids about Angela's condition and their plan to visit her this morning. There would be a better time to have that difficult conversation.

***

Luke called Bill Samuelson and asked if this was a good time to visit. He thought it would be polite to give him a heads-up instead of just ringing the doorbell.

"Sure, y'all come on over," Bill said. "Penny had to go to class today, and Jennifer is flying back from Austin tonight, but Angela's parents are here. I'm sure they would be happy to see you. Just come on in."

"Okay, we'll be right over."

Luke and Kara walked in the Samuelsons' front door without ringing the bell. They'd donned their work clothes and forced smiles. Bill had moved Angela's bed into the living room, near the front door on the first floor. It was easier for Bill and the caregivers not to go up and down stairs all day, and Luke sensed that Angela didn't want to be alone. The room was warm, with a faint hospital smell and a mix of cleaning chemicals.

Angela was lying on an adjustable bed that elevated her, watching *Good Morning America*. An IV cart was next to the bed, with several hanging bags providing constant drips. The morning sun from the eastern windows lit up the room, and the day seemed as encouraging and optimistic as ever. Luke wondered what the room looked like in the evening, when the sun was setting on the other side of the house, and darkness crept across the floor before the long night. He was keenly aware that Angela didn't have many more sunrises and sunsets to appreciate.

Kara reached for Angela's hand as she approached the bed. "How are you doing?" she asked.

"Just living the dream, Kara. Actually, I don't know what it feels like to feel good anymore." Angela's face was taut, and her eyes sunken. She had lost weight since last week. Luke was once again struck by the unfairness of it all.

"Oh, Kara, you look so good," Angela said. "I've never understood how you stay so fit. It must be your Asian genetics. Nebraskans don't have genes like yours, you know. We get bigger and bigger and look like pears after a while."

Luke smiled and patted Angela's shoulder. There was nothing pear-shaped about her now. She was nothing but taught skin and bones.

"I guess I'm lucky. My mother never weighed more than 115 pounds. We ate fish and salad all the time growing up. But I'm tired of that now," Kara said.

"It was barbecue and corn on the cob in Nebraska." A faraway look entered Angela's eyes. "It sure was good."

She met Luke's eyes, then turned toward Kara. Her expression grew serious now, all traces of the past, gone. "Please keep an eye on my daughters and make sure they find the right husbands and live good lives."

Luke had no words. He rubbed Angela's shoulder again.

"We will. You know we love Jennifer and Penny as though

they were our own daughters. We've watched them grow up, go through middle school and high school. I can't say I ever liked that boyfriend that Jennifer had back then."

Luke managed to nod. Kara was so much better at this than he was.

"You and me both," Angela said, with a hint of her old sparkle. "I'm going to miss you guys, but I'm sure we'll see each other again someday. We'll have coffee together and talk about our kids and cooking."

"I'm sure we will." Kara didn't miss a beat. "You scope heaven out for us, okay? Find all the cool places to hang out."

Luke started to lose his composure and, after giving Angela another quick squeeze, he quietly walked away. From other emotional talks over the past weeks, he knew that Angela understood. Kara's compassion and strength reminded him why they'd quickly become inseparable when they'd met nine years ago. His wife was amazing. Always.

He went to the kitchen, where Bill and his father-in-law, Gary Carter, sat at the table.

"Hey, Gary, it's good to see you again. It's been a long time. I hope you and Claudia are doing okay." *What a stupid thing to say, but what else is there to say?*

"As good as you can expect, I guess. I appreciate you asking. The Lord's been good to us over the years, with our family farm and the corn crops, so I can't complain about that."

Gary was wearing jeans and a flannel shirt with suspenders. His protruding belly strained the buttons on his shirt, and he wore his local Wahoo, Nebraska co-op hat, which cast a shadow over his well-trimmed, short, gray beard.

"This cancer stuff is so unfair, you know. Angela never smoked and lived a much cleaner life than me or her mother ever have, and here she's the one that's sick. It just ain't fair. Parents aren't supposed to outlive their children," Gary said, shaking his head.

"I...I don't know what to say, Gary. I can't imagine how you feel," Luke said. The man's thoughts echoed his own. He couldn't imagine how painful it would be to outlive Nathan or Kaylie. He pulled in a slow, deep breath.

"I still think it has something to do with all those pesticides we used on the farm, when she was just a child. We had all sorts of stuff back in the late fifties and sixties. If you are exposed as a small child, they say it can affect you later. You know, we used that on our soybean crops for many, many years." The older man shook his head. "We'd get it all over us, and joke about how we'd never get a bug bite again. I gotta believe that had something to do with Angela's cancer. I should have been more careful. I take the blame for being so sloppy."

Bill put his hand on Gary's shoulder. "It's not your fault, Gary. We all did what we thought was right at the time."

"Don't beat yourself up over DDT, Gary. There is no conclusive data that indicates DDT causes cancer," Luke said. It was surprising how often his professional knowledge as an environmental consultant crept into casual conversation. "It's really more of an ecological problem than a human health problem. I know there's been a lot of talk, but we haven't actually found a link between DDT and cancer. I've never told you this, Gary, but my younger brother, Charlie, died of leukemia when I was ten. My family lived in Los Alamos, and my parents worked at the national lab. When Charlie got sick, everyone assumed it had to do with radiation at the lab or something like that, even though my parents worked in the administrative building, pushing paper around, as my mother would say. Charlie never went to the office, and I know that because we didn't have security clearances." Luke laughed at his own joke, having told the story to others and finding the bit of humor helpful. "Everyone was convinced it was radiation poisoning that got him sick, when it was probably just a childhood DNA mutation. A stroke of bad luck."

"I'm sorry to hear about your brother, Luke, I hadn't heard that before," Gary said with a small smile. "But I've read a lot of stuff that says women have a higher chance of getting breast cancer, especially in middle age, if they were exposed to DDT as infants and children."

Luke nodded. "You can say that about almost everything we eat or come in contact with. Truth is, we're exposed to so many things every single day that it's hard to pinpoint just one thing that might cause cancer. Maybe you can draw that conclusion if a person smokes five packs a day—that's certainly a big contributor. But sometimes cancer is genetic, and you can't do much to avoid it, especially breast cancer."

After a long pause, Gary leaned forward. "I'm gonna insist on an autopsy to see if my girl had any DDT in her body." His determination was clear, despite his lowered voice. "If her cancer is the result of DDT exposure, I'm gonna file a lawsuit against those bastards."

Luke didn't respond. He'd learned long ago that, no matter what scientific data he presented, he was unlikely to change someone's mind regarding cancer and other human health risks from chemical exposure.

"Gary, let's not cross that bridge right now. According to what I have learned from Luke over the years, almost all of us have DDT in our livers or fat. It bioaccumulates there and doesn't break down, but it doesn't necessarily cause health problems," Bill said.

"What is it you do, that you know so much about DDT?" Gary asked Luke.

Luke was relieved to have a question that didn't involve cancer and death. "I work for an environmental consulting firm, Webber Environmental, and manage remediation projects. That's a fancy name for the cleanup of polluted sites. As it happens, we're cleaning up the country's largest DDT manufacturing plant, in Torrance, California. Guadalupe Chemical made DDT until '82, ten years after the EPA banned its use in the US. It was banned mostly for ecological reasons, not human health reasons. For example, the peregrine falcon faced extinction because their eggshells became too fragile, due to the DDT in the fish the falcons were eating."

"Oh, yeah, I remember hearing something about that," Bill said. "I thought it was bullshit, until years later. What's left of the plant now? Is that where you go when you fly out to California?"

"I go to a thirteen-acre, paved parking lot with a razor wire fence around it. You'd never know there used to be a DDT manufacturing plant on that spot. We refer to it as the 'site' now. That allows us to assess the contamination and do cleanup work, without a bunch of looky-loos and attention from the public."

"So, is there DDT in the LA drinking water?" Bill asked.

"No," Luke said. "The DDT sticks to soil in the groundwater and doesn't move much at all. Don't get me wrong, though; there's tons of it under the old plant site. DDT dissolves in chemical solvents like chlorobenzene as part of the manufacturing process, but it's those solvents that dissolve into the groundwater and move downhill toward the ocean. So, we monitor for chlorobenzene in the groundwater and try to clean it up. We sample the groundwater every three months to monitor changes in the concentration of all the contaminants and track where the groundwater contamination is moving."

"What about all the DDT that's in the dirt?" Gary asked. "We sprayed it on the crops for years."

"Good question, Gary. A lot of DDT dust blew into the yards around the plant site over the years, and many of the neighbors were plant employees who used DDT in their yards. We're doing soil sampling in people's backyards to confirm how much DDT is in the soil. We already know it's there. It's just a question of how much."

"What do you do if people have a lot of DDT in their back-yards? Do you have to go dig up their backyards?" Bill said.

"Maybe," Luke said, with a faint grin. "You can have a lot of DDT in your backyard, but if you don't eat the dirt or kick up a lot of dust because you have grass, you don't get much exposure, right? Now, if it's been sprayed on everything, like in a Nebraska soybean field, you see more exposure."

"That's what happened on the farm. I'm telling ya, we got it all over us. Breathed it in, swallowed the dust, and rubbed it in our eyes. You name it; we were around it all the time," Gary said.

Luke nodded but remained silent. The morning's emotional stress was beginning to take its toll. He'd never seen someone dying of cancer before, and he couldn't imagine how wiped-out Gary and Bill were, confronted by it 24-7.

"Hey guys, I need to get to the office," he said, longing for the distraction of work. "The grind never seems to end, you know. Gary, it's good to see you. I'm sorry it's under these circumstances."

Gary stuck out his big, calloused hand and Luke shook it. "Don't work too hard, Luke," the older man said. "And, don't forget about the enjoyment of living. It can come to a screeching halt at any time."

Luke told Bill he would call him later and returned to the front room. He was relieved to hear Kara and Angela talking about cooking. He wasn't sure he could handle more talk of cancer and death, so he gave Angela a long hug. Luke told both women he had to go to work and gave Kara one more smile before leaving the house. He paused on the wide front porch, gripped by the sudden fear of losing Kara, terrified by the thought of a life without her. *How would Nathan and Kaylie get through this at such a young age? How would I take care of them on my own?*

Wiping the tears from his eyes, he climbed into his Civic and drove to the office.

2

It was nearly 11:00 when Luke parked on the street several blocks from his office, knowing the parking garage would be full by now. He had his weekly noontime lunch meeting with the Guadalupe project team, and as the project manager, he wanted enough time to prepare. Luke was usually one of the first people in the office in the morning, and showing up so close to lunchtime made him feel guilty, even though he had a good reason to be late. Avoiding the elevator, he quickly climbed the four flights of stairs, entering his office through the rear door, hoping not to be interrupted.

He had a corner office with a view of the mountains west of Denver. The season's first snowfall covered the peaks. The dull gray office walls needed painting and were full of tiny pinholes and drywall anchors left over from previous occupants. Several of his project maps hung on the walls, and textbooks, reference manuals, and journal articles filled his bookshelves. Draft reports cluttered his desk, almost obscuring the 3x5 photo of Kara and the kids that sat beside his computer screen. The office was his home away from home.

The visit with Angela had left him distraught, and he struggled to focus on the meeting's agenda. Thank goodness he'd remembered to have his assistant, Cindy, reserve the Longs Peak conference room in advance. *This year, I'll recommend her for a nice Christmas bonus for keeping me organized and thinking ahead.*

He got a good ten minutes' worth of emails answered before Nancy Webber knocked on his door. Nancy owned Webber Environmental, the company she'd started eighteen years before after working for business owners who kept all of the company profits for themselves. She was in her fifties, just over five feet tall, with short brunette hair that shimmered with gray streaks she refused to color. It was common knowledge that Nancy spent her free time working and writing papers for publications instead of exercising or socializing, and she expected others to do the same.

Despite her workaholic expectations, Luke had nothing but respect for his boss. She'd earned a PhD in contaminant hydrogeology in the early '80s, and had been one of only a few experts in the business when the Comprehensive Environmental Response, Compensation, and Cleanup Act (CERCLA), commonly known as "Superfund," had been enacted to clean up the country's most contaminated sites. Nancy was an expert who knew how chemicals such as DDT and chlorobenzene moved in groundwater and where they would ultimately end up.

"Hey, Nancy. How are you? Are you going to make our meeting today?"

While Luke looked over at her, he observed the clock above the door, strategically placed so he could see the time while still maintaining eye contact with somebody standing in his doorway.

"I can't make it today, Luke. We have a potential client coming in for a visit who has a big problem with a chlorinated solvent plume in the groundwater right here in Denver. It could be an interesting project and worth a lot of money. Wouldn't having a project right here in our backyard be nice?"

"That would be awesome. It beats flying across the country and having clients who refuse to pay for our time wasted in airports and planes. Sign me up!"

"So, EPA wants to have another public meeting out at Guadalupe. When was the last one? It seems like it has been forever. Any particular reason, do you think?" Nancy asked.

"I've been wondering why as well. I suspect there is something the EPA is not telling us. They may be trying to get some public support or want us to do more groundwater investigation work. What better way to make Guadalupe do more work than to announce to the public that it will happen? We'll find out."

"I assume you are going to present the results from the latest rounds of groundwater and soil sampling and the status of the groundwater treatment facility."

"Yep, that's the plan," Luke said. "Chad is doing the quarterly groundwater sampling with his crew as we speak, and he'll be there next week. Of course, we won't have the new results yet, but we'll have results from the last three quarters. The concentration of chlorobenzene and the other solvents in the groundwater hasn't changed much in the last year, and every one of the backyard DDT soil samples shows concentrations below the cleanup levels. We've sampled over eighty backyards adjacent to the plant. Nobody seems worried about DDT in soils, so I think it will be a non-issue."

"Who do you think will attend the meeting? How many people from the EPA are going to show?" Nancy asked.

"Antoine Watson, the new EPA Project Manager, will be there, for sure. This public meeting will be his first site visit. Remember, he was assigned to the project only three months ago after Carla, the previous manager, got reassigned. I talk to Antoine about every day, but I've never met him in person. He seems like a good guy, though. He's pragmatic and wants to get things done in a hurry. It will be helpful for us to give him a tour of the site.

"Simone Delgado, EPA's contract toxicologist, told me she would be there. I assume the usual neighbors will show up, wanting to know what's going on, as well as those that just come for the snacks." Luke grinned. "But it's a Tuesday night, and the Lakers are playing at home, which will likely reduce interest."

"Who's going from our side?" Nancy asked.

"Our budget is getting a little tight, so probably just Rudy, Debbie, and me. I'll let Rudy cover the investigation results, and Debbie and I will cover the groundwater treatment facility. Of course, Earl Kemp will be there to open the gates and serve as the Guadalupe site representative. He's the only Guadalupe plant employee left, you know?"

"Make sure Rudy doesn't get carried away with his maps and graphs. He tends to put people to sleep and be a little condescending when he drones on about investigating a site. Don't tell him I said that. He is very good at what he does. He just wants everyone to know it," Nancy said.

"I'll keep him in line at the meeting, although putting the public to sleep at a public meeting is not a bad strategy. Remember, I did plenty of Navy briefings to impatient captains and admirals, so I can speed him up if necessary."

"Do the best you can, Luke. I'll support you if it comes to that. Are you going to fly commercial or take your plane?" Nancy asked.

"We'll see how the weather looks. This time of year, you can have some great and not-so-great days to fly over the mountains. Also, I can't afford to miss the meeting, so I'll likely be flying commercial."

As he spoke, Luke decided he definitely wouldn't fly himself, much as he loved being in the cockpit. There was simply too much work to do this time. He had to arrange an hour-by-hour schedule for the site visit and subsequent meetings, beginning with a client dinner the night before.

He knew his clients, Caroline Woodson and Bob Burrows, would want to fly into LAX the night before the EPA and public meetings to have dinner with Luke and his team to prepare and strategize. Caroline, Executive Vice President at Guadalupe, was responsible for all environmental concerns. She always traveled with Bob Burrows, Senior Legal Counsel. Bob worked at Guadalupe for fifteen years after practicing as an environmental attorney for a large law firm. His expertise was Superfund. The former DDT manufacturing plant was designated as a Superfund site, which placed it under the jurisdiction of the federal EPA. Bob and Caroline worked on several Superfund sites for Guadalupe and understood how to negotiate with the EPA and the various stakeholders, including environmental consulting firms like Webber Environmental. As a result, Bob and Caroline would never get too close to consultants like Luke and his project team. They believed that consultants worked harder if they always feared being fired.

****

Luke sat at the eight-person conference table in the windowless Longs Peak conference room and immediately began devouring his turkey avocado sandwich without waiting for the others. The emotional stress of the morning had increased his appetite.

"Hi, Luke."

Mid-bite, Luke nodded a greeting to Josh Crandall, the GIS

mapping expert. In his mid-fifties and of average build, Josh was more at home with the maps he created than he was with people. His office resembled a military command center with little natural light, four computer screens of various maps and colors, and classical music playing in the background. Luke considered both the man and his maps invaluable to the team. The maps showed the contours of chemical contamination concentrations in soil and groundwater and were essential for visually telling the story of chemical contamination, past and present.

Beth Longoria, their new chemist, came in next. Fresh from the University of Wyoming, this was her first job. In her early twenties, she still dressed like a college student, in tight-fitting jeans and a pink sweater. Attractive, with short blonde hair and blue eyes, she had caused quite a stir in the office.

"How do you like your job so far?" Luke asked as the young woman sat down beside him.

"It's great. I've learned a lot in the last six months that I never learned in school."

Luke smiled. "That's usually what happens. School gives you the tools to build on, and you continue to learn for the rest of your career. You're doing great."

"Thanks, I appreciate that. It's funny. Working here, facts that I learned in school pack a greater punch. Like, I learned that DDT has a half-life of around ten years or so before it breaks down into other, daughter products, which last just as long or longer. Some of these compounds have a half-life of 150 years, and when you start looking at actual sites and talking to people, you realize this stuff will be around for a long time," Beth said, with a combination of excitement and concern.

"You're right about that," Luke said, with a glance at his phone. He prided himself on beginning meetings right on time.

He gave everyone a smile. "I know Rudy's still MIA, but let's go ahead and get started. This public meeting is coming up fast. Oh, before I forget, Debbie couldn't make it today because she is at a client lunch. She'll give the EPA a tour of the groundwater treatment facility and deliver a short presentation. I'll get with her tomorrow and sort out what she needs to bring."

Luke spent the next several minutes going over his proposed agenda for the upcoming meeting.

As usual, Rudy Gallegos came in ten minutes late and sat down without apologizing for his tardiness.

Luke couldn't hold back a little good-natured ribbing. "My watch must be ten minutes fast today. Let me reset it to noon."

Beth and Josh grinned.

Rudy's perpetual frown deepened. "I had to use the restroom, Luke. That's what happens to men over fifty. You young Navy flyboys can hold it for a long time, but older civilians like me can't make it that long."

Rudy's technical abilities and effective presentation skills enabled him to get away with perennial lateness and prickly comments. He'd been Nancy's university classmate, and the two relied on each other for technical quality.

"Okay, give us the shorthand version of the remedial investigation and what happened last year," Luke asked.

Rudy took a deep breath and wiped the mustard from around his mouth. "I'll start by talking about chlorobenzene, since it's the primary contaminant of concern at the site. It's been almost a year since the last public meeting, so I plan to show a map of the chlorobenzene concentration in the groundwater a year ago and a map of what it is today. It will be obvious how the chlorobenzene plume has migrated south, toward the ocean, and under several new neighborhoods."

Josh clipped two of his maps to the wall. They showed the migration of the chlorobenzene plume toward the Pacific Ocean.

Rudy ate another bite of his sandwich and continued with his presentation. "As you can see in the two maps, chlorobenzene continues to migrate horizontally in the groundwater toward the ocean, and vertically downward into the Silverado aquifer, a water supply aquifer for the LA basin. This downward, vertical migration hasn't happened before. Historically, chlorobenzene only affected the shallower aquifers that aren't used for drinking water."

"Why does the chlorobenzene keep sinking deeper? Shouldn't it dissolve in the shallow aquifers just below the surface?" Beth asked.

"Good question, Beth, but I'll bet nobody asks it at the public meeting," Rudy said, with what was, for him, a hint of a smile. "The short answer is, when chlorobenzene is dissolved, it stays in the shallow groundwater and moves horizontally. But, in this case, there is so much chlorobenzene that it displaces the groundwater instead of dissolving in it and moves downward because it's denser than the water. It's called a 'dense non-aqueous phase liquid,' or 'dean-apple' for short." He raised a hand and began counting off with his fingers.' "'D-N-A-P-L.' We're figuring out how to remove it without causing a bigger problem. If it were gasoline from a leaking gas station, it would float on the water, making it easier to clean up. Sites with DNAPL are much more difficult to clean up. There are tens of thousands of gallons of DNAPL under this site, and every time you move it by pumping, the DNAPL moves downward to the cleaner, unpolluted aquifers. It's still hard to believe there is actually that much, but it's undeniable."

Beth snapped her fingers. "I get it now! Without the chlorobenzene, the DDT stands still."

"You got it. The chlorobenzene acts like a ferry boat for the otherwise stagnate DDT. I wouldn't expect a chemist to come to that conclusion on his own," Rudy said, throwing his hands and fingers out from his head like a lightbulb.

"On her own, you mean." Beth sat straighter in her chair. "So, Luke, how many people attend a public meeting?" she asked.

"The last meeting only had about fifteen locals, plus a few students from the nearby university who were interested in environmental science. I think this one, too, will be fairly routine. It was a fun meeting last time, with easy questions. It gives us a chance to show off what we've accomplished in the last year."

3

Luke returned to his office and shut the door, where he immediately began typing an email to Simone Delgado at EPA in San Francisco.

Simone, will you be attending the Guadalupe public meeting next week? We should talk beforehand if you are going, or even if you are not.

Simone was a toxicologist by education, specializing in the risk to human health from various toxic chemicals. She was currently a contractor for EPA Region 9 in San Francisco and an expert on acute and chronic effects of chemicals on humans and animals. As a former EPA employee, she knew the agency's internal workings and often provided Luke with valuable insight.

They also had history. He leaned back in his comfortable, ergonomically approved office chair and gazed out the window at the mountains, reflecting on their college days. They'd been classmates their first year, and when she'd needed a place to live as a sophomore, Luke invited her into the rental house he shared with two other male engineers. It had worked so well they'd remained housemates for the remainder of college. They enjoyed many of the same activities, such as hiking and camping. She never complained about muscle pain or camping inconveniences, like some of his college girlfriends had. She was always positive and fun-loving. Their unique relationship had come close to being more, but ultimately never ventured beyond platonic. His desk phone rang, and Luke came back to the present. He picked up the receiver.

"Luke Graham here."

"Hi, Luke! It's Simone."

His chair snapped forward as he straightened once more. "Hey, Simone. You must have read my email. How's the new job going?"

"The job is going well, though it tries to cut into my free time with Alison. Can you believe she's six now?"

He chuckled. "Our kids are growing up fast too. Nathan is now in second grade, and Kaylie is five. We camped in the backyard last week, and they had a blast. So far, they both like the outdoors. Maybe we can find a way to go camping sometime with the kids. Let them get to know each other."

"Maybe," she said, after pausing for a moment. "I was talking with my former coworkers at EPA, and they said they have new test data that indicates EPA should lower the cleanup level for DDT concentrations in the soil from 150 milligrams per kilogram to fifty, because the human health effects of DDT are probably greater than originally thought."

Luke suddenly rose from his chair and reached for his coffee mug. "Simone, c'mon. How does EPA come up with these new cleanup levels after all these years of DDT testing? This change will have an enormous impact on DDT cleanups everywhere. Sites that weren't considered hazardous before will now require cleanup."

"I know that, but the agency has done more animal testing with what they believe to be more accurate results."

"You mean rat testing, right? Somehow, that's supposed to simulate humans?" Luke couldn't keep the sarcasm out of his voice. They'd had similar conversations before, but she'd never been able to convince him the EPA tests had a scientific basis.

"It may seem like we are comparing apples to oranges, but believe it or not, Luke, rats and mice are similar to us biologically in many ways."

Luke chuckled. "We know a few rats, don't we, Simone? I wish we could use them as test animals."

"I wish we could too. The data would be much better if we could test humans, but we can't go out and give people doses of DDT."

"You know, in some ways, we have human data. I was talking with the old plant manager last week, a guy named Earl Kemp, who has worked at Guadalupe his entire career. You'll meet him next week. He's in his late sixties now, and except for acid burns on his arms and face, he sure seems healthy."

"I'll admit. Comparing rats to humans is where the science gets fuzzy, Luke. When somebody gets cancer, and you look back over the last thirty years of what they may have been exposed to in their daily lives, it's difficult to draw definitive conclusions as to the cause of their cancer. I mean, we're exposed to all kinds of stuff all the time, right? We usually resort to epidemiological studies at this point. But, as I've said before, we have to use something quantitative regarding cleanup levels, and this is still our best method."

Luke thought of Angela and Charlie for a moment while he did a little mental math. "Well," he said, at last, "if the cleanup level is lowered, some of the homeowner's yards that we considered clean will be flagged as hazardous. I'm not sure if you know this, but most former employees lived near the plant and could take home all the DDT they wanted, for use in their yards. And the houses around the plant, especially those downwind, had DDT dust blown into their yards for years."

"I know it can seem irrational how we come up with rules and cleanup guidelines, but there is a scientific basis."

"Okay, Simone. Neither one of us ever really wins this argument, but thanks for calling me back. It's always great to hear your voice."

"You too. We'll see you at the project meeting, right?"

"I'm going to be there, and so will my project team, plus Caroline and Bob from Guadalupe."

"By the way," Simone said, after a few beats of silence had passed. "I've never told anyone that you and I have a personal relationship that goes back so many years. I think we should keep it that way, to avoid any perceived conflict."

Luke pondered her request. He'd never brought it up, either, but not from fear of any questions their shared past might raise. "You make a good point," he said. "Let's keep our friendship quiet for now."

4

The sun had not yet risen on Saturday morning when Luke woke to find his son, Nathan, staring at him. Nathan was dressed in his yellow snow pants and blue poly ski shirt, ready to hit the slopes.

"Dad, Dad, it's six o'clock. You told me to wake you up, if you were still asleep. Come on! We have to get going, or we'll be late," Nathan whispered.

"Okay, buddy," Luke said through a yawn. "I need you to let Columbo out in the backyard for ten minutes, then feed him and make sure he eats his breakfast. Shut the door on your way out, and we'll get dressed."

Nathan left the room and shut the door. Luke jumped out of bed and locked the door. Then, before the room's chill could reach him, he crawled back into the bed, cuddling next to Kara's warm body. He wrapped his arms around her, cupping his hands over her small breasts. Nathan would be knocking on the door again in fifteen minutes. *Do I pursue Kara's warm, silk pajama-clad body or get more sleep?* Deciding there would be time for Kara later, he opted for another fifteen minutes of shut-eye.

When he entered the garage after a quick breakfast with a hot cup of coffee for the drive, Nathan was already sitting in the car with his seat belt on. Luke was glad they had loaded their ski gear into Kara's Land Cruiser the night before, as the morning's mayhem was time-consuming and chaotic enough as it was. Unlike her brother, Kaylie was still half asleep and more interested in returning to bed than skiing, so she took some prodding. A missing mitten resulted in a ten-minute search. Finally, they rolled out of the driveway and headed toward Van's house.

Luke and Van Russo had been friends since their years at the University of New Mexico. He lived in a small house on the west side of Denver with his six-year-old tabby cat. He was transferred to Denver from his company's headquarters in Washington, DC, six months prior, where he worked as an analyst for a military security company. His yard looked immaculate compared to his neighbors, and the house was in excellent condition. All the curtains were closed, and two satellite dishes on the south side of the house stared at different geosynchronous satellites.

Van was standing on the sidewalk with his ski gear. He stood well over six feet and weighed at least 230 pounds, with short black hair and a neatly trimmed beard. He looked more like a ski lift operator than a skier, in his brown Carhartt overalls and a black Gore-Tex jacket.

He loaded his gear into the SUV and attached his skis to the rack on the top before folding his long frame into the backseat behind Kara.

"I hope you haven't been standing out there too long?" Kara asked.

"I just got outside. I knew when you were going to drive up." He turned to the kids. "Hey, rug rats, you ready to shred some powder today? It's the first big snow of the year. I can teach you how to get some air and do spread eagles and back-scratchers this year."

"I'm not a rug rat," Kaylie said.

"I want you to teach me how to get some air, Mr. Van," Nathan said. "We don't have to ski with Kaylie; she's a chicken anyway."

"Oh, shut up, Nathan. You're stupid."

The bantering continued for another minute before Nathan asked, "Mr. Van, why don't you have a wife and kids to go with us?"

Luke burst into laughter and exchanged a quick glance with Kara.

"I promise I didn't set that one up, Russo," he said into the rearview mirror.

Van took a minute to answer, "Because I haven't found a woman like your mother yet. When I do, I'll marry her, and we'll have some kids that you two can hang out with."

After a few more miles, Nathan asked another question, "Mr. Van, did you grow up with my mom and dad?"

Van smiled. "I sort of grew up with them. Your dad and I were friends in college. We got in a lot of trouble, mostly because of your dad. Hasn't he told you all these stories yet?"

"Whoa, don't believe him, Nathan. Van was in a fraternity and goofed off when all of us engineers were studying. Ask him about the time he pulled the electrical breaker at the football stadium on Saturday. He shut down a college football game."

"No way! Really?" Nathan asked, with a mix of admiration and astonishment in his voice.

Van chuckled. "It wasn't all fun and games. Your dad and I were in the Reserve Officers' Training Corp, ROTC, in school, and after we graduated and got commissioned, we both ended up in Iraq in the first Gulf War. Your dad flew around in a nice, air-conditioned reconnaissance plane, while yours truly here was in the desert, getting shot at and picking up angry prisoners."

"Did you guys win?" Nathan asked.

"We survived, Nathan, if that is what it means to win. And it will probably happen again, because Saddam is still stirring up trouble. We should have taken him out when we had the chance."

"Did you ever kill anyone, Mr. Van?" asked Nathan.

"Nathan, that's not a question you want to ask someone," Kara said.

Van paused and replied, "We can talk more about that someday. I mostly spent my time camping in the desert, asking Iraqi soldiers what they were doing and where they lived. Pretty boring stuff."

Luke turned up the radio, figuring Van had enough interrogation for today. He glanced in the rearview mirror to see Van admiring the snow-capped mountains and blue sky.

They soon arrived at the Loveland Ski Area, just an hour's drive in good weather. The sun was out, and the temperature was in the teens, making for a perfect, crisp morning. Fresh snow had fallen in the last two days, and the early-year ski conditions were excellent. Luke was excited about being in the mountains with his family and quickly forgot about the Gulf War and Angela.

Luke agreed to take Nathan and Kaylie to ski school while Van and Kara made some early runs. Kara was a better skier than Luke, and he understood he slowed her down. She'd learned to ski when she was young and enjoyed skiing aggressively, although she was always mindful of others on the slopes. She could ski in the moguls and make it look effortless.

On the other hand, Van skied hard and fast, and his happiness was measured by how many vertical feet he skied in one day, with complete disregard for his big body and other skiers who got in his way.

***

After a warmup run, Kara and Van caught the chairlift to the top of the mountain. With no other riders on the chair, Kara found it a good time to fill in some gaps in Van's past. She raised her goggles and shot Van a penetrating look.

"What did you mean in the car this morning when you said you just asked prisoners what they were doing?"

Van squirmed and adjusted his hat. He looked her in the eyes. "I did what I was ordered to do, Kara. We didn't do anything as bad as the Iraqis did to the Kuwaitis and some of our soldiers. Most of the Iraqis we captured were willing to tell us a lot of information without us having to force it from them. I was in the Army Special Forces for three years before I went over in '90, as part of Operation Desert Shield. We spent most of our time collecting intel and putting battle plans together. It wasn't until early '91 that the war started, and we began getting information from prisoners."

"Where were you when the war started?"

"After the Iraqis invaded Kuwait, we were assigned to Khafji, near the southern Kuwait border in Saudi Arabia. We interviewed a lot of Kuwaitis as they fled the country, and then the Iraqis invaded us in early '91. We got pushed back, and a few of us hid in the desert for days. I won't sugarcoat that. It was scary. We dug into the sand and hid ourselves under plywood and more sand. Eventually, the Army and the Marines pushed the Iraqis back into Kuwait. We took hundreds of prisoners and collected intel that saved a lot of lives during the following month. Intel was everything, Kara, and it still is today. That's why I'm in the business."

Kara nodded. "So, that's how you got into the security business. I never really knew."

"There's more to it than just the Army. My dad was a private investigator in South Chicago. He tracked down cheating husbands at first, and then later, he started working on bigger cases involving hardened criminals and drug dealers. He started giving me some of his research and analytical work when I was in my early teens. I really enjoyed it, and my dad was a good teacher. At first, it was mainly a bunch of library work, but every so often, he'd have me sit outside someone's apartment in a playground, watching the place for activity. When I turned sixteen, he started taking me to talk to suspects." Van shot her a smile. "I was already approaching six feet and wrestled 184, so I must have looked intimidating for my age. He even bought me a Smith & Wesson .44 magnum revolver, just like Dirty Harry had, with the long barrel. It was clear to anyone we talked to that I was carrying a big gun, and it usually helped us get the answers we were after. I never had to say anything."

They were nearing the top of the mountain, so she straightened her skis and replaced her goggles. Van lowered his goggles as well.

Kara didn't hold back her astonishment. "Isn't it illegal for a minor to carry a weapon?

Van's smile became a full-on laugh. "Big time. Dad never loaded it, but he had some bullets in his pocket to give me if everything went to hell."

"Did that ever happen?"

He gestured toward his skis. "Time to get off the lift, Kara. We can finish this conversation later. Let's hit the first run and have some fun!"

***

Kara and Van skied another run and rejoined the lift line again. It had grown longer as usual, now that the morning hour was later. An older man, flaunting a long, gray ponytail and shiny new skis, edged ahead of them as the skiers converged.

"Excuse me, sir, but I believe you just cut in front of us," Van said in an authoritative voice.

Kara leaned closer to Van and said in a low voice, loud enough for the man to hear, "Some people just think their time is more important than mine." She thought about adding, "You must be from Texas," but reconsidered, knowing that there were probably other Texans in the line who might take unkindly to her comment.

"I do tend to get out of control once in a while and run over people. These Carhartt's don't get torn up very easily."

Kara decided to change the topic once they were on the chairlift together and probe further into Van's life.

"Have you ever had a serious girlfriend, Van? I never hear you talk about any woman other than some of your coworkers. I'd think a guy like you would be married by now."

Was it her imagination, or was Van fidgeting again? Kara decided to push just a little more. She'd known him for years but had never asked such pointed questions.

"I got involved with a girl after I came back from Iraq. Her name was Susan, and we got along super well and had a great time together. But it only lasted for a year or so."

"That's actually a long time. Why did you break up?"

He raised a shoulder. "Our relationship just got boring after a while. She wanted to spend more time with me and do all sorts of time-consuming, mundane things, like shopping and walking. I found myself looking forward to Monday and going back to the office. It was more enjoyable to work than to be around her."

"Do you think you'll be a single guy forever? You're terrific around our kids, you know."

"I'll find someone, but I'm too busy now to look very hard. As for kids, I don't know. I might get bored, which scares me because it wouldn't be fair to them. I like doing my own thing and working."

"I know you manage data and information for the Navy. Do you know where all our ships and submarines are?" Kara teased.

"It's kinda like that. The military wants to know everything about everything and everyone, so there's never a shortage of data to collect and analyze. And what I find out is pretty interesting," Van said, with a smile.

When they reached the bottom of the mountain, Kara took off her skis and leaned one in a nearby rack that held hundreds of other skis. Van took one of his skis and placed it next to hers, then took the other mismatched set and put it on another rack closer to the restaurant. It was an old trick most skiers used to keep their skis from being stolen.

"Why don't you pick up the kids from ski school, and I'll meet you inside. I'll find us a table," Van said.

Luke arrived a few minutes later after being relieved from

ski school duty by Kara and found Van devouring his peanut butter and jelly sandwich, which he had carried in the breast pocket of his overalls. "How's the snow?" Luke asked.

"Pretty awesome morning, Rattler," Van said, using Luke's naval aviator call sign. "We got in over thirteen thousand feet vertical already, and I only fell twice. Kara didn't fall at all. She's an amazingly smooth skier."

"Kara said she would watch the kids, so I can go with you this afternoon. Let me get a hamburger. I'm starving. Watching kids makes a man hungry."

"You know they charge a fortune for those, and if you overeat, it'll slow us down," Van said, his dark eyes locked in on Luke.

"We'll see who slows us down," Luke replied.

****

Luke found Kara at the end of the day with Nathan and Kaylie, who looked exhausted despite the smiles on their faces. Van arrived and said, with a tinge of disappointment, "We could have made thirty thousand feet vertical if Rattler hadn't stopped so many times. It was that hamburger he had at lunch. He didn't believe me."

Luke ignored Van's jab and loaded the kids and skis in the SUV for the ride home. He started the engine and the heater as the early winter sun hid behind the mountain and the temperature dropped. Kara and the kids were in the back seat, just about to doze off, when Luke's car phone rang. He answered the phone over the car speaker to hear Bill Samuelson's voice, and felt a knot in his stomach, anticipating what was next.

"Luke, I just wanted to let you and Kara know that Angela

passed away this morning," Bill said, his voice matter of fact. "We were all there and with her to the end. It was peaceful. She was ready, and she's in a better place now."

"We're so sorry to hear that," Luke said. "We'll come by when we get back from skiing. How are you all doing?"

"We're getting by. How was the skiing? The weather and snow sound great," Bill said.

"It was a good day," Luke said, with tears in his eyes. In the back seat, Nathan and Kaylie began to cry. Luke's tide of emotion made him short on words.

"Luke and I will be there in a few hours. Thanks for giving us a call," Kara said. Luke hung up, and the car was silent for several miles.

"It's not fair!" Kaylie said, through her sobs. "How come Ms. Samuelson had to die? She didn't do anything wrong. Why did she have to get cancer?"

In the rearview mirror, Luke saw Nathan poke his sister and say, "She got sick because of something called DDT." Nathan's eyes widened as he met Luke's reflection. "You're not going to get sick, are you, Dad?"

The question surprised Luke into silence. He and Kara would have to be more careful when discussing sensitive subjects in the future.

"No, Mom and I are fine," Luke said, with extra emphasis. "And we don't know why Ms. Samuelson got cancer. Sometimes it just happens." As responses went, it wasn't his best, but it appeared to satisfy Nathan.

5

Luke drove to DIA Monday morning while the moon still hung in the western sky. It promised to be a long day. His back was stiff from skiing, and his nerves frayed from the emotional toll of Angela's death. As far as he knew, he'd managed to tiptoe out of the house without awakening anyone else. His years in the Navy had accustomed him to odd hours and a sleep-when-you-can attitude. He grabbed a coffee and a *Wall Street Journal* and headed to the underground train.

Debbie Sparks was waiting for him at the gate. She also appeared sleep-deprived and older than her twenty-seven years. Her wire-framed glasses were slightly askew, and she wore her conservative blouse buttoned to the top.

"Hey, Debbie. Did you have a good weekend?"

"It was a great weekend. Too bad it ended at four o'clock this morning and will go even later tonight with the time change. It's gonna be a twenty-five-hour day."

Luke smiled. "You'll survive. Lack of sleep never killed a real consultant. It's a badge of honor that you'll brag about someday. Besides, the EPA will be impressed with your groundwater treatment facility. It's your chance to shine and, the air looks smooth over the western US."

"Good, I don't like turbulence. You're probably used to it, but I'm not."

"Planes never fall apart in the air. It's like driving a car on a bumpy road. You do that all the time and never think twice."

The look on Debbie's face ended the conversation.

Throughout the flight to LA, they discussed how to best present the groundwater treatment facility to the EPA, who would be touring it today for the first time. The running conversation kept Luke alert and lifted his spirits.

They pulled up to the former plant site in Luke's rental car and found Earl Kemp's '82 green Ford Bronco. Luke had listened to Earl brag about how he had logged over 210,000 miles in the Bronco, and it seemed to know its way to the site. Earl was cleaning something at the treatment facility, and Luke assumed Earl had already completed his routine inspection duties, including checking the perimeter razor wire fence for holes. Luke gazed across the empty, asphalt-covered, thirteen-acre site and imagined the former DDT manufacturing plant. The plant's history and contamination were paved over before his eyes.

Earl was now in his mid-sixties and looked every bit his age. His forearms were bleached and spotty, with a variety of skin pigmentations. Luke had dared to ask once, but Earl didn't know if the scars resulted from chlorobenzene and sulfuric acid exposure, or his years in the sun. It was likely a combination of both.

"Earl, how are you doing?" Luke said, reaching out to shake Earl's hand.

"Couldn't be happier, Luke," Earl said, with a mix of sarcasm and honesty.

Debbie stepped up and gave Earl a big hug. They had spent months together, overseeing the construction of the groundwater treatment facility. Luke, who was fond of the older man himself, had been glad to see they had hit it off and developed a mutual respect for one another.

After some small talk about the traffic on the 405 and the infrequent change in weather, Luke and Debbie started the tedious process of putting on the slick, white, Tyvek suits and gloves, as required by the Webber Environmental Health & Safety plan.

"Make sure you get that duct tape on there, good and tight, Debbie. You never know. Some DDT might get in your sleeve, and we'll have to cut off your hand," Earl said, as they wrapped the heavy-duty, all-purpose tape around their wrists and ankles.

Debbie laughed and replied, "It's an EPA day, Earl. We must be on our best behavior, which means you too."

"If you say so. I'll have to try real hard not to be a smart-ass, but I'll do it for you."

Luke smiled. Earl had made it clear on previous trips that he didn't feel the need to comply with Webber's strict health and safety requirements. He wore safety glasses and steel-toed boots, which made sense to him, but he'd been exposed to chlorobenzene and DDT for the last forty years without any apparent health problems, so why should he change his ways now?

"I'm with you, Earl," Luke said. "These suits are overkill in situations like this. Can you imagine suiting up to spray worm killer on your lawn at home? I swear, my garage is as bad as any chemical storage facility. I've got pesticides, insecticides, solvents, industrial cleaners, and so many other toxic shit that I've bought over the years that I can't even remember what I have. They sell it in such big plastic bottles, I'll never use it all. I get more exposure at home than I ever get out here."

Next to arrive was Chad Purcell, from Webber Environmental, and his groundwater sampling assistant. Luke admired Chad's easy-go-lucky attitude and how he got his job done without ever seeming stressed.

"Hey, Boss Man, I like the sound of the Bronco these days. Did you finally adjust the timing chain?" Chad asked Earl.

"Only you could hear that difference, Chad. I'm impressed. You are a real gearhead."

"You know I work on small plane engines in my spare time, to earn a few extra bucks. We're talking about performance with those turbocharged engines," Chad bragged.

"How many more groundwater monitoring wells do you have to sample?" Earl asked.

"We've sampled forty-seven so far this week. Eight more to go today, then we'll be done for three months when we do it all over again."

"How many more groundwater monitoring wells are you all gonna drill, Luke? It seems to me that we already have a pin cushion all over Torrance," Chad said.

"No idea. I'm not the one who makes that decision."

"All I know is the more wells you drill, the more work I have, and I keep my job. Plus, I'll get more overtime. You know what I'm saying?" Chad said.

"Chad, you remember the EPA is coming today, right?" Earl said, now becoming more serious. "When they show up, I need you to come over to the groundwater treatment facility and answer any questions. Don't start bull shittin' them like you do to me. They'll see right through it. These two regulator types coming in today are pretty smart cookies."

"You got it, Boss Man. I'll lay off the BS and speak nothin' but facts, nothin' but facts," Chad said, with a gleaming, over-whitened smile.

***

Luke followed Debbie as she meticulously performed routine maintenance on the groundwater treatment facility. He was impressed with her attention to detail, and it reminded him of going through an airplane checklist. He was aware of the sun rising higher in the sky and the hotter temperature, which made the Tyvek suit even more uncomfortable. Finally, a brand-new Chevrolet Suburban drove through the gate. Luke spotted Simone in the passenger seat.

"You must be Antoine," he said to the tall, broad-shouldered man who stepped out of the Suburban. Luke stuck out his hand. "I'm Luke. Great to finally meet you in person."

Luke had created an image of Antoine Watson in his mind that was not too far off the mark. Antoine was in his mid-thirties, with brown skin and bluish-grey eyes. He had a first-impression air of likability that was hard to resist.

Luke knew Antoine was a bit of a wunderkind at the EPA. He had risen quickly through the ranks because of his ability to manage multiple projects simultaneously and work well with the diverse, often hostile, stakeholders associated with a complex Superfund process.

Luke stepped back and admired the Suburban. "Nice wheels. Is my client paying for this, or the US taxpayer?"

"Yeah, yeah, yeah." Antoine's wide grin showed he'd taken the teasing as Luke had intended. "I gotta get here somehow. It's all they had left to rent. It's nice to meet you too. Thanks for getting me out of the office. It sucks, sitting behind a desk and commuting to the office five days a week, in San Francisco traffic." He looked around, sniffing the air. "Did you buy me a big cup of coffee, or does it always smell like coffee out here? Where is that wonderful smell coming from?"

Luke jabbed a thumb in the direction of the ocean. "There's an industrial coffee brewing house next door. They've been here for at least forty years, and there are some big ovens where the beans are roasted. The smell beats the hell out of the LA air."

Simone stepped out from behind the Suburban, and her eyes met Luke's. It had been seven years since they last met, and he was unprepared for the surge of emotion that swept through him. Luke wanted to hug her but was mindful of their last conversation, so he shook her hand like a stranger instead. He hoped there would be time for getting reacquainted in the next two days.

He made introductions while Earl reluctantly pulled on his white Tyvek suit after receiving the evil eye from Debbie. Luke wanted to ensure that Antoine and Simone saw firsthand the groundwater treatment facility Guadalupe had constructed as part of the judicial consent decree, agreed upon with EPA.

"Okay, Antoine and Simone, I'll let Debbie and these guys describe the facility, how it works, and what they do to maintain it. They are the ones who designed it, installed it, and make sure it works every day."

Debbie stepped forward to begin the tour she was practiced at giving. Luke knew she was proud of this treatment facility and wanted to convey that pride to Antoine and Simone. The tour was going well until Antoine, standing close to Debbie, asked her a simple question and smiled. Luke could see their eyes meet and sensed the attraction between them. Antoine was an attractive man, and Debbie briefly lost her train of thought and stumbled over a response. Did Antoine do this on purpose to control the conversation, or was it just a natural gift he had with women?

"As described in our monthly status reports, we pump ground-water up from ninety-five feet below the surface and run it through the treatment facility," Debbie said. "That's the depth with the highest concentration of contaminants of concern. Our goal, of course, is to remove as much chlorobenzene as we can. We like to say it's 'groundwater,' but the truth is, there's a lot of pure chlorobenzene and dissolved DDT in this area. The carbon in these two vessels adsorbs the chlorobenzene, DDT, and other organic molecules and removes them from the groundwater. It's the same carbon process used in your home water treatment system. I hope everybody has one. We get over 99.99 percent removal of all organic contaminants in the groundwater. In other words, you can drink the water coming out of the carbon vessel. It's that clean."

Luke knew it was a pilot-scale facility that only treated the same volume of water that someone would get from a garden hose at home. Based on the operating results of the pilot facility, a much larger, full-scale facility would be designed and installed.

"How often do you have to replace the carbon vessels?" Simone asked.

"Great question," Debbie replied. "We only replace one vessel at a time. We operate the vessels in a series, one after the other, and test the groundwater between the two every week for chlorobenzene and other organic chemicals. When we detect an unacceptable level in between, we know that it's time to replace the first vessel with a clean vessel. Then, we run the groundwater in the opposite direction, so we always have a clean vessel on the discharge side. The carbon vessels only last about six weeks. We haul off the contaminated vessel to Louisiana for recycling, where the carbon is cooked at a high temperature and incinerates the chlorobenzene and DDT."

"Have you had any problems operating the facility?" Antoine asked.

Obviously excited to finally have a say in the conversation, Chad grabbed a piece of PVC pipe clogged with a white, crystalline scale material and presented it to Antoine and Simone. "Here's a piece of pipe I replaced last week because the scale material plugged it up, so we couldn't get much groundwater to flow through the facility."

They all gathered around the pipe and examined it closely. Antoine held it up to the sun to see if he could see through the pipe from end to end before banging it on the ground. Some of the scale material was sprinkled out onto the asphalt. The remaining crusty material was cemented to the inside of the pipe.

"Do you know if it is DDT? Have you had it analyzed?" Simone asked.

Luke had been waiting for Simone to ask that question, since she was a scientist and never assumed a conclusion.

"I sent samples to the lab last week," Chad said.

Earl stood back, watching the highly educated group examine and pontificate about the white scale in the pipe. Luke knew exactly what Earl was thinking. Earl had been around DDT his entire adult life, and no one else in the group had worked in a chemical plant or had "real plant experience," as Earl liked to say.

In their protective white Tyvek suits, the scientists and engineers continued to make guesses about the white scale material and why it deposited in the pipe. Luke watched as

Earl finally stopped the guessing by stepping forward and sticking his finger in the pipe, where he gathered some of the white deposit. He rubbed it between his ungloved fingers as the others watched and hesitated to say anything about his lack of concern. He then licked his fingers clean.

He spit it out of his mouth and stepped back, a knowing glint in his eyes, relishing the shock factor. "Sure as shit, that's DDT," he said. "I know DDT when I taste it. I've been breathing it and tasting it for years."

Luke held back his desire to laugh when he saw Antoine and Simone shake their heads. Even Debbie's face paled a bit.

"Why waste money on a laboratory analysis when you have Earl around," Luke said, to muffled laughter from the group. "Sorry, Earl, but we're taking a sample to the laboratory anyway. There might be something else in there that your taste buds don't know about. You need some water to wash that down?"

"Where does the treated groundwater get discharged after it goes through the carbon vessel?" Simone asked, changing the subject.

"The treated groundwater goes from here to the storm sewer, which discharges it into the ocean," Debbie said. "Chad takes the official confirmation sample every month to verify that the chlorobenzene concentration is less than the one part per billion limit agreed to in our federal surface water discharge permit."

"That's like finding one red ping pong ball in two Olympic-sized swimming pools filled with white ping pong balls," Chad said, with his gleaming smile.

Antoine and Simone were nodding, and Luke could see Debbie doing the math quickly in her head to determine if Chad was correct.

"Thanks for that visual, Chad. I can't say I have thought about parts per billion like you just did," Luke said.

Eventually, the tour and questions ended, and the conversation drifted toward dinner arrangements and tomorrow's schedule. "Debbie and I have dinner with Caroline and Bob to prepare for tomorrow's meetings. The client sets the schedule, you know? So, let's have drinks tomorrow night, after the public meeting. We'll probably have a lot to talk about then," Luke said, with a grin.

Luke pulled Earl aside, while Antoine and Simone drove away from the site. "What do you think of these EPA folks, Earl?"

"They seemed interested and asked good questions. Antoine seems pretty level-headed and pragmatic. Simone seems to know her chemistry, plus she's kind of cute," the older man said, winking.

"She's too young for you, Earl, but I agree."

***

Luke went back to his hotel room and cleaned up for dinner. He had a few minutes before meeting Debbie in the lobby and decided to call Kara. He liked to talk with her and the kids daily while traveling. After several rings, the phone was answered, "Graham residence, Claire speaking."

"Claire, it's Luke. I was looking for Kara."

"Oh, hi, Luke. Kara called, said she had a client dinner, and asked if I could babysit the kids. Fortunately, I was open."

"This must have been a last-minute thing?"

"Yeah, some client dinner. Kara thought it would go until nine or ten tonight."

"Oh, okay. I'm glad that worked out for you. You must

not be watching your grandchildren tonight. Can I speak to Nathan?"

After a few muffled sounds, Nathan came on the line. "Hi, Dad. Claire's making us dinner, and we're going to watch a movie. When are you coming home?"

"I'll be back Wednesday. How's Kaylie doing?"

"She's good. Dad, you're not going to get cancer like Ms. Samuelson, are you?"

"I'm not going to get cancer, Nathan." Luke frowned. His son had become preoccupied with this fear over the past few days. He assumed it was a natural reaction, given Angela's recent death, but it was disconcerting all the same. "Everyone's okay. Don't forget to let Columbo out, and make sure he has some food."

"I will. See you, Dad." Click.

His son was not much for a conversation on the phone, but it made Luke happy to speak with him. Nathan had reminded him of Angela's passing, and Luke had yet to fully process his grief. But that would have to wait until this trip was over. Kara hadn't mentioned a dinner today, but it wasn't too unusual for her to have last-minute client meetings. The kids were in Claire's good hands.

Minutes later, Luke raced down the stairs to avoid the slow elevator and met Debbie, who was waiting for him in the lobby. "You're going to love this restaurant, Debbie. It's on the marina in Redondo Beach and has awesome seafood. It's Bob Burrow's favorite place and he somehow always gets the best table."

The drive was short, and Luke and Debbie arrived at the restaurant located just a few miles from the former DDT plant. Luke paused in the parking lot to admire the view of the ocean and the setting sun. He saw the smile on Debbie's face and watched as she took a deep breath of the ocean air blowing onshore from the west. Surfers were riding the final waves of the day. The restaurant was crowded with a boisterous, well-dressed clientele and colorful drinks. Luke couldn't understand how they all afforded such a lavish lifestyle on a work night. They must be on expense accounts like him or had jobs that paid more.

The hostess escorted Luke and Debbie to the corner table where Bob Burrows and Caroline Woodson sat. Bob and Caroline had flown in from Boston, home to Guadalupe's headquarters. Luke was glad that Rudy Gallegos had also arrived, and he and Bob were already working on martinis. Bob looked relaxed, wearing an untucked short-sleeved shirt and khaki cotton pants with Top-Siders. Caroline was sitting next to him with a glass of white wine and a confident smile on her face. She wore her favorite beige blazer and light-weight wool pants with black, low-heeled pumps that reinforced her executive role at Guadalupe.

"Debbie, this is Caroline Woodson, vice president of environmental management," said Luke. "I'm sure you have seen her name on various documents. Caroline is Bob's supervisor and responsible for every environmental legal case against Guadalupe. I don't think you two have ever met in person."

"Great to meet you, Debbie. I've heard wonderful comments about your work and the groundwater treatment facility. I'm glad y'all can join us tonight," Caroline said, in her charming Southern accent.

"It's great to meet you and be here, participating in everything," said Debbie. "This is nice. I could get used to California."

"I still prefer Atlanta. That's where I come from. Fourth generation. The pace is a bit slower than out here. I received my law degree from Emory, and someday I hope to retire back there," Caroline said.

"How long have you been with Guadalupe, Caroline?" Debbie asked.

"Since 1980. I worked for a regional law firm in Atlanta for about ten years after I passed the bar and got tired of watching less competent men get promoted to partner ahead of me. So, I went to work on the other side of the table and became their client." Caroline gave Debbie a look of satisfaction. "Oh, here I am, dating myself again. Tell me more about yourself."

"I was born in Riverton, Wyoming, and spent the first ten years of my life there. Not too exciting, and I'd rather not retire there. My parents were both engineers in the oil and gas business. No surprise I became an engineer, huh?" Debbie said, with a small snort in her laugh. "The oil business was in bad shape when I was in college, but the environmental business was taking off, so I studied a lot of environmental science and went to work in that industry. That's how I got hired by Webber."

The arrival of a calamari appetizer cut their conversation short, and they all began to eat.

Luke decided to get to the business discussion before the next round of drinks and food arrived. Bob and Caroline were on East Coast time, and he knew he would lose his audience soon. "The EPA liked our treatment facility and gave us kudos for getting it up and running, but they want it to be expanded to treat about ten times the current volume and make a material impact on removing the chlorobenzene and DNAPL source," said Luke. "I explained why we didn't want to pump groundwater faster and potentially worsen contamination of the deeper aquifers, but they kept pushing. We never discussed the cost increase of a bigger treatment system, and I never brought it up."

Caroline interrupted Luke in an uncharacteristically loud voice, "Luke, you need to make damn sure that EPA doesn't give us a Unilateral Administrative Order and require anything more than what we are already doing. We have a limited budget from our insurance company, who is paying, you understand."

Luke had an immediate flashback to higher-ups in the Navy with inferiority complexes, who were empowered by the rank on their shoulders and the alcohol in their bloodstream. He leaned into the group at the table and responded directly to Caroline. "I'll handle it, Caroline. I am sure that Antoine is getting pressured to do more and move faster. We'll talk and find common ground. We always have."

Caroline smiled at Luke and waved at the waitress.

"Just so everyone knows, I saw Brooke Burr in the lobby of the Hilton when I was checking in," Bob said, changing the subject. "For those who don't recognize the name, she founded Environmental Freedom & Justice, a nonprofit, environmental legal activist organization. She started it about ten years ago and has made Guadalupe a target. We first heard of her in the late seventies, when she was an activist with Environmental Life Force. 'ELF,' as they were known then, used incendiary devices to burn up crop duster airplanes parked on tarmacs overnight. She worked with the guy who later formed Earth First."

"At least a decade ago, Brooke was arrested outside of our pesticide manufacturing plant in Louisiana, when she chained herself to the plant's front gate," said Caroline. "It was one of those long, heavy-duty, industrial sliding gates. Somebody activated the gate, and it started to open with her chained to it.

Lucky for her, a security guard stopped the gate, or she might have had her arm ripped off by the fence post."

"A month later, our plant superintendent went missing and was presumed dead. His fishing boat ran into an offshore oil platform about five miles from Port Fourchon, with a fishing line in tow and no one onboard," said Bob. "If the boat hadn't hit the goddamn platform, it might have gone out in the Gulf until it ran out of fuel. There was an extensive search for his body, and finally, it floated to the surface. The authorities concluded he fell off the boat and drowned. There were rumors that some protestors, including Brooke, may have had something to do with it, but no charges were ever filed."

Bob took a slow sip of his martini, and Caroline jumped in to finish the story of Brooke. "We lost track of her for several years, then learned she earned her environmental law degree from Lewis & Clark Law School in Oregon. From there, she went to a big, nonprofit environmental law firm in San Francisco before breaking out on her own and starting EF&J. I suspect she is in the hotel because she plans to attend our public meeting tomorrow night. She could upset the apple cart."

"That's the first I've heard about EF&J. What do they focus on, besides taking out chemical company executives?" Rudy asked.

"I think they focus on taking out consultants too," Bob said, tipping his glass at Rudy.

Caroline smiled at Bob and said, "To answer your question, Rudy, EF&J desires to eliminate virtually all synthetic pesticides from our food chain, especially organochlorides like DDT. They have three or four attorneys that are experts with FEPCA. That's the Federal Environmental Pesticide Control Act."

Debbie piped up, "I had to write a college paper on FEPCA in my environmental regulations class. FEPCA goes way back to the Federal Insecticide Act of 1910, and has been amended several times since. It requires EPA to monitor and update registered pesticides."

"That's impressive, Debbie. I'm beginning to like you more and more. Have you ever thought about being a lawyer? It pays more than an engineer," Caroline said.

Luke and Rudy glanced at each other without saying a word. Luke knew Caroline believed lawyers ruled the world and no greater profession existed. She once commented to Luke that "anybody could do technical work because it's just formulas and calculations and doesn't require much intellectual thinking."

Why am I always working for an attorney or mid-level business person who makes more than me?

"These enviro companies print money by showing pictures of sick birds and dead fish. It tugs at people's heartstrings and brings in more dough for the attorneys to live on—and I say that as an attorney," Bob said. "Then, those same attorneys file lawsuits and slow everything down. They have the patience of saints. I remember one enviro company that killed a land development project when I was a contractor in that business. I needed to use dynamite to break up a granite outcrop, and this attorney brought it all to a screeching halt by filing a lawsuit saying it was the mating season of a rabbit that was an endangered species several miles away. I couldn't believe it! The science was flimsy at best, and the comment period would take years, so we finally just gave up and went elsewhere."

The waitress returned to the table to take everyone's order. Luke ordered salmon, and Bob ordered the California spiny lobster special. "Luke, the lobster is superb here; you should try it," he said.

"Salmon sounds better tonight. My wife, the marathoner, says I need the Omega-3, and who am I to argue with her?"

Luke loved lobster but had his reason for not ordering it, which he didn't want to discuss at dinner. He'd learned recently that as many as fourteen million gallons of DDT-laced acid were legally dumped off the coast of Long Beach in the Santa Monica Basin between 1947 and 1961. Bob and Caroline had never mentioned Guadalupe's ocean dumping to the Webber team members but were surely aware of it. Luke would not consider eating crab or lobster from around Long Beach.

Bob winked at Luke. "I know they've released all kinds of crap about California ocean dumping in the fifties and sixties by Guadalupe," Bob said. "But I've been eating crab and lobster out of these waters for years." He shut his menu with a snap. "I say to hell with it. I'm getting the lobster!"

Rudy nodded his head. "Me too!"

But it didn't sway Luke away from his original choice. He was sticking with the Alaskan salmon.

Luke and Debbie returned to the hotel immediately after dinner, leaving Rudy and Bob to discuss football playoff projections. Luke wanted to prepare for tomorrow's meetings with the EPA and the public. It would be a long day, and he had said nothing to Caroline and Bob about the EPA's intent to lower the soil cleanup levels in the neighborhood. He thought it best to let Simone present this tomorrow instead of subjecting himself to Caroline's and Bob's wrath.

Luke thought about calling Kara, but it was getting late, and she was probably already asleep. Instead, he called Van.

"Hey, Russo, I need some help with people's background intel."

"I thought you would never ask, Rattler. Who is it? Tell me some more, and don't hold back on me."

"Can you do some digging on a woman named Brooke Burr and the Environmental Freedom & Justice organization? Things may be starting to heat up out here."

6

Rudy was the first person to enter the hotel conference room in the morning and begin setting up his presentation materials for the meeting with the EPA. Luke and Debbie arrived soon thereafter and offered to help. "I shouldn't have had that last martini," Rudy said, as he rubbed his temples. His necktie with a small stain was on the table, the knot already tied.

"Do you need another coffee?" Luke asked in a loud voice. "I'm going to get one."

"Please. This hotel coffee sucks. I just need to arrange the chairs how I want them, Luke. I've been doing hydrogeology presentations for years, and there is a certain way it needs to be done to keep the audience engaged." He filled a glass with cold water and chugged it down before arranging his maps on the table.

Antoine and Simone arrived a half hour later, followed by Bob and Caroline. After some tension-reducing small talk about the prior evening, Rudy said, "Let's get started. According to Luke's meeting agenda, I'm up first and will summarize the latest groundwater sampling results."

Rudy pointed at his map showing chlorobenzene concentration in groundwater near the former plant site and began the presentation he had practiced with the Webber project team. Since Antoine was relatively new to the project, Rudy decided to start at the beginning. "In the last twenty years, the 'plume' of chlorobenzene has traveled almost ten miles south of the former plant in the shallow aquifer toward the Pacific Ocean. In addition to chlorobenzene in the groundwater, the Consent Decree negotiated with the EPA defines other contaminants of concern, including 1, 2 DCA, DDD, and DDE. I know it sounds like toxic soup. These compounds are mostly the natural degradation products of DDT, and they're found at lower concentrations in the groundwater. Unlike chlorobenzene, which moves easily, these compounds don't travel as far."

"These compounds may be less prevalent and at lower concentrations, but how come we haven't been more focused on them?" Antoine asked.

"I agree that these compounds should be cleaned up. Our operating assumption has been that if we can clean up the chlorobenzene, which is the most prevalent compound, the other compounds will also be cleaned up, and then we'll…"

Antoine interrupted Rudy. "Why aren't you cleaning up the source area, where chlorobenzene concentrations are the highest? Can't you pump more groundwater out of the ground than you are now? As long as the source area exists, the chlorobenzene plume will keep moving until it hits the ocean. It seems like this could last forever."

"You're right. It will probably take thousands of years for the chlorobenzene to dissolve away on its own, but pumping it causes the pure chlorobenzene, or DNAPL, to migrate deeper, since it is heavier than water. Then, it could contaminate the clean drinking water aquifers below. We have yet to find a good solution. Luke and Debbie are working on a solution in the groundwater remediation feasibility study process," Rudy said.

He finished his presentation, and the group took a break for lunch, which included sack lunch sandwiches and a chocolate chip cookie. Luke and Debbie discussed groundwater remediation ideas, and the meeting continued into the afternoon. Finally, Luke closed one folder and reached for another. "If there are no more questions on the groundwater remediation feasibility study, let's move on to the soil sampling results."

Rudy stood up again and arranged his soil sampling maps on the table. "Here is the map of DDT concentrations in neighborhood soils from the sampling round two years ago. Samples were collected from residential yards where contaminated soil from the former plant was used for fill material during the residential development. We took five more soil samples in the last six months, so we have forty-six sample locations. You can see that the DDT concentrations in neighborhood soil samples are between one and a max of 143 milligrams per kilogram, which is lower than the 150 milligrams per kilogram cleanup objective. We recommend no further action regarding neighborhood soils."

Rudy collected his maps and sat down to take a long-awaited sip of his coffee and eat Debbie's cookie. Luke and Debbie were next on the agenda to discuss the groundwater treatment facility.

"Before we move on, Simone has some new information to present on the soil cleanup levels for DDT," Antoine said.

"Thanks, Antoine," said Simone. "As you all know, the cleanup level for DDT in residential soils has been 150 milligrams per kilogram since it was first established years ago. The EPA recently performed toxicology studies to determine if the cleanup level needs revision. We do this periodically to incorporate new epidemiological information. These studies include using rats and feeding them various concentrations of DDT to determine the LD50, the lethal dose of DDT at which 50 percent of the rats die quickly from eating the DDT. The LD50 measures acute toxicity, not to be confused with chronic, or long-term, toxicity. Think of something like cyanide, for example. If you swallow an LD50 dosage of cyanide, you may die instantly. If you take a much lower dose, you would probably be able to take that dosage every day for years and never die from cyanide poisoning. As we say in the toxicology business, 'the dose makes the poison.'"

Luke knew where Simone was going next with the new soil cleanup levels and the reaction she would surely receive from Bob and Caroline. Guadalupe was not going to take kindly to lower cleanup levels for DDT and the associated cost of more residential yard removals. He felt bad for allowing Simone to walk into the fire, but defending the EPA's policies was not up to him.

Simone continued, "Based on the LD50 of DDT on rats, we have determined, using widely accepted toxicological practice, that the new soil cleanup level for DDT in the neighborhood properties should be 50 milligram per kilogram instead of the previously determined 150 milligram per kilogram. Obviously, this will designate many of the residential yards as hazardous and require soil remediation. Do you have any questions?"

Luke admired Simone's confident and straightforward delivery. He was also impressed with her knowledge of human toxicology. She had come a long way since their days at college. He smiled as she concluded but knew she had unleashed a surprise attack on Guadalupe. *Maybe I should take a small dose of cyanide every day for the rest of my life so that I can prove a theory of human toxicology.*

There was a long pause in the room as Caroline and Bob

looked at one another in astonishment. Caroline spoke first. "Thank you for your presentation, Simone. That was well done, and it's clear that you know your subject matter. It appears that you, I mean the EPA, are recommending neighborhood soil be removed and replaced with clean soil because the concentration of DDT in the soil is now at a level that could, based on your new studies with rats, potentially cause risk to humans."

"That is correct," Simone said.

Bob finally closed his mouth and took a deep breath through his nose. "Simone, first of all, you presuppose that rats and humans are the same, toxic... toxicologic... toxicologically speaking, and that someone can precisely derive a soil cleanup level from an LD50 test. Secondly, we already know someone must ingest contaminated soil regularly for twenty or thirty years to receive a chronic dosage. I realize little kids may eat soil once in a while, but they aren't going to eat soil for thirty years because, at some point, they become adults, and adults don't eat dirt!"

Simone responded quickly. "You would be surprised how much dirt you inadvertently ingest every year, just by breathing dust and particulates in the air. It's not a pretty thought, but it's a lot. We have to come up with something to use as a cleanup level, and this is the best we can do."

"DDT is not considered a carcinogen. It's not even bad for humans," Bob said, waving his hands.

In an apparent attempt to get control of the meeting, Antoine said, "I know this all sounds like overkill, but we have new epidemiological studies that appear to tie increased levels of breast cancer to DDT exposure at an early age. More importantly, we must follow consistent methodology at every

Superfund site, or else we have no legitimacy for what we require the responsible parties to clean up."

Luke immediately thought of Angela. He had not heard of any recent studies potentially linking DDT to breast cancer. Maybe there was something to Gary's supposition about his daughter's cancer after all.

"Antoine, can we back up a minute, please?" asked Caroline. "It's never been confirmed that the DDT found in residential back-yards is attributed to fill material taken from the former plant site. Employees sprayed DDT in their yards of their own volition. As we have made clear to the EPA, Guadalupe is not responsible for DDT contamination when the homeowner willingly used it on his own property."

"We agree with you, Caroline. Guadalupe is not responsible for a homeowner's actions, but the distribution of DDT in the neighborhood is consistent with aerial photos showing the grading of fill material from the former plant site for housing development," said Antoine. "I will also add that we have reviewed the soil data more closely and found a second chemical called beta-hexachlorocyclohexane, or BHC. BHC is a byproduct of manufacturing the pesticide lindane, which was produced at the plant in the late fifties and early sixties. Lindane was not given to employees for personal use, and its concentration in the soil is consistent with DDT's. Therefore, the EPA has concluded that lindane and some of the DDT in the residential soils must have originated from the fill material from the former plant site."

Luke had seen the soil reports before and the presence of lindane, but he had never put the puzzle pieces together and concluded that fill material from the former plant site must have been used. He wondered if Bob and Caroline knew this all along.

Bob leaned back in his chair and crossed his big arms across his chest. "Okay, then. Based on the new information, what is the EPA recommending that Guadalupe do to take care of this situation?"

"Before I answer that, I have to tell you that the situation is worse than just high concentrations of DDT in the soil. During our field investigation, we found several large chunks of pure DDT buried in some backyards. If children had found these and either ingested or touched the DDT, it could have been very serious or even fatal. Therefore, the EPA is preparing an Administrative Order for Guadalupe to remove and replace the contaminated soil in the neighborhoods."

"You must be kidding," said Caroline, standing up from her chair with her hands outstretched. "We'll need to excavate forty or fifty homeowner yards and replace them with clean soil. That will cost millions of dollars, especially since the excavated soil is hazardous and must be disposed of properly. And what will we do with the residents during the cleanup?"

"The homeowners will need to be relocated to a hotel, or extended stay suite, for the duration of the removal action," Antoine said.

"It appears that there are still a lot of details to be ironed out," Caroline said, after an awkward silence. "We'll wait for a draft of the Administrative Order from the EPA and go from there. Will you have a draft soon?"

"We're working on it right now," said Antoine. "But as you know, there is not much 'draft' in an Administrative Order once the EPA's legal team approves it. It is usually final by the time you receive it."

"I assume we are not discussing removing residents' yards in tonight's public meeting, right?" Luke asked. "This action will undoubtedly set off the neighbors, and we're not yet prepared to discuss the removal of residential yards and the relocation of residents." He glanced around the table. The others, including Simone and Antoine, nodded in agreement. "With that said, I suggest we end our meeting now and find our way over to Van Kirk Elementary School. It's about twenty minutes away. The public meeting starts at six, and we need to get set up beforehand."

***

Luke, Rudy, and Debbie squeezed into Luke's economy rental car and went through a drive-up a few blocks from the elementary school. Luke parked in the back of the parking lot so they could have a few minutes to eat and vent about what they had just heard from the EPA.

"I can't fucking believe this!" said Rudy. "Can you imagine people evacuating their homes for months while their yards are completely dug up and replaced? Hell," he said, gesturing toward the school building, "even this school will have to be closed for months. The DDT has been here for decades! This is so ridiculous. Simone and the toxicologists are so wrapped up in their science projects they can't see the practical side of this. Groundwater is what we ought to be focused on. It's a much bigger problem in the LA basin than the soil. The chance of getting cancer from drinking tap water or breathing air pollution next to the freeway around here is so much higher than sniffing or eating dirt. Have fun explaining this to the residents, Luke."

"Why should I have to explain it to the homeowners?" said Luke. "This is the EPA's problem. We're the ones who think it's overkill."

"Are you kidding? Because you are the project manager, Luke," Rudy said, shaking his head.

"Have you guys met Jimmy Mendoza?" Debbie asked.

"I remember the name. What about him?" Luke said, exhibiting interest as he navigated to the elementary school.

"He's the paving contractor who did some work for us at the groundwater treatment facility. Jimmy's kind of a community leader. He lives down the street in one of the nicer houses with a well-kept yard. He can be a bit of a badass, intimidating guy. I can only assume he probably won't like having his yard dug up." She tapped a finger against her chin. "Maybe Chad can help us with Jimmy. They hung out a lot when Chad helped with the construction of the treatment facility. Jimmy would be a key guy for us to get on our side, if we can."

"We're going to need all the help we can get to make this acceptable to the homeowners," said Rudy. "That is, if it happens. These things have a way of getting delayed or canceled after everyone gets bent out of shape. We'll see."

The three gobbled their fast food and left Luke's rental car to enter the main door of the elementary school. Luke saw Earl and Chad waiting at the front door. He asked them to help move chairs and tables around the cafeteria and greet attendees as they arrived. Earl was a natural at this and knew many of the residents. Luke noted the older man had brought several packages of cookies and a case of plastic water bottles. It was enough, but not too much. When hungry and waiting for dinner, attendees were less inclined to stay around and ask questions.

After the tables and chairs were arranged in the cafeteria and Earl and Chad were stationed at the front door, Luke walked through in his mind what would happen next. He watched as the parking lot and street started to fill up, faster than he expected. Cars were showing up earlier than usual for a routine public meeting. Several people had gathered outside in small groups. He watched a large Hispanic man with a larger-than-life personality, who he thought was Jimmy Mendoza, walk in with a few friends and immediately start chatting with Earl and Chad. Jimmy's arms were crossed across his large chest, and he wore a frown on his bearded face. Luke decided to join the conversation.

"Hey Jimmy, Luke Graham. I think we met last year at the treatment facility. How are you?"

The man turned his angry eyes in Luke's direction. "I'm good, Luke, but I'd be better if I wasn't being forced to move out of my house and have my yard ripped up. I put a lot of work into that yard, you know? But other than that inconvenience, I'm doing great. How about you?"

Earl and Chad looked at each other, then at Luke. He read the confusion in their faces. Obviously, the EPA's recommendation to clean up neighborhood soils had been leaked. Luke wasn't entirely surprised. His Navy experience had taught him the value of secrecy and the reality of leaks. He decided to try bluffing. "What are you talking about, Jimmy?"

Jimmy cocked his head to one side. "Don't act dumb, Luke. Everybody knows that the EPA wants to dig up our neighborhood while they screw around moving dirt from here to there. Don't get me wrong, the Torrance Suites is kinda nice, with their happy hour and free snacks, but I'd rather live in my own home."

"That's what we want, too, Jimmy. The EPA thinks and talks big, but it's not a done deal until the ink is on the paper, and that may never happen. This is just the normal course of regulatory sausage-making. We'll see where things go in the next six months," Luke said.

He didn't bother to ask Jimmy about his sources of information. It must have happened a few days ago for the attendees to be so well informed. It must have come from someone in the EPA.

Hoping he had diffused the situation, at least for the short term, he returned to the sign-in table and noticed that Brooke Burr and Amy Nunez had signed in. He looked at the women sitting in the audience, wondering which ones might be Brooke and Amy. Bob had told him that Brooke focused on avian and aquatic species. Soil contamination in a neighborhood was not her focus. So why was she here?

Luke stepped out into the hall and walked to an empty second-grade classroom. He took out his cell phone and dialed Van's number from memory. His friend answered after the first ring. "Hello, Van here."

"Russo. It's Luke. What did you find out about Brooke Burr? She's here with another woman, Amy Nunez."

"Man, she's definitely an activist. A smart one, and, by the looks of her most recent picture, good-looking too. She founded Environmental Freedom & Justice in '88, after getting a law degree from Lewis & Clark in '83. They've produced quite a few environmental attorneys. Before all that, she was part of Earth First! and did some activist type things that got her in legal trouble. Based on some of her law enforcement records, she has no regrets and is proud of her activist work. Oh, yeah, she seems to focus on the peregrine falcon and the bald eagle popula—"

Luke cut him off. "The peregrine falcon was the biggest ecological problem resulting from DDT. Eggshells from the exposed falcons were too thin and broke when the mother sat on them. They were almost extinct before DDT was banned. So, this makes sense to me now. Brooke is focused more on the ecological side of DDT than the human health side. Can you get me some intel on Amy Nunez? I need to know what her role is in all of this. She looks mean and mad at the world. Thanks, Russo. You're part of the team now!"

7

As Luke walked down the hall toward the cafeteria, he noticed the local TV station van parked outside. Who had called the media? It was probably either Jimmy Mendoza or the EPA employee who had leaked the soil removal plan in the first place. Someone from Guadalupe would have to talk to the reporter and get ahead of the coming crisis. Speaking to the media was against Webber's corporate policy unless Nancy approved it in advance. Of course, he could always plead his innocence and claim the press had cornered him, forcing him to make a comment or appear complicit. He'd been interviewed many times while in student government in college. He'd always enjoyed the challenge, equating it to a verbal chess game.

Antoine and Luke made their way to the stage in the front of the cafeteria as attendees continued to file in. Luke saw fifty-one names on the list, and several intentionally didn't sign in. Attendees stood in the back, and the room grew louder with every new entrant.

Antoine called the meeting to order and asked everyone to stand and recite the pledge of allegiance. Luke thought it was his way of getting everyone's attention and admired the way it worked. Antoine then made introductions and briefly walked through the agenda.

Somebody shouted from the back of the room. "I don't see anything on the agenda about evacuating me from my house. Are you guys going to talk about that?" A few others in the audience voiced their agreement, and the murmuring in the room became louder. Antoine raised his hands to get control of the meeting.

"Let me answer the question. Please be quiet so I can answer the question. We were not planning to address soil cleanup tonight because the EPA is still evaluating the potential risks to the residents and whether or not any cleanup is necessary. I realize that some of you may not be aware of what I am referring to, so I suggest we add time at the end of the meeting to open the floor for public comments. We'll let anyone wanting to speak three minutes of uninterrupted time. Let's return to the agenda so we are not here all night. I'll turn the meeting over to Luke Graham with Webber Environmental, who is leading the investigation and cleanup of the site for Guadalupe Chemical."

Luke introduced Rudy, who presented the results from the latest round of quarterly groundwater sampling, which drew little interest from the audience. Debbie followed with a description and pictures of the groundwater treatment facility that appeared to meet with more interest yet only drew a few questions from the audience.

"Ma'am, do you know how much DDT is in the groundwater you are pumping?"

Debbie glanced in Earl's direction before replying, "We are still waiting on formal laboratory analyses of samples from the groundwater. The results will tell us the concentration of DDT. However, we have empirical data indicating a substantial amount of DDT in the piping and the groundwater." Earl smiled at Debbie and winked.

Antoine cleared his throat. "If there are no more questions for Debbie, I recommend we give you some background on the residential soil contamination issue before we allow time for public comments. Keep in mind that we are not prepared to go into an exhaustive discussion of the issue at this time, but we want to give you some background in light of all the concerns. I'll let Simone briefly describe the new toxicology results on DDT that the EPA has obtained."

Simone gave the attendees the same toxicology background she had detailed at the EPA meeting earlier in the day. There were mixed reactions from the attendees in the room when she presented rat testing and LD50 results. Several people gasped when she revealed the lethal doses of DDT and preliminary indications of increased breast cancer cases. Others shook their heads and chuckled.

A woman in the front row stood, pulled a piece of paper from her purse, and began reading. "Ms. Delgado, thank you for being here. I have a question for you. I have read that DDT can cause breast cancer in women, like you just said. My mother died last year from a long battle with breast cancer, and I am now more and more convinced that she got it from the manufacturing plant. How can I be sure that this plant caused her cancer?"

Luke glanced over at Bob and Caroline. They sat stoically in their chairs, and Luke hoped they both continued to hold their tongues. There was little they could say or do to favor their case at such a public meeting. If the conversation needed to go in another direction, it would be best if Luke stepped in and did it, since he was neither an EPA nor a Guadalupe employee.

"First of all, I am sorry for your loss," said Simone. In her career with the EPA, Luke knew she'd often answered questions like this and knew she could handle herself. "It's challenging to determine why someone gets cancer, especially breast cancer, because that can be caused by so many different environmental exposures, as well as basic genetics. With all cancers caused by chemical sources, there has to be an exposure pathway. Namely, you'd have to be exposed to DDT through inhalation, ingestion, or dermal contact. Now, we know DDT is not easily absorbed through the skin. It usually enters the body through the ingestion of contaminated food. I don't know the specifics of your mother's situation, but I would happily talk with you after the meeting. Did your mother live in the area?"

"My mother lived in Fresno, but she came to visit quite often. She must have been exposed at my house, though."

Luke knew Simone had family farmland near Fresno, and DDT had been widely used there for many years. There were many questions about the woman's mother: Where did she live? Did she work on a farm? Did she smoke or have other risk factors tied to breast cancer? Simone, ever the consummate professional, knew better than to go down this path in a public forum.

She ended the exchange and passed the meeting back to Antoine. "Before we go to public comment, let me just say that the EPA will likely perform more soil sampling in the area to get an accurate determination of the locations of high DDT concentrations. This sampling will determine if, or how much, soil will need to be excavated and replaced to protect your health."

***

It was time for public comments. Antoine reiterated that anyone in the audience was allowed three minutes of uninterrupted time to comment on the investigation and cleanup of the site and that all comments would be included in the official record. "Please state your name, address, and occupation before your three minutes begins," Antoine said.

Jimmy Mendoza was the first to step forward, followed by four others, who formed a line behind him, waiting their turns to speak. He cleared his throat and looked directly at Antoine and Luke. "I'm Jimmy Mendoza, and I own Mendoza Paving and Concrete. I live at 1350 204th Street. I heard the EPA recommends that our yards be dug up and replaced with 'clean' dirt. First, I want to know if this is true, and if it is true, when will this happen, and how will I be compensated?" Jimmy continued, his voice booming. "I've lived in my house for over thirty years and raised three healthy kids. My wife and I are both as healthy as can be expected for people our age, and it makes no sense to me that our yard needs to be dug up and replaced. I don't know anyone in the neighborhood who's had cancer in the last ten years other than Bobby Carr, but hell. He smoked three packs a day for his entire life and died of lung cancer. As far as I know, he didn't eat any dirt from his yard." Jimmy pulled in a lungful of air. "I work with big trucks all day, and I can't imagine dump trucks driving up and down our streets all day. The dust and traffic hazards alone are huge. Has anyone at the EPA thought about that?"

Antoine looked at his watch that he had removed from his wrist and displayed prominently on the table.

Jimmy continued, almost ranting. "If you're gonna move me out of my house, it better be somewhere nearby and convenient. My wife and I have a business to run. And you better re-landscape it too. I spent thousands of dollars making my yard look nice over the years. My neighbors can vouch for that." Jimmy looked around, prompting a few nods. "It's the stupidest thing I have ever heard of." Jimmy pointed a finger at both Antoine and Luke. "Don't be surprised if some heavy equipment breaks down or ends up in Mexico."

Luke glanced at Debbie and Rudy. *How the hell did I end up in the middle of this action? It's the EPA's decision, not mine.*

The next twenty minutes was filled with similar speeches from Jimmy's neighbors and friends. When the line to speak dried up, Antoine asked if anyone else had comments to present. After a moment, the woman in the front row rose again and reluctantly approached the podium.

"Hello, my name is Jennifer White, and I live across the street. I am an Administrative Assistant at Hughes Aircraft. As I said earlier, my mother died of breast cancer last year. I am very concerned that this area is polluted with DDT and is a health risk to me and my children. I think the EPA, or whomever—maybe Guadalupe Chemical—should clean up the soil, since we all know DDT is in it. My mother was a wonderful person. She always cared for me, and watching her die slowly of cancer for all those years was painful for me and the family. DDT was obviously the cause of her cancer, and I am afraid it will kill me someday."

Jimmy stood up. "Jennifer, with all due respect, you're afraid of your shadow half the time! I'm surprised you ever leave your house."

For a moment, Luke thought Jennifer might cut and run, but after a steadying breath, she held her ground.

"You know, Jimmy, you are always the one bullying us around. Just because you're on City Council, you think you can rule the world and tell us what to do. I'm tired of it, and I want my property cleaned up."

Others in the audience started mumbling approval for what Jennifer was saying. Luke shot Antoine a pointed look when Jimmy moved toward the microphone again.

"Okay, everybody, let's have some order in here and get back to public comments," Antoine said, raising his hands. "You can take these conversations outside after the meeting, if you promise to be civil with one another." Jimmy turned and sat down in his chair.

A man named Keith Cole stepped up and introduced himself. "As a residential real estate broker, I'm concerned about our property values. Try selling your house with contamination in the yard. I helped my neighbor, Roger, sell his house last year, and he had to disclose that his property was contaminated with DDT and that he knew it. He said the DDT levels were safe, based on what the EPA folks told him. That probably helped him sell it, although he had to reduce his price. But, if I understand Ms. Delgado correctly, our yards are now considered to be unsafe. Each of us would have to disclose that to a buyer if we attempted to sell our houses. It's the law. So, I believe we have no choice but to have the yards removed and replaced, whether we believe them to be contaminated or not. I'll be the first volunteer. That's all I have to say." Keith turned and sat down.

The ensuing eruption of chatter threatened to end the meeting. Luke was surprised by the number of homeowners who supported removing their yards and replacing them with clean soil. The comments about perceived health risks and improved real estate values made sense to him, although he had to walk the line between Guadalupe and the residents professionally. But, despite the uptick in support from the homeowners, the anger in Jimmy's eyes told Luke the man wasn't about to go quietly. Once again, Luke found himself as a peacekeeper, but this time he wasn't in uniform.

***

Antoine's commanding voice quieted the room. A few attendees had slipped out the back door, but most of the crowd remained intact.

"Are there any more comments from anyone?" Antoine said. "If not, we can adjourn."

"I have a comment to make." In the back of the room, a woman rose and walked confidently to the podium in stylish jeans and a tight, white blouse that highlighted a nice figure. Swinging her long brunette hair back over her shoulder, she flashed a brilliant smile and held the microphone close to her mouth.

"My name is Brooke Burr, and I live in San Francisco."

Uh-oh. Luke kept his expression professional as he waited to hear what the environmental activist had to say.

"I am the founder and owner of Environmental Freedom & Justice, an environmental advocacy firm. It is a travesty that, over the course of many years, Guadalupe Chemical recklessly contaminated your neighborhood and has yet to clean it up. I have been involved personally in the negotiations and cleanup of numerous Superfund sites around the country, just like this one, and it is usually the stakeholders—all of you in this room—who are the ones that pay the price in so many ways."

Brooke turned the full force of her gaze on Bob Burrows. "Everyone here must hold Guadalupe responsible for its past and present actions. From day one, they have shown a complete disregard for human health and the environment. You also need to ensure the EPA takes immediate action and that legal maneuvers by Guadalupe don't go on forever, which is a strategy that most complicit companies take."

"Hold on a minute, missy," Bob said, shaking his head. "We've been working on this site for many years, and we would be much further along if it weren't for you and other environmental 'advocates' who keep filing frivolous lawsuits and slowing down the investigation and cleanup process. Why don't you let the people in this room decide how they want to move forward, instead of telling them what to do? You can't just walk in here—"

In his usual, calm voice, Antoine interrupted, "That's enough for now, Bob. Ms. Burr has the floor for the remainder of her three minutes."

Luke smiled to himself. He was now one up on Bob. The man should have kept his mouth shut, and Luke wouldn't hesitate to remind him of this outburst when the time was right.

Brooke gave Bob an exaggerated wink before continuing her comments. "What Guadalupe has not disclosed to any of you today is the massive offshore pollution this manufacturing plant has caused. It's only a few miles from here. They have also failed to accurately inform you of how much of our country's farmland is polluted with DDT and its impact on the environment and your health. This pollution has now contaminated our food supply, which causes more harm than living on contaminated soil under our grass."

Brooke switched the mic to her other hand. Unlike Bob, whose face had flushed to an angry red, she appeared cool, calm, and collected. "For twenty years, Guadalupe discharged DDT waste down the sewer to the treatment plant in Carson City, where it was eventually discharged into the Pacific Ocean via a pipe about one mile from the shore of the Palos Verde

Peninsula. According to several researchers, DDT has polluted an area around that pipe that's about the size of San Francisco. In addition to the sewage outfall, Guadalupe has disposed of at least five hundred thousand barrels of DDT and acid off the coast and in the deeper water off the Palos Verde Shelf. Thanks to Guadalupe and other companies, this area has become a chemical dumping ground.

My point in being here tonight is to make sure you know who you are dealing with. Guadalupe will continue to deceive you and do as little as possible regarding the site's cleanup. They will express their economic pain and how they don't have enough money to do what is necessary and right. They will argue that the benefits of DDT outweigh the costs to the environment and human health, and on and on. With that, I will stop. Feel free to talk with me after the meeting. Thank you for listening, and enjoy the rest of your evening," Brooke finished in a charming voice.

Antoine leaned forward into his mic again. "Please be advised that the previous comment regarding offshore contamination of DDT is not part of the Guadalupe Superfund site effort that we are discussing tonight. The offshore contamination is being investigated under another action by the EPA," he said. "Since our comment time has expired and no one else is in line to speak, this meeting is now adjourned."

Luke gathered his notes and materials and watched as the young television reporter and her cameraman approached Caroline. He didn't envy that conversation. Haewon Lee, whom he'd seen several times on the local news, was a tenacious young reporter who wasn't afraid of asking tough questions. It was clear she was adept at moving quickly through a crowded room, utilizing her smile and petite size. Her cameraman, who appeared to double as her bodyguard, could not keep up with her. Luke was interested in Caroline's responses, but several attendees were waiting to ask him questions.

The next half hour flew by. When Luke headed to the parking lot, he was talked out. Small groups still lingered between the handful of cars. As he passed, Luke heard snatches of conversation. Some discussed the removal action, while others went on about next week's high school football game.

Jimmy was waiting for him near the rental car. "Luke, you need to stop this goddamned insanity. Digging up yards is crazy. You know as well as I do the health risk is non-existent, no matter what that illogical, arrogant EPA woman says."

Luke ran a hand through his hair. He was tired and hungry and should just walk away. But something about the man's manner got the better of him. "Jimmy, just let the EPA clean up your yard. After some inconvenience, you'll be better off at the end of the day. The value of your house will be higher, and the DDT will be a non-issue in the future."

Jimmy stared hard into Luke's eyes. "You're either with us or against us. You need to decide. If you are not with us, get the hell out of the way, or we'll get you out of the way."

Jimmy turned and stormed away. Luke stood, car keys in hand, and pondered the man's threatening words. Jimmy was a hothead. Did it go any further than that? He was still wondering when Rudy and Debbie joined him a few minutes later.

"Time for a debrief at the bar," Rudy said.

"I second that," Luke said and unlocked the car.

8

uke returned to his hotel room to make two calls before meeting the others in the bar. "Russo, how's it going? I know it's getting late in Denver, but I also know you never sleep. Brooke Burr gave a three-minute comment that was the best comment of the evening. I must say, she's good at her game. She's attractive, convincing, and can command an audience. Kinda comes off as arrogant to me, though. I'm not sure how to read Amy Nunez. Like I said before, she seems intense and a bit out there. I get the impression that Brooke doesn't let her talk."

"I found some arrest records on Amy," said Van. "She has several arrests for civil disobedience at environmental protests. She's done a lot of community service. She's probably good at picking up trash on the highway. What I found most concerning was her arrest last year for breaking and entering a chemical storage and disposal facility in Louisiana. The police searched her car and didn't find anything stolen, but they found some C-4 explosive residue. That's an impressive report for ordinary police officers because they don't usually run across C-4 or, for that matter, even know what it is. Brooke helped with her legal problems, so we know they've been working together. Amy was ultimately convicted of misdemeanor criminal trespass and did some jail time, but overall, she's gotten off light, considering her criminal history. The C-4 residue raised some concerns and put her on the FBI watchlist. C-4 is such a high-powered explosive that it isn't often used outside the military. It's usually not good when someone has access to it."

Luke whistled. "What's Amy doing with C-4? Is she looking to blow up a bulldozer? She wants our cleanup work to take place." He shook his head. "No, I'm just not worried about Amy, Russo. She's a nobody. My bigger concern is Jimmy Mendoza, one of the neighborhood residents. He was threatening me for not taking a stand against soil removal. He's an opinionated, angry kind of guy, and he worries me."

"Sounds like you're starting to have some fun now, Luke," Van said.

"But why threaten me? I'm just an environmental consultant—the guy in the middle of everybody else, trying to do what my client wants me to do and earn a living in the process. If you're going to threaten someone, you should threaten Bob. He makes the decisions for Guadalupe and pushes the legal limits."

"Luke, it's not smart to threaten attorneys," said Van, laughing. "Believe me, I've tried. Threatening you, on the other hand, makes all the sense in the world. You have the ear of the EPA and Guadalupe and can influence both of them, which you are good at. Watch your back. I'll check into Mendoza for you. You're going to introduce me to this guy, right? It's fun to go on the offensive and turn the tables on pricks like him."

Luke hung up and made his next call. "Hey Babe, how are you? How are the kids?"

"We're all okay. The kids had a good day at school. How are you?" Kara asked.

"I just got out of a public meeting that wasn't what I expected, and it got a little out of control. Caroline was interviewed by KKAT, the local TV station. I never even thought the press would be here." Luke decided to keep Jimmy Mendoza's threat and Van's briefing to himself.

"That sounds exciting. When are you back tomorrow? I need to get my training run in. I get behind when you are on these trips."

"I have a morning flight, but I need to run by the office on the way home. I can probably leave early and get home around five. Does that work?"

"That would be great. I'll see you tomorrow. Love you."

"Love you too," Luke said.

Luke laughed as he set the phone down. It wasn't hard to figure out how their son got his dislike of phone conversations. Kara never stayed on for more than three minutes, tops.

He checked his email for anything urgent and headed to the hotel bar.

***

Luke walked into the bar and looked for the others. He found Antoine and Debbie sitting beside each other in the dark corner of the hotel bar, drinks in hand, enjoying themselves—perhaps a little too much—after the anxiety of the public meeting. The paneled walls and dim lighting made for an intimate setting.

"Oh, hi, Luke. What did you think of the meeting tonight?" Debbie said as Luke approached the table.

"I was going to ask you the same thing, Debbie, since it was your first public meeting. What was your impression?" Luke pulled a chair up to the table.

Debbie sat up and became serious. "I was surprised by the intensity of the audience and how everyone had a different opinion about the soil removal plan. It seems like no matter what we do, we'll be liked by some and hated by others. Honestly, it feels like a no-win situation. What do you think, Antoine? You go to these meetings all the time."

"This is par for the course," said Antoine. "I remember a project in San Diego, where a woman was convinced her husband had died of cancer from a Superfund site. There was no physical pathway for contamination in the air or groundwater that could have impacted her husband, but you couldn't change her mind. She brought a bag with dead plants from outside her kitchen and passed it around. We all took a whiff out of respect for her loss, but it was obviously a biological sewage smell, not a chlorinated solvent smell. I think she had a leak in her kitchen drainpipe, under the house's foundation. We empathized with her and agreed to take a few samples outside her home, by the kitchen, to verify our olfactory assessment. People usually calm down over time, and the issues fade away, but they never change their minds. This meeting was tense but not as bad as some. Occasionally, someone gets agitated and wants to tear your head off."

Simone arrived, looking more relaxed than she had during the meeting. Her hair was down, and she'd removed her suit jacket. She glanced around the dimly lit room. "Where's everybody else?"

"Bob and Caroline took the red eye back to Boston. They never like to stick around and waste the next day traveling," Luke explained. "Rudy might join us later, but he has another deadline he is working on."

The waitress finally came to the table and took Luke's and Simone's orders before flirting with the two single guys at the adjacent table. Luke was ready for the cold draft beer he'd ordered, and this delay was eating into his already short evening. Eventually, their drinks arrived, and each played back the meeting repeatedly, giving their impressions of the comments and attendees.

"Someone must have leaked the EPA's plan for soil removal," Simone said.

Luke wasn't sure if Simone was insinuating that he had leaked the information. He had only known about the lower DDT cleanup levels for a week, since his call with Simone, and he hadn't told anyone.

"I recently heard of the offshore dumping issue that Brooke Burr mentioned," said Luke. "It sounds like a big deal. Is it being investigated by the EPA?"

"Off the record, Bob and Caroline are well aware of the offshore dumping, and it's getting more and more attention within the EPA," said Antoine. "I told them it is now on the CERCLIS list and will become an official Superfund site someday. Brooke Burr was pretty accurate in her description of the number of barrels and where Guadalupe dumped them. Remember, it was legal to dump barrels of waste offshore for decades. However, the barrels were supposed to be dumped in the deeper water off the Palos Verdes Shelf. Disposal boat companies often went out at night and dumped the barrels much closer to shore to save fuel and labor costs. The boat hands would take hatchets and cut the barrels open so they would sink. So, most of the contamination is closer to shore than was ever intended."

"This is an interesting case. Isn't Guadalupe in the clear? I mean, it sounds to me like it's the disposal companies' fault because they dumped the waste, knowingly, in the wrong locations," Luke said.

"You're partially correct. Under Superfund, the disposal companies are PRPs, potentially responsible parties. However, Guadalupe cannot avoid liability since they manufactured the product. Good try, though, Luke," Antoine said, smiling.

Luke chuckled. "Okay. Just make sure the next time you talk to Caroline and Bob, you tell them I attempted to get Guadalupe out of the offshore problem," he said.

There was a part of Luke that was offended that he hadn't heard more about the offshore dumping, but he wasn't surprised. He'd learned, within a few short years of being an environmental consultant to Guadalupe, that he was told only what he needed to know. Yet, Caroline and Bob expected him to be one step ahead and always on the lookout for their best interests. He assumed it might be different if he was an actual employee of Guadalupe. This trip had confirmed his suspicions that the only way to stay ahead of his client was to rely on Van Russo's non-traditional methods of gathering information.

Simone and Debbie had started a side conversation about careers and the workplace, so Luke turned to Antoine. "How did you get into the EPA? Was this always your passion?"

"I don't know if it was my passion, but I was always interested in chemistry and saving the environment. My high school chemistry teacher suggested a degree in environmental science. So, I went to Cal State, Fullerton, and got one!" He grinned. "That's the short version, anyway. The California Department of Toxic Substance Control was hiring back then, and they offered me a job. Don't tell them I said this, but if you think the EPA is bad, just be glad this isn't a site administered by DTSC, or you would have to turn the entire residential area into a wildlife preserve."

"Did you grow up around here?" Luke asked.

"No, I grew up in Sacramento. My dad was a high school English teacher. I was taught the value of an education from day one, and my parents were strict. Probably because I was the second of four kids, and my older brother was a real fuckup. He ended up in prison. I became the senior sibling, so to speak."

"Whew, my upbringing was pretty tame, compared to that," Luke said. "So, do you expect this soil removal action to happen, or can Guadalupe shut it down?"

Antoine shrugged his wide shoulders. "There's always a chance, I guess, but I think it's procedural at this point. Caroline and Bob know this. The concentration of DDT in the soil is higher than the human health standard, so it qualifies as an emergency action by statute. Guadalupe will go through the motions to try to stop the removal, but I'm pretty certain it will move forward. They are probably on the plane right now, trying to figure out how to get their insurance carrier to pay for the removal and disposal of soil. You know damn well, Luke, that the EPA is not going to pay for it unless we are the absolute last resort."

Antoine and Debbie stepped away and went to play pool in the adjacent room. Luke thought about watching Debbie in action. Everyone at Webber knew she had grown up with a pool table in the house and was always eager for a game of pool if the opportunity arose at a party or bar. Luke also felt a paternal obligation to keep Debbie from falling prey to Antoine's good looks and charm. Still, their close friendship might pay dividends later with confidential information. After all, they were both single adults.

In the meantime, Luke finally had a chance to speak to Simone without the risk of being overheard. "It's wonderful to see you in person. You look as beautiful as ever. How's life treating you?" he asked.

"Thank you for the compliment," she said with a smile. "Life's going okay. It's just jam-packed, you know? Alison makes it a lot of fun, though. I enjoy being with her and watching her grow up. I must admit, going to work every day gets in the way."

"Did your husband ever ask you how you got that tattoo on your butt?" Luke asked, chuckling.

Simone shook a finger at him. "Listen. He thinks I got it in Mexico, while I was on spring break with a few sorority sisters. There are some things he doesn't need to know," she finished with a laugh.

Luke went to the bar for another round of drinks and asked to have one of the TVs tuned to KKAT. "Maybe we'll see Caroline on the ten o' clock news. I'd like to hear what she had to say. Speaking of soil removal, how did Jimmy Mendoza know about the plans to excavate and remove the residential soil?"

Simone arched a brow. "Are you accusing me of telling him what the EPA plans to do?" Her tone wasn't entirely playful.

"Nope, just asking. But somehow, Jimmy knew what was coming. Hell, I just found out last week from you. And, what's more, he knew details, which bothers me. There's a leak somewhere, and that can only cause us problems."

Simone sipped her draft beer. "Well, I can count on one hand the people I've told, and Jimmy isn't one of them."

Luke nodded. "Are you convinced that DDT is carcinogenic in humans? Has anyone ever studied the health of plant workers to see if there is elevated risk? Based on Earl's stories, he swam in the stuff back in the day, and he's never been sick a day in his life." He took a sip of his second beer. It was just as icy cold as the first. "Earl told me he had his liver biopsied and tested for DDT a few years ago. He volunteered for a study. The tests confirmed that the concentration of DDT in his liver is so high it qualifies as a hazardous waste. Now, that may be hyperbole, but Earl told me it was true and, what's more, he's quite proud of it. Someday, when he dies, the question will be, can he be buried or cremated legally, or will he be disposed of in a Class I landfill, or incinerated in a hazardous waste incinerator?"

They both laughed.

"I've met old-timers like him before that seem to live forever," Simone admitted. She finished another sip. "But, back to your question. At this point, the EPA relies on studies from other agencies or institutions, such as the National Institutes of Health. Like I said earlier today, there is epidemiological evidence to support higher rates of breast cancer in women, and insulin resistance in the children of those exposed to industrial quantities of DDT. One of the biggest problems we have researching the damn stuff is that it takes a long time to break down in the liver and our fat cells. It can take decades because it is such a stable molecule. I'm sure you and I have DDT in our bodies. In fact, I've read studies that show, during the widespread use of DDT, the average American had seven milligrams per kilogram of it in their body fat."

Luke didn't bother to hide his shock. "Good God. If we have that much DDT in our bodies, why are we worried about cleaning people's yards to less than 50 milligrams per kilogram? Shouldn't we be more worried about our food supply?"

Simone looked at Luke as though he had lost his mind. "That's not my specialty, Luke. That's a regulatory question. But to answer your original question, I don't think DDT is bad for the average person. Not when it's compared to many of the other twenty million organic molecules out there. DDT is an ecological problem. You do remember what happened to the peregrine falcon?"

That reminded Luke of Brooke Burr. "What do you know about all this offshore dumping of DDT and sulfuric acid? I'd never heard the details, or maybe I haven't been paying attention."

"Brooke Burr is an activist. She gets people fired up, sometimes to the point where they take extreme action. Having said that, the EPA has been studying the offshore dumping issue and trying to determine if DDT is a problem in marine life. We've measured DDT at elevated concentrations in fish off Palos Verdes. Those little fish that feed on the ocean floor are eaten by the bigger fish that we eat, so DDT still finds its way into our food supply."

"One more reason not to eat fish from around here," Luke said. "But if DDT is more of an environmental concern versus a human concern, where does that leave us?"

"If we can clean up places that we know are contaminated, then we should. If it's too difficult to clean up or a waste of social resources, like the offshore contamination, we may have to wait for the DDT that's out there now to naturally break down and disappear over time. The EPA has a lot of contaminated sites in this country, with all sorts of chemical contamination. It's all about prioritizing, Luke."

Luke pointed to the TV over the bar just as Haewon Lee's news segment began. "We'd better watch this."

HAEWON: "We are here at the Van Kirk Elementary School in Torrance for the public meeting on the cleanup of the former Guadalupe Chemical Company DDT manufacturing plant. The EPA informed the public tonight that most of this neighborhood I am standing in now will be scraped and cleaned because of toxic levels of DDT in the yards and houses. It appears that the EPA has changed its mind from years ago when it gave this area the green light that it was safe to live in. Let's listen in to some of the public comments."

The first clip was of the lady in the front row, teary-eyed over her mother's terminal breast cancer and her fear of living in the neighborhood. This was followed by a clip of Jimmy Mendoza ranting about bulldozers driving all over and massive dust clouds. Lastly, Brooke Burr's impassioned statement about the five hundred thousand barrels of DDT and acid dumped off Palos Verdes was aired. The news story then panned back to Haewon's interview with Caroline.

HAEWON: "I am here with Caroline Woodson, Vice President of Environmental Management for Guadalupe Chemical, who is in charge of the cleanup for Guadalupe. Ms. Woodson, what is your reaction to the meeting tonight and the fears from the neighbors about toxic levels of DDT in their yards?"

CAROLINE: "Thank you for the question, Ms. Lee. Being here tonight and listening to the neighbors' concerns is important. We take the comments very seriously. Guadalupe Chemical closed the plant in 1982, almost twenty years ago, and we have sampled this area extensively. The EPA determined there was no health risk to people living here from the former plant. Now, the EPA has changed its mind based on questionable science and says there is a slightly higher risk to residents, which requires extreme measures. We will discuss this with the EPA, and our very qualified team of scientists will look at the facts. Over the last twenty years, the DDT concentration in this area—and everywhere around the world, for that matter—has decreased every year, because DDT breaks down over time and essentially disappears. So, I question whether we should believe there are elevated risks to the residents here tonight."

HAEWON: "Ms. Woodson, can you tell us your plans to clean up the offshore contamination?"

CAROLINE: "As the EPA explained in tonight's meeting, the offshore issue has nothing to do with this neighborhood and the residents here. Like many other companies, Guadalupe legally dumped waste into the ocean for several years before the government banned offshore dumping in the late seventies. We supported the ban on offshore dumping and found ways to treat our waste at the plant because we believed it was the right thing to do."

The KKAT news anchor returned and moved to the next story about a surge in oil drilling activity in Long Beach.

Luke made a face. "Looks like you're the problem, Simone. You knew someone had to be the scapegoat, and it wouldn't be Guadalupe."

She shook her head. "As usual, I'm the bad girl, and you're the 'very qualified scientist.' I thought you were a Navy pilot. How did you get to be a 'very qualified scientist'?"

"I learned toxicology from you. I'll give you credit someday, I promise, but not yet."

Simone patted Luke's hand under the table and gave him a big smile. "I miss you, Luke. You keep me motivated in some strange way, and I want our friendship to last forever. Let's make sure we see each other again soon." She kissed him on the cheek, then stood up and walked away without looking back.

9

uke arrived at DIA and drove directly to his office. He again avoided the elevator and climbed the four flights of stairs, entering his office through the rear door. He was mad at himself for letting his cell phone battery die and immediately plugged it in and went to his voicemails. Listening to each, he deleted a few and prioritized the others. Caroline's voicemail was at the top of the list.

"Hi, Luke, Bob and I were talking on the way home last night, and we want you to delay this removal action as long as you can. Aside from the fact that it makes absolutely no sense to dig up and replace perfectly nice yards, the EPA will send us the bill and demand reimbursement. Our insurance company will balk, like always, and refuse to pay it, and lawsuits will start flying. Please have your team calculate how much you think this fiasco will cost. If we can't stall, we don't want the EPA to remove this soil without our oversight. They'll spend twice what it should cost and we'll get in a big fight over it. Put some thought into all this, and we'll talk tomorrow. We're counting on you, Luke, but if you are uncomfortable with this, we'll find someone else."

Then treat me like I'm on your team and quit threatening to replace me all the time. You could show some appreciation too.

Based on what Antoine had said at the bar the night before, the EPA would move forward on the soil removal action regardless of Guadalupe's desires. He thought he had a month or two, at least, before the EPA and Guadalupe agreed to a soil sampling plan, and the actual sampling would take another two months. Bidding and contracting with a removal contractor would take at least another two months. Any unknown delay would add another month. Luke relaxed, assuming the urgency would fade as usual, and continued to return calls.

***

He walked into his house a few minutes after four in the afternoon, feeling guilty for arriving late and leaving early to get home. Kara was dressed in her running gear and stretching by the front door. She kissed him on the cheek and was out the door. The kids were excited to see him, and he was happy to be home. They proceeded to tell him everything that happened in the last two days, and the ensuing chaos was enough to allow Luke to forget about his job for the moment.

Later, he and Kara relocated to the couch after the kids and Columbo were in bed. As he massaged Kara's calves and thighs, he ignored his email until the morning. After pouring two glasses of wine and flipping on the gas fireplace, Kara retrieved a blanket from the closet. They pulled the blanket over themselves and began to shed just enough clothing that a kid wouldn't overreact if they were seen.

After a restful night, Luke arrived at the office early and informed Nancy about the events in California.

"If EPA demands another round of soil sampling, Luke, we need to create the sampling plan and perform the work.

I'm sure we can be cheaper than EPA's subcontractor, and our sampling crews need work," Nancy said, with her usual concern for billable hours.

"I really can't make that pitch right now to Guadalupe because they want me to try and convince EPA that more soil sampling is unnecessary," Luke said.

"You need to learn how to do both, Luke. Argue with EPA, and then when they prevail and sampling has to happen, you moan and groan and demand to do the work," Nancy said with a grin. "That's how you do what Caroline wants and get the sampling work at the same time. It's a form of consulting art, Luke. You'll figure it out, and then you'll bring in loads of business."

Luke returned to his office to check his email and found a note from Van at the top of the list. "RESPOND ASAP" was all it said in the title block. A red exclamation point designated it as "urgent." Van regularly sent so-called "urgent" emails which could usually wait a day or two. However, Van's obsessive sense of urgency was one of his greatest strengths because he acted fast and never procrastinated.

Van picked up the phone before it rang, surprising Luke. "Hey, Russo, what's going on so early in the morning? Are you going to share some top-secret security stuff with me that I'll need to keep quiet about for the rest of my life?"

"Don't make jokes like that on an unsecured line, Luke. What I've learned is most important and relates directly to you and your family's safety."

Luke tensed. "Okay. Go."

"I dug deeper into Mendoza's past. He's done a lot of bad things, like assault and battery on his first wife. He spent some time in the slammer for that. I thought maybe he had gone to Vietnam and had PTSD, since he was born in '52, but he got lucky, and his number never came up. You'll love this, Luke. He was born on October 24 and was draft number 196. Everybody with a draft number before 196 was sent to Vietnam. Those with 196 or higher stayed home. He missed it by that much! Had he been born on October 25, he would have gone. Makes you think about a higher being calling the shots, huh?"

"Yeah. He's a lucky bastard for sure. What else? What makes him a threat to me and my family?"

"His business partner died about ten years ago in a paving accident. Fell into a hot asphalt tank. Mendoza was suspected of foul play in the case but never charged, and the case is still cold today. He took over the business after giving his partner's wife a lousy settlement for her half. Even better, Mendoza killed a guy in a bar about five years ago. Witnesses say the other guy started the fight, and Mendoza had to defend himself. He grabbed a broken beer bottle and cut the guy's throat. It was ruled self-defense, so he got off."

Luke forced his muscles to relax. Mendoza was a bona fide nasty dude, but he was several states away. "Sounds like I'd better not piss him off, huh? But Russo, how many consultants like me get thrown into a hot asphalt tank? I've never heard of it."

"I've never heard of consultants like you getting snuffed out either, but then again, there's a first time for everything. I'm going with you on your next trip to California, no matter what you say. You're going to need another set of eyes."

***

Luke woke early to see Kaylie standing in the doorway. It was 4:32 a.m. Luke was a light sleeper, and it didn't take much to wake him.

"Dad, my stomach feels funny."

"Are you going to be sick?"

"I don't know. I don't think so, but maybe."

Kara woke up while Luke led Kaylie toward the toilet, just in case. They didn't make it. Last night's dinner came up and spewed onto the carpeted floor. Kaylie began to feel better after a few minutes, and Luke took her back to bed while Kara cleaned up the carpet.

"I really need to go to the office today. I have a client coming in for a three-hour strategy session. Can you stay home with Kaylie? Hopefully, Nathan won't get sick too," Kara said as they climbed back into their bed for the remaining hour before the alarm rang.

"Sure, it should be a quiet day, and I can try out this new VPN system. It works with our internet and supposedly will let me log in to the office server, get my email, and move files around. We'll see if it works."

Once he'd seen Kara and Nathan off, and Kaylie was feeling better watching TV with Columbo, Luke settled into his home office in the unfinished basement bedroom. "Office" was a stretch—just an old wooden desk and folding metal chair. He planned to replace it with an ergonomic office chair but hadn't got around to it yet. Van worked at home most of the time and had a comfortable office that Luke had seen once, only for a few seconds. Perhaps it was time to get some home office advice from Van. Maybe this weekend.

He messed around with his desktop computer for a couple of minutes, following the instructions for the VPN connection, which he half expected would fail. Much to his surprise, it worked on the first try. The familiar bell announced that he had an email. It was from Caroline, with an EPA Administrative

Order attached and a note setting a conference call for later in the day. Luke opened the legal document and read the EPA's official request that Guadalupe perform another round of soil sampling at the plant site and throughout the neighborhood. The EPA wasn't wasting any time, which was fine by him. He forwarded the email to the project team and asked them to get together before the conference call, both to discuss the soil sampling effort and stay one step ahead of Caroline by having answers before she asked questions. Then he headed upstairs to check on his daughter.

"How are you feeling? You're not as pale as you were." He placed a hand on her forehead. "I don't think you have a temperature. Do you feel up to going to my office for a few minutes?"

She didn't take her eyes off the television screen. "Not really. I'd rather stay here and watch TV."

Luke resorted to blackmail without a twinge of guilt. "We can get a snack and a scoop of ice cream in the cafeteria. We'll only be there for a few hours. C'mon, grab your blanket, a book, and a video game. Dads are supposed to bring their daughters to work now and then." Preferably not when they were sick, but he had no other option. If only Angela was around and could help in a work crisis like she had done before.

Both Nathan and Kaylie had been to his downtown office several times before, and she knew the drill. She sat in the swivel office chair, spun around a few times, and then started coloring in her favorite coloring book. She'd kept down her hard-boiled egg breakfast earlier that morning, or he wouldn't have brought her in.

"If you feel like you're going to throw up again, you can always use the trash can."

Kaylie peered into the plastic-lined can. "That's gross."

"It's better than on the carpet, but you'll be fine. Cindy's just outside if you need me."

He grabbed his notes and headed to the conference room. He was the last to arrive. "All right, team," he said, after shutting the door. "We have an hour to conceptualize a soil sampling plan for the neighborhood soils before we get on a conference call with Caroline. I'll throw out the first question: How many samples should we take, and where should we take them?"

Rudy stood and approached the soil sampling map pinned to the corkboard wall. His dress shirt was wrinkled and coming untucked in the back. It looked like the same shirt he had worn in California days earlier.

"That's actually two questions, Luke, but I'll let that go for now." He pointed to the previous soil sampling locations. "This sounds simple to me. I would take samples in the same locations we did last time to confirm our earlier results and see if the DDT concentrations have naturally declined. We might be able to demonstrate that natural degradation of DDT is happening in the yards, and they are now below the cleanup level, making this entire, stupid removal action unnecessary."

Luke hid a smile in his hand. It was always clear where Rudy stood on an issue. He never held back his opinion.

"I think the objective is different this time compared to the first sampling round years ago," Beth stated. "Our objective now is to determine how many yards need to be removed. I can't understand why we would remove someone's yard if it has never been sampled. I think they all need to be sampled."

"That would cost a fortune," Rudy pointed out. "Guadalupe will never go for that. Isn't there some way we can approach this more statistically and take fewer samples?"

Chad, who had returned from Torrance, weighed in. "I'm guessing I'll be the one going door to door, telling people we're going to dig up their yards, unless one of y'all wants to be there with me. Safety in numbers, you know."

Luke chose not to respond to that. "Josh, can you create a map of the area to sample and let us know how many yards we're talking about?"

Josh was silent for a moment. "I can't draw the removal area boundary if I don't know which yards are clean. It sounds like you need to keep sampling until you find where the concentration levels drop off. Then you can define the boundary."

There was another, longer silence before Beth spoke up. "We might reduce the costs if we run a modified analysis instead of the full EPA Method 8081, since all we are looking for is DDT. Method 8081 detects about thirty organochlorine pesticides and costs much more. It sounds like overkill to me, and we might run across other pesticides out there that would create new problems. I can check with our laboratory contractor to see if we can save money."

"Great idea, Beth. Look into it," Luke said. "Rudy and I will take the call with Caroline, but if you have any new ideas before the call, let me know."

Luke took Kaylie to the cafeteria just before it closed for the day and, as promised, bought her a scoop of ice cream.

"Can I have a hot dog too?"

"Umm, sure, I guess. You haven't had much to eat in the last twelve hours. You must be feeling better, huh? I'll split it with you, though," Luke said, not wanting her to overeat. "Eat it slowly, Sweetie. We don't want it coming back up."

"Let's not talk about that anymore, Dad. It's pretty gross."

Luke smiled. "One more meeting, and then we can leave,

okay? Tell your mom you had a great time at the office, and don't mention the hot dog."

Luke and Rudy joined the call with Caroline and Bob and presented their thoughts and concerns. Right on cue, Caroline began to complain about the cost of the sampling, and Bob started exploring ways to reduce the number of yards requiring sampling.

"Luke, you and Rudy need to put a plan together and make sure it doesn't cost a fortune and reduces the number of yards removed. The yellow iron digging up the yards will incur the real costs, so more sampling costs are probably worthwhile if it leads to less digging. When we get our sampling results back, we'll be better positioned to argue our case about leaving the neighborhood soils alone." Caroline ended the call after an hour of back and forth that resulted in no agreement.

10

He was overworked, underpaid, and got all the shit work, Chad thought, as he pulled his cell phone from his pocket. Over the last several days, the team had isolated thirty residential yards around the site, and access had to be obtained from as many residents as possible. As he'd predicted, he was tasked with contacting homeowners and asking for their permission to take a soil sample from their yards.

He took a deep breath and dialed Jimmy Mendoza's number. He'd saved this conversation for last, because he knew it would be explosive. Jimmy didn't disappoint.

"Chad, do you really think I am going to let you take a goddamned sample from my yard unless I know the concentration of DDT is going to go down instead of up? That's like putting a witness on the stand and not knowing what the hell they will say—and I have experience with that, by the way."

"Look, you have nothing to lose by having your yard sampled," Chad said, launching into what was, by now, a practiced argument. "Just think about it, Jimmy, the DDT results might come in lower than before, and your yard won't be removed. I don't understand why you won't let us take the sample. It seems like a no-brainer to me."

"If I let you guys sample my yard, it implies that I agree with what the EPA is doing, and that's wrong."

The line fell silent. Chad let Jimmy have the time to collect his thoughts. Hopefully, the truth of his words would change the man's mind. It was just a stupid sample, after all.

"We need to get together, Chad, and have lunch," Jimmy said, finally. "My treat. I have an idea I think you will like."

Chad breathed a sigh of relief. That was a one-eighty he hadn't expected. "Sounds good to me. I'll take every free meal I can get. I'm on *per diem* this month, so every meal I don't have to pay for is money in my pocket."

***

Chad pulled the company truck into the parking lot of Sylvia's Diner and took the last parking spot, between two other contractor trucks. The old diner was only a few blocks from the former DDT manufacturing plant. He knew from past conversations that Sylvia had owned the restaurant ever since she'd lost her job at Guadalupe, back in the eighties, when the plant was shut down.

"What's up, *señor*? Haven't seen you in a few weeks. You doing good?" Sylvia asked. Chad was impressed she could work the cash register and maintain conversations with two customers simultaneously.

"*Muy bien*, Sylvia. Just living the dream, and your green chili is part of that dream. Bring me a Diet Coke, would you please? Have you seen Jimmy today? He said he was going to buy me lunch."

Sylvia chuckled. "I hope you have some money in your

pocket, *amigo*. That guy gets busy and forgets about things like lunch meetings."

Despite Sylvia's dire warning, Jimmy opened the door a few minutes later and plopped down beside Chad at the end of the bar. He was dusty and sweaty, likely from laying hot asphalt. He ordered an iced tea and gulped down half in one try. "Whew, it's warm out there for January. Glad you could make it today, Chad. It's been a while since we had lunch together."

"Thanks for the invite. I usually eat in my truck. This is a step up for me." Chad raised his Diet Coke in a silent toast.

"How many people have given you access to sample their yards? I figure a few pricks like me out there won't agree."

Chad hedged. He probably shouldn't divulge too much information. "Most people want their yard sampled, so they know what's in it. I think the real estate value discussion hit home. They want it sampled now, so the EPA will pay for the removal. Otherwise, they'll have to do it themselves someday, to meet the real estate disclosure requirements at a sale. I don't care why they sign, as long as they sign. You know what I'm saying?"

"It's all about getting that signature on the access agreement, huh? You're all about getting the job done. That's what I like about you, Chad. When do you think you'll start sampling yards?"

"It'll be a few more weeks at the rate we're going, then probably two weeks of sampling. A few people have gotten their lawyers involved, which slows me down. A lawyer has to make a change to prove his worth, you know, and then I have to send the agreements back to Denver for review. It usually requires at least two visits with the homeowner, and a week or two of faxing documents back and forth."

"I have more experience with those goddamn lawyers than anyone should ever have," Jimmy said.

Chad nodded. "Yeah, they make all the money, while people like us do all the hard work." He gave Jimmy a smile. "You know, I thought about going to law school. I could be a lawyer today sitting in a cushy, air-conditioned office, but my dad told me I was too stupid, so I just gave up, and now it's probably too late."

A waitress interrupted them, and Chad ordered his green chili bowl. Jimmy ordered a green chili cheeseburger with fries. The conversation drifted to asphalt mixing, the upcoming Super Bowl, and Sylvia's new waitress, who was wearing a skirt much shorter than the other women in the diner.

"Tell me how you go about getting these samples," Jimmy asked. "Do you just dig a hole and gather some dirt for the lab?"

"It's kinda like that, although the EPA has a sampling procedure I have to follow. It's easy to do, because we're sampling for DDT that's not volatile, so it doesn't evaporate when you dig it up, like gasoline or chlorobenzene. If we are in somebody's yard, we scrape off the grass and the roots, then take our hand auger and pull a six-inch plug out of the ground." Chad made a lifting gesture with his hands. "I pour the sample onto a stainless-steel plate, divide it into four piles, mix each one around, and then recombine it before I pour it into an amber jar. Then, I seal it up, put a label on the jar noting the time and location, and pack it in a cooler with dry ice. It gets overnighted to the lab. Of course, I have to change gloves every time I get a sample and wash the plate thoroughly, to prevent cross-contamination. The procedure is the procedure. You know what I'm saying?"

Jimmy rubbed a dirty hand over his stubbled chin. "So, if the DDT is in the grass or roots, you won't detect it?"

"Probably not, because we put that stuff aside."

"Do you do all this by yourself?"

Chad shrugged. "Chuck's out here with me for the sampling. You met him, I think. I usually have him do all the other things while I collect the samples."

"How big is the sample jar?"

"We use a standard, five-hundred-milliliter jar. Why are you asking, you want to come help me?" Chad laughed loudly at his own joke.

Sylvia—whose skirt was shapeless and long—set their food down on the table. Jimmy took a big bite of his cheeseburger and chewed it with a thoughtful look on his face.

"You know, Chad," he said, after he swallowed, "I never was a math genius, but it seems to me that if you filled half of the sample jar with clean dirt, then the DDT concentration would come back from the lab at half the concentration that it really is. Did I do my math right?"

"You're a smart man, Jimmy" said Chad said with a smirk. "We call that 'dilution.' Like they say in our business, 'dilution is the solution if you want to lower a concentration.'"

"You two need some refills on your drinks?" said Sylvia. "Customers come first, you know."

"You bet, Sylvia. And by the way, who's the new waitress?" Chad asked.

"She's my niece, and don't get any ideas. As it says on the door, honey, I have the right to refuse service."

She walked away, taking Chad's empty cup with her. Jimmy turned and stared at Chad. "So, it wouldn't be that hard to dilute those samples, would it?"

Chad swallowed. Was Jimmy suggesting…? "No… it wouldn't."

"I can make it worth your while, Chad. Wouldn't it be nice to drive a new truck, or spend a week in Hawaii? You do like the beach, I understand."

Chad's chest tightened. He should tell Jimmy to go to hell, but some extra money right now sure would be nice. God knows he deserved it. He worked his ass off and got zero thanks for it. Turning, he stared at his reflection in the smudged window, debating. It would be easy to do, and the chances of his getting caught were virtually nil. None of the higher ups paid attention to what he did. He met Jimmy's eyes again.

"Why should I trust you, Jimmy? You get what you want, and I take all the risk."

Jimmy pulled an envelope from his jacket pocket and slid it across the table. "The second half will come when you get the sample results back from the lab."

Chad looked at the thick envelope for a moment, then grabbed it and quickly shoved it in his safety vest pocket. He wanted to count the money at the table but knew he would have to wait until he got in his truck.

"Good choice, man," Jimmy said, giving him a wink.

Chad thought about how thick the envelope was. *If it's full of Franklin's, I'm in good shape. If it's full of Lincoln's, I just got screwed. What the hell? I can always demand more.*

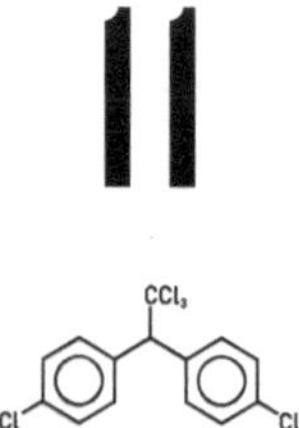

As soon as Luke answered his phone, Bob began ranting. "Environmentalists are ideological idiots who don't understand the real world and are scaring people to get into their wallets. Get yourself prepared for another turn of events, Luke. Legal ones, I might add, and all the fun that goes along with them."

"What are you talking about, Bob?"

"Environmental Freedom & Justice, including our attractive friend Brooke Burr, has decided to raise the bar on us and everything we do. EF&J filed two civil lawsuits this morning against Guadalupe in the US District Court for the District of Oregon. Why in the hell is it always Oregon? All the enviros live in Oregon, I guess. There must be something in the water there, because they never file in places like Texas or New Jersey."

Luke smiled to himself and pondered the irony of Bob's statement. The groundwater in Oregon was relatively clean compared to the numerous, contaminated groundwater sites in the more industrial areas. "What are you, I mean Guadalupe, getting sued for? Is Brooke claiming we did something illegal?"

"The first lawsuit claims that Guadalupe is colluding with the EPA and purposefully going too slowly on the cleanup of the manufacturing plant, thus violating the intent and requirements of the damn Superfund law. They assert that removing the neighborhood yards provides negligible health benefits and is a stall tactic for the overall site cleanup, including the offshore contamination. I agree with her on the neighborhood soil, but how are we colluding with the EPA? Is she claiming that we are too close to the EPA? Holy shit! I've never been accused of being too close to the EPA by anybody in my entire life. Talk about wasting time and money. Now, I have to draft a response, hire outside counsel, and manage another legal effort. Hold on, Luke, let me see who is on this other call."

Luke took a deep breath and thought of his relationship with Simone. He had years of email threads with her and wondered if they would be discovered by EF&J in a case of colluding with the EPA. Bob came back on the phone. "How in the hell do these salesmen get your goddamn phone number?"

"What's the second lawsuit?" Luke asked, hoping to divert Bob from discussing colluding with EPA.

"EF&J claims that Guadalupe is the primary party responsible for the offshore contamination because our offshore disposal companies dumped too close to shore in an effort to cut costs. That conspiracy theory has been around for a long time, and we've gone through every document that existed at the plant and never found any evidence to that effect. Even the old-timers dispute it. The Department of Justice deposed several of them a few years ago."

"Unless the former employees are lying, to save their asses." Luke regretted the words as soon as they left his lips. He could almost hear Bob's head explode.

"Luke, remember who is buying your meal ticket. Don't even think that way. Of course, some former employee could have lied to me and then gone to EF and fucking J behind my back. But there has to be ironclad evidence to support the claim. Otherwise, it's gossip and bullshit and won't make it into court."

"I understand, Bob. What happens next? Will I be subpoenaed at my house and deposed? Should I tell Kara not to answer the doorbell?" Luke asked, in an attempt to lighten the conversation.

Bob didn't slow down. "You'll make a good witness for Guadalupe. You're just trying to get things done and reach a compromise between Guadalupe and the EPA. Unless there is something I don't know about? I'll coach you before you talk to them. In the meantime—I'm sure I don't need to say this—be careful what you say and write going forward. Get your records straight and shred old drafts and chicken scratch, because you'll probably get a subpoena demanding otherwise. You're always charging me for file maintenance, so I assume you're already on top of that. I'll let you know if anything changes and what our outside counsel suggests."

Luke hung up the phone and gathered the project team for a short meeting to describe what Bob had just told him. He couldn't help but notice Debbie kept her eyes glued to the floor the whole time. He didn't imply any impropriety between her and Antoine. If the lawsuit had described their mutual flirting, Bob would have filled him in already. As to what came out going forward, only time would tell.

***

Luke received a call from Earl a few days later. It was unusual, if not a first. "How are you doing? What's going on out there in beautiful southern California?"

"Luke, sorry to bother you, but I was watching the KKAT

news last night before bed, and right there in front of my eyes was a video of you and Antoine at the public meeting. It was followed by a comment from Haewon Lee about Guadalupe getting sued by EF&J. I almost called you last night, but figured I'd wait until this morning, with the time difference and all. I'm afraid you're a local TV star out here."

"Oh, that's just great," said Luke. "So much for anonymity. Maybe I should go on *Star Search* with Ed McMahon—see if I can be an environmental TV star."

"I guess Caroline and Bob make all the decisions, and you get blamed. I feel for you, just so you know."

"Thanks, Earl. I appreciate that," Luke said.

"I will say, there seems to be more interest in the site since the public meeting. It's hard to explain, and maybe it's just a feeling, but I lock the gate to the site behind me now when I'm there and keep looking over my shoulder. Plus, Chad's started taking samples in people's yards, which has raised some eyebrows. I know that reporter gal is trying to make a name for herself, so I don't know what to believe. Are the lawsuit rumors true?"

Luke described the two lawsuits, paraphrasing what Bob had told him.

"That's unfair," the old man said. "We followed the rules every damn time. The press is making this whole thing much worse than it is—even the offshore stuff. DDT in the ocean will get buried in the mud over time and degrade before we know it. I know this molecule, Luke. I know it well, and it's not bad for humans."

"EF&J is after publicity. Whether they win the lawsuit or not doesn't matter. Their goal is to draw attention to the on-shore and offshore contamination and how bad pesticides like DDT are for the environment. Before long, the donations will pour in, and they'll all be taking home a nice, fat Christmas bonus."

"I'm waiting for KKAT to figure out who I am and interview me. I'll plead the fifth before I say something that makes the evening news. Chad hasn't been interviewed, which surprises me. It's just a matter of time before they figure out what he's doing. He'll sing like a songbird. You guys better make sure he knows what to say and what not to say."

"I hadn't thought about that, Earl. That's good thinking. I'll call him after we hang up and give him the legal lecture."

"One more thing I'd like to mention, Luke, if it isn't out of line."

"Yeah, what's that?" Luke asked.

"I've been watching Chad bring soil samples from the yards back to the site, where he does all of the chain of custody paperwork before he sends them to the lab. He's got that doofus helper of his, Chuck, running around, cleaning tools and putting things away, so he's by himself most of the time. I was in the guard shack, doing my usual paperwork, and I spotted him, way over on the other side of the site. I had my binoculars with me—not that I spy on folks, but they come in handy when protecting thirteen acres of asphalt. I watched him open a sample jar and put something in it from a bucket in the back of the truck. I swear, it looked like he added more soil. Now, I know you sometimes add reagents in the field with liquid samples, but you don't need to do that with soil samples. I suppose it could have been a control sample. Anyway, it seemed kinda odd to me."

Luke straightened in his chair. "I'm sure it's nothing, Earl, but I'll talk to Beth when she returns from vacation. She's our project chemist. Don't let any biased TV people find you and try to get an interview. Thanks for the call. I appreciate it."

12

Luke's cell phone vibrated. The caller ID showed Bob Burrows' number. He let it go straight to voicemail. If his friendship with Simone was now in the open, Bob would likely let that slip in the message. That would give Luke a few minutes to prepare for a return call.

"Luke, I need to talk with you about these goddamn lawsuits."

There was a pause, and Luke pictured Bob taking a long drag from his cigarette before he began again.

"I'd like us to go to Torrance and meet with Earl and Lenny Donahue. Lenny is the barge operator that dumped a lot of our waste offshore. Legally, I might add. We need to talk with them and get some facts straight before going further. Call me as soon as you can."

Luke breathed a sigh of relief. The voicemail had nothing to do with his friendship with Simone or whatever might be happening—or not—between Debbie and Antoine. Bob's request was a new task in the project, which wasn't all bad. Not only was it an additional scope of billable work that would make Nancy happy, but it was litigation support that he'd never done before. It sounded intriguing. Maybe Caroline and Bob had more trust in him than he thought.

"Hey Bob, I got your voicemail. I'm sorry, but I was in a meeting and couldn't answer."

"Let's get out to Torrance next week on Tuesday and meet first with Earl, then with Lenny. We've had a non-disclosure agreement with him for several years, so he'll converse without a lawyer sitting beside him. I'll set that up for Tuesday afternoon."

"I assume the purpose of our meeting is to learn what and when waste was dumped offshore?"

"Basically, that's it. Earl can add some specifics to what we know from our files, since he was responsible for designing and building the sulfuric acid recovery plant. That plant eliminated the need for offshore dumping and sewer discharges."

"What do you mean by sewer discharges? I thought they just dumped barrels in the ocean."

Bob cleared his throat. "Sorry, I guess you're not in the loop about that. We wanted you to focus on remediating the site, not the offshore issues. Some DDT waste went down the sanitary sewer and discharged about a mile offshore, around the sewer outfall. That's a separate issue we'll need to investigate someday, but it's all part of the same offshore problem. I assume you can make it to California early next week? Caroline gets all worked up about lawsuits like this and wants us to act quickly. It will also be good for me to get out of the office. Caroline's gnawing at my ass as soon as I step foot in the place. I can't even go to the goddamn bathroom without her chasing me down the hall. Get there Monday night, and I'll give you more background on the offshore problem."

***

Luke and Bob were already seated and sipping coffee when Earl arrived at the restaurant. "This must be pretty damn important for the lawyer and the engineer to come all the way out here, just to see me. I know you can't fire me 'cause I don't work for either of you."

Luke smiled at Earl, hoping he didn't look as tired as he felt. He hadn't slept well on the soft hotel bed, and the lack of sleep was beginning to take its toll.

"Well, Mister Earl, what can I get you to drink this morning?" The waitress gave the older man a beaming smile.

"I'll take my usual, Betty," Earl said, handing the woman his menu. "Coffee, bacon, and eggs the way I like 'em."

The waitress glanced in Luke's direction. "Mister Earl, this looks like the young man I saw on TV the other night." She shook her head. "Looks like someone's got himself in some hot water," she said before heading toward the kitchen.

Luke's mouth fell open. If Betty remembered his face, how many other people would too? So much for being anonymous in Torrance, California.

"I'll cut to the chase," Bob said. "Our lovely friend, Brooke Burr, at EF&J, sent two lawsuits our way. The first focuses on our involvement in the offshore dumping, and the second on our supposed lack of action, collusion to be specific, in the site's cleanup. Luke and I are here to get your historical knowledge of the plant operations. I know we have talked about it before, but I need to hear it again, and Luke needs to hear it for the first time."

"Sounds like I'm gonna be on the witness stand someday soon," Earl said.

"I hope not, but you'll probably get deposed, and we'll have a chance to spar with Brooke verbally." Bob grinned, revealing a mouthful of nicotine-stained teeth. "That's the fun part. What do you remember about the offshore dumping in the early days?"

Earl's forehead wrinkled. "Let's see. Back in '63, when I started with Guadalupe, I reckon we were dumping about 150,000 gallons a month of spent acid off the coast."

Luke knew "spent acid" was a mix of DDT and sulfuric acid. The two compounds couldn't be completely separated once combined.

Earl raised a finger. "Mind you, it wasn't illegal then, and they'd been doing it since '47, when Guadalupe built the plant." He grinned. "Those were the good old days. We were saving the world from mosquitoes and malaria."

"What was in the acid? Was it mostly DDT or something else, and why so much?" Luke asked.

"Let me tell you how we made DDT 'cause this will help you understand the waste issues. Basically, we mixed chloral with monochlorobenzene and cooked it in concentrated sulfuric acid at a high temperature. The DDT floated to the top of the reactor column and got scraped off and sold. The lousy shit at the bottom of the column was sludge. We tried to recover the sulfuric acid and use it again, but that didn't work, so the sludge got sent offshore and dumped, 'cause we didn't have a use for it."

"That sounds messy, Earl."

"It was! Why do you think I have all these spots and different colors on my hands and arms?" Earl rolled up his sleeve. "It wasn't the DDT that did this. It was the sulfuric acid and chlorobenzene."

"So, most of the waste that was dumped in the ocean was sulfuric acid? That's no big deal. Doesn't acid neutralize in salt water? I remember that from high school chemistry." Luke said.

"You're right, Luke. The problem was the DDT in the acid, not the acid itself. About one percent of the acid waste was DDT. It may not sound like much, but over fifteen years, it added up to about six hundred tons of DDT. That's why the plant manager, Mr. Wright, tasked me with designing a sulfuric acid recovery plant to eliminate, or at least reduce, our waste volume. We got the acid recovery plant running in '63, and no longer needed to dump offshore." Earl grinned again. "The company gave me a big raise because we'd saved money and reduced waste. I was the local hero."

Bob, who had been eating throughout Earl's recollections, pushed his empty plate into the middle of the table. "To your knowledge, did anyone at Guadalupe ask the offshore disposal company to dump waste closer to shore?"

Earl leaned back in the booth as Betty set both his coffee and his breakfast down on the table.

"Anything else, hot shot?" she asked.

Earl eyed his meal with an eager look on his face. "Nope. This will do me."

Betty nodded and walked away.

Earl took a sip of his steaming coffee before he resumed talking.

"Not that I know, Bob. Of course, I was still a young engineer, focused on the task at hand. I didn't have anything to do with offshore dumping. Wright was a great manager, and a stand-up kinda guy. He promised me I would get a raise and promotion if I got the acid plant up and running, and when I did, he came through. I can't speak to anything else."

"The records from the plant show that about ten to fifteen million gallons of acid with DDT were disposed offshore," said Luke. "That seems unrealistic to me. Does it make sense to you?"

"If you do the math over fifteen years, I guess it makes sense. The barge guys may have some better records."

"We're talking to Lenny Donahue after lunch, and we'll see

if—" Bob's cell phone started to buzz. "Excuse me, guys, I need to take this call." After exiting the booth, Bob stepped outside, most likely to have a cigarette.

Luke made a pretense of checking his own phone for a few minutes, giving Earl time to finish his breakfast. Once the old man had finished, Luke pocketed his phone once again.

"When did DDT production start to decline?" he asked.

Earl shook his head. "I remember it so well. The decline started after Rachel Carson came out with her book, *Silent Spring*, in '62. It was before your time, Luke, but I'm sure you've heard about it. Somebody sent a copy of the book to my house, in fact. It took aim at organochlorine pesticides like DDT and how they affected the environment. We were naturally defensive about it and didn't want to believe any of it. But we already knew insects were building up a resistance. The effectiveness of DDT on mosquitoes had dropped by about 50 percent by then. The pressure on us only got worse when the data on the peregrine falcons and bald eagles came out. They finally banned it here in the US in '72. That's when the business died. We tried to develop other pesticides, but nothing worked out. We shut down in '82 and shipped the plant to Indonesia, where DDT was still legal. I've heard it's still running today."

"You disassembled the plant and shipped it to Indonesia?" Luke asked, with wide eyes.

"Yeah. We labeled the pipes and parts, took them apart, and put them on a ship. Pretty simple, really."

Luke hesitated. "I guess so." Ever since his phone conversation with Bob, he'd vacillated between curiosity and caution. Curiosity won. "What's with the sewer discharge contamination? I just heard about that last week. Between you and me,

Bob and Caroline like to keep me in the dark, like I'm a spy or something."

Earl chuckled. "I feel for you, Luke. That's how we disposed of the off-spec DDT. We sent it right down the sewer. Nobody said we couldn't."

"How long did this go on?"

Earl shrugged. "At least twenty years. I've read an EPA estimate that states over one hundred tons of DDT was sent to the wastewater treatment facility in Carson, and ultimately discharged a mile offshore at the outfall."

"Wow, that's a hell of a lot of DDT. There is no way for us to distinguish where the DDT in the offshore sediment came from, since it came from both the sewer and the offshore dumping."

"I know it sounds like a lot of DDT in the ocean, but one hundred tons here, and five hundred tons there—that's nothing compared to the eight hundred thousand tons we produced over the years. We shipped it all over the world."

"I can see it already, Earl. The barge guys will say the DDT came from the sewer outfall, and Guadalupe will say the DDT came from illegal dumping by the barge guys."

Earl laughed. "You're catching on fast. That's how this environmental business works. Everyone points fingers at everyone else and tries to avoid responsibility. But at the end of the day, everyone pays for the cleanup. It's just a question of who pays more."

"By the way, we're supposed to get the results from the soil sampling of residential yards next week. I talked to Beth about your concerns with Chad and how he sampled. She says we'll be able to tell from the results if he did anything funny."

"Thank you, Luke. There's just something about Chad. I like the guy, and he works hard, but I don't trust him for some reason. I can't explain what it is. I'll be interested in hearing what you find out."

***

The LA traffic was heavy around the Port of Long Beach. The arrival of a cruise ship made it even harder to navigate. Bob seemed to be lost, driving in circles around the port terminals.

"Do you know where you are going, Bob? I've seen this diner at least two times now. It's starting to make me hungry," Luke said, even though he had no appetite after the large breakfast.

"Do not worry, my son. I know I'm close. It's been a couple of years since I was last with Lenny. I remember he had two tugboats and a salvage barge that were easy to see from the road."

"Why were you here back then?"

"The EPA was interviewing Lenny. He shared his offshore disposal logs and compliance reports. The EPA was searching for volumetric data to start their remedial investigation of offshore contamination. There was nothing about criminal activity or illegal dumping then, just records review."

"Lenny must be getting up there in age if he was involved in the offshore disposal in 1947. Did he start this company?" Luke asked.

"No. The company was started by Lenny's dad in '46, after he returned from the war. Lenny's dad was a submariner in the Pacific, on the USS *Croaker*. When you have more time, Lenny tells a great story about his dad. Like so many ex-Navy guys from the war, his dad went to work in the shipping business or the ports."

"Oh, there's Croaker Salvage," said Luke. "Just over the railroad tracks."

Lenny was waiting for them at the door to the tiny pilot house on the salvage boat and seemed to fill the doorway. Although he was only of average height, he had broad shoulders and was solid, like a wrestler. He smiled a thin smile and reached out to shake Luke's hand.

As they shook Luke could tell that Lenny was missing a finger, but he kept his gaze on Lenny's face. Lenny invited them in, and Luke and Bob sat across a metal desk in the only two chairs available to guests. The leather armrests were cracked and patched with duct tape. An old, yellow sofa, with a threadbare blanket and a saggy pillow, was pushed against the wall behind them. Pictures of his Sertoma club buddies and various community and economic development pictures decorated the wood-paneled walls. Several dumbbells of various weights were aligned neatly on the floor.

"Welcome to my home away from home, gentlemen. I'd offer you some coffee, but I quit drinking it last year to reduce my stress. You know my dad died when he was sixty-two, from a heart attack. He was piloting one of our tugboats out of the harbor. Ran it aground a couple of hundred yards from here. I've got a feeling it was all the shitty food that did it. That, and the stress of a 24-7 job. Every day, it was bacon and eggs for breakfast and a cheeseburger and fries for lunch." Lenny smiled. "I don't think he ever ate anything green. Two packs a day on top of that. Bless his heart."

Bob squirmed in his chair and linked his fingers across his protruding stomach. Luke wondered if all this talk about poor health and bad eating habits made Bob uncomfortable. Lenny's father was about the same age as Bob was today when he died.

"Are you the only one that uses this office, Lenny?" said Bob. "Where is everyone else?"

"My bookkeeper works at an office in Long Beach, and my employees stay in the tugboats. I keep this place to myself. It's my sanctuary, where I can get away from everyone and have meetings like this."

"Right. As I mentioned on the phone last week, Environmental Freedom & Justice claims that Guadalupe told your employees to dump waste close to shore to save money and that your employees did it. Based on depositions from Guadalupe employees a few years ago, this 'close-in' dumping never happened. I believe that's true, but it would help to have some further proof to support our position."

Lenny frowned. "I've heard this bullshit a lot in the last few years. People don't understand what goes on at a port. We have the Coast Guard watching us constantly and the Port Authority logging when we leave and when we return. They have records on everybody, you know. If our barges hadn't gone where they were supposed to go, the authorities would have been waiting at this door when we returned, asking why.

"The EPA tried to get those records from the Port Authority, but it's been so long ago, most of them have been destroyed." Lenny shook his head. "It's just my word against theirs, who-ever 'they' are. The Palos Verdes sewer discharge and ocean currents could have caused DDT to deposit close to shore. Nobody knows the answer, but everyone is after me like I'm the evilest person on the planet."

Bob's chair gave an ominous creak as he shifted his weight forward. "We just need more evidence to support our side of the story. Let's keep looking and thinking about who or what can support our case."

Lenny looked from Luke to Bob and back again. "Yeah, sure. And in the meantime, I'll continue to get death threats. What if someone blows up my barge? I just bought a terrorism rider on my insurance policy. Everything Dad and I did was perfectly legal for all these years. If you don't like that we dumped DDT, go have words with Pat Brown. He was the damn governor in the days when the dumping happened. Nobody gets mad at him!"

"Didn't he die a few years ago?" Luke asked.

"I don't remember, and I don't care if he's dead or alive. Either way, I'll bet he doesn't get death threats like I do!" Lenny said.

Luke paused, hoping Lenny's words were indicative of a dry sense of humor. "Lenny, let me change the subject slightly. How was the DDT loaded on your barges back then?"

"Bob knows this, but I'll repeat it. We had tanker trucks show up from the plant with about three thousand gallons of acid, and we pumped it onto the barge into our holding tanks. Once we were full up, we went to the designated disposal site and opened the valve into the ocean. It was concentrated sulfuric acid, so we had to be careful. We insisted our guys wear rubber suits and safety gear."

"Did you ever dispose of drums with DDT?"

"No. The DDT always came by tanker truck. We did dispose of drums, though. Most contained oil waste, PCBs, and some low-level radioactive stuff from other companies."

"I read that the drums wouldn't sink, and you had to punch holes in them or shoot them. Is there any truth to that? I'm just curious."

Lenny raised his eyebrows. "Oil is lighter than seawater, Luke. I'm not saying it happened, but can you think of a better idea?" He turned to Bob. "Do you think EF&J will come after me with a lawsuit?"

"I doubt it right now. EF&J knows that Guadalupe has deeper pockets than Croaker Salvage, and we're a higher visibility target to go after. But we'll probably have to depose some of your former employees."

"You'd better hurry up, Bob. There's only a few men left who were around in those days, and most can hardly remember their names anymore."

They all shook hands again, and Luke knew it was now or never. "So, Lenny, I must ask how you lost your finger. Was it an accident on the barge?"

Lenny gave him a sheepish grin. "I'm glad you asked, Luke. People want to ask but seldom do. No, I didn't lose it in a cleat while bringing in a line or handling salvage. It was a dumb ass mistake I made at home. My garage door wasn't working right, so I had to close it by hand. As I pulled it shut, I got my index finger in between the door panels. It smashed the bone quite slowly and hurt more than anything I'd ever experienced. The worst part was, I couldn't file for Workers' Comp because I was at home."

***

As they headed south toward LAX, Luke was glad he and Bob had allowed extra time for traffic on the 405. As usual, it was a parking lot during rush hour, but Luke didn't mind as much as he might have on another day. The captive time in the car with Guadalupe's lawyer gave him the opportunity to get Bob's honest perspective on the lawsuits.

"How can EF&J prove that acid and DDT were illegally dumped close to the shore? Without any damning testimony from employees, the Port Authority, or the Coast Guard, it seems almost impossible to make the argument, especially with the sewer outfall being in that same area."

"Of course it's difficult to prove, but EF&J doesn't care if they win or lose. The case will be described on their website soon, if it's not already, and they will use it to raise more money by talking about DDT in our food chain and how it causes cancer. They will milk this lawsuit for as long as they can by claiming that big corporations have more money for lawyers and that EF&J is the underdog trying to protect the people. Dying birds are bad and make for good pictures on their website, but the fear of cancer really raises money."

Luke fiddled with the car radio, trying to get the latest traffic report. "I'm surprised the DDT is still hanging around in the ocean mud after all these decades, based on what Earl says. I guess the big fish eat the little fish that feed on the ocean bottom, and shit out the DDT that settles to the bottom. And the process starts all over again until birds or people take the fish away."

"You just simplified a very complex ecological process," Bob said with a crooked smile. "You should read about that stupid little white croaker fish that everyone around here likes to catch. I thought Lenny's dad named his company Croaker Salvage because of that fish until I heard about his submarine experience. Anyway, the croaker is a bottom feeder with lots of body fat. Fat stores DDT, and that damn fish has the highest levels of DDT around here by far. The state says you shouldn't eat them at all."

Luke nearly threw up his hands in surrender. He and Kara had vowed to eat less red meat and more seafood. *What are we supposed to eat now? Everything is bad for you.*

"I assume EF&J is busy looking to find evidence to support their case. Won't they be talking to Lenny, the Port Authority, and the Coast Guard, trying to find old records?" Luke said.

"That's what most plaintiffs would do. But EF&J isn't typical. It has an activist element, and it wouldn't surprise me if someone there was sending those death threats to Lenny. I mean, look at Amy Nunez and her criminal record. That woman's off her rocker! She's incapable of making the connection between the use of pesticides and producing enough food on the planet to feed six billion people. She'll go to extremes to convince others she's right. Brooke is a bit like that, but she knows when to stop pushing. That's the difference between them."

"But really, what do they gain by threatening Lenny and his business? He hasn't been in the offshore disposal business since 1972."

"The first thing that comes to my mind is you scare him so much he sells his business. Then EF&J can hang a guilty tag on him. Or, EF&J is simply vindictive and wants retribution for everything Croaker Salvage has done. It doesn't matter to the ignorant types if everything they did was legal at the time. That's what pisses me off, Luke. These assholes, like Brooke and Amy, play armchair quarterback and blame everyone else for doing what they thought was right at the time."

It was apparent Bob was getting wound up over the whole business. He was riding the car's bumper in front of them, so Luke gave him a moment to regain his composure and focus on driving. Luke toyed with the idea of telling Bob about his history with Simone. It might be better to get it out in the open. Or it might not. If it became an issue later, he would ask for forgiveness.

Luke said goodbye to Bob, and they headed to their airport

gates. Luke found an empty seating area that was relatively quiet and called Kara.

"Hey there! I am at the airport and just got to my gate. It's on time, so that's good. It was an interesting day. How was yours?"

"I spent the entire afternoon dealing with Columbo. When I left for work this morning, he didn't look very good, so I came home at lunch to check on him. I could tell he was in pain, so I took him to the vet. They gave him something to make him throw up. Sure enough, he threw up a few rubber toys, which he swallowed whole. It's kinda funny. I have them in a bag. Unfortunately, I missed a client meeting this afternoon. Why does this always happen when you are out of town?"

Luke ignored her rhetorical question. "Is he okay?"

"Oh yeah, he's fine. It's my job that I'm worried about, not the stupid dog."

"You're great at what you do. They'll never fire you. I'll see you soon. Love you."

Luke hung up and made his next call. "Russo, how's it going? Have you found any national security breaches lately? Wait, don't tell me. This is an unsecured line."

"Don't be a smart ass, Rattler. I can lose my job over crappy jokes like that. Why are you calling me? You don't just call to say 'hi.' What's going on?"

"I met this guy, Lenny Donahue, today. He owns a company called Croaker Salvage. They operate out of the Port of Long Beach and were the primary company that Guadalupe hired to dump DDT and acid off the coast. He was complaining about some recent bomb threats. People seem to hate him now because of the offshore dumping Croaker did in the fifties and sixties, which was perfectly legal at the time. Isn't there some way to track these threats and see who they are coming from? Why can't we figure out who these people are and deal with them?"

"It takes time and resources to track them down and build a criminal case. That's if Donahue has gone to the police. Some folks don't. I'll do some digging and ask a few favors. Let's talk when you get back to Denver." Click. Van was gone.

13

Luke returned to his office early the next day, and before he had a chance to grab his first cup of coffee, his phone rang.

"Good morning, Luke. I thought I would catch you before your day gets going. If you're anything like me, I get so much done from 5:30 to 7:30, before everyone else gets here and starts bothering me," Antoine said.

"I guess that's a career advantage you get from being single, without kids in the house," Luke said.

"You're right. But being childless can be a career disadvantage, too, when everyone's sharing kid stories all day, and I have to nod and laugh. Fortunately, I have nieces and nephews, so I can talk about them and sound like I fit in. The primary reason for my call is to find out from you when the lab will deliver the soil sample results."

"Beth told me she expects the results anytime. We can summarize the results in a report within two weeks after that and send you a copy."

"Hmm," Antoine paused. "I think we'll request Guadalupe provide us the raw data as soon as you guys get it, so we can start looking at it sooner. There's so much at stake, and I think pushback from the community on the removal action is inevitable after hearing from the public. I want to draw my own conclusions sooner."

Luke had not thought much about Earl's suspicions in the last few days. *What if Chad tampered with the samples at the site, and the results came in with lower DDT concentrations, eliminating the need for soil removal? Would we accept the results, or would I admit I was concerned about the sampling based on what Earl had told me?*

"One other thing, Luke. I heard through the rumor mill, and we have a pretty good one here in San Francisco, that EF&J has filed a few lawsuits against Guadalupe. I know you can't tell me anything specific, but do you see these 'rumored' lawsuits impacting our investigation and remediation of the site?"

Luke smiled. "I assumed you would eventually learn about these 'rumored' lawsuits, which I will neither confirm nor deny. I will say this, though. You and I should take personal notes every time we converse, as though we will be featured on *60 Minutes* next Sunday evening. Any personal stuff should be off the record and definitely not in an email. That applies to anyone else you talk to at Webber." Luke assumed Antoine would pick up on his innuendo, which was about as subtle as a sledgehammer. "To answer your question, I think any lawsuits will bring more attention to the offshore Palos Verdes contamination issue than the site cleanup. Site cleanup is a local issue, but offshore Palos Verdes contamination could affect many more people in the LA basin because of the food supply concern. Ultimately, the winner will be EF&J, who will gain more fundraising dollars."

After they'd finished the call, Luke went down the hall to Debbie's office. She sat behind a large computer monitor in a windowless room, barely visible from the door. Pictures of family and friends and her two cats cluttered her desk.

Textbooks and technical reports filled the bookshelves, and the smell of fresh flowers filled the air. He ignored the flowers and gave her the same spiel about document control and the likelihood of being deposed.

"Assume that all of your emails will end up in public view, in front of a jury, or in front of a judge. If you want to make sure the opposing counsel has nothing to dredge up in a lawsuit, choose your words carefully in emails, be strictly business, and take careful notes when you have conversations. This advice applies to personal email accounts as well."

Debbie turned away from Luke's gaze and stared at her computer, trepidation evident on her face. "I guess it's alright to delete old emails today, so as not to run out of storage space."

"That's just good corporate housekeeping practice," Luke said. "Electronic storage space is always in short supply, and cleaning up our computers is a corporate requirement."

Luke left the office and took a quick walk down the block to grab a cold turkey sandwich for lunch. It was starting to snow, and he knew Kara would be grumpy when he got home because she couldn't train for her marathon for a few days. She'd have to use a treadmill at the gym instead. Then, he switched gears, remembering Debbie's flowers and wondering whom they were from. The arrangement was pretty and provided some spring-like cheerfulness in the middle of winter. He decided to stop by the flower shop on his way home. Maybe flowers would improve his wife's mood.

Luke returned to his office to find a note from Beth stuck to his computer monitor. *Results are in — need to talk.* He called Rudy and then took his sandwich to the conference room.

Beth wore a quizzical look as she paged through the sample results. "These results are interesting." She clipped a map on the wall, showing the soil sample locations and results from two years ago. "Can one of you read out the location and the DDT concentration from today's lab report? I'll write it next to the yard sample from two years ago, and we'll see what the difference is."

Luke read off the DDT concentrations, and Beth wrote them on the map next to the previous sampling round results. It was immediately apparent that the new DDT concentrations were much lower than the earlier ones.

"Huh." Rudy stood, frowning at the map. "Without doing the math, I would say, just by looking at the data, that the new DDT concentrations are about half the previous ones. Does DDT break down that fast, Beth?"

"DDT does not break down that fast, and even if it did, we would see more metabolites—the daughter products—like DDD and DDE, in the results. These results show that the concentrations of DDD and DDE have gone down as well. That doesn't make sense."

Luke looked at Rudy, who had a bewildered look on his face.

"Wow, I just noticed something else. This is fascinating. We have positive hits for aldrin in the sample results," Beth exclaimed. "Aldrin is another pesticide that test Method 8081 detects. The Method picks up aldrin, DDT, endrin, heptachlor, dieldrin…"

"What does that mean?" Rudy asked.

Beth shook her head. "I'm not sure. I can't explain it. We've never had hits for aldrin in any of our soil samples to date. I doubt these homeowners all went out and sprinkled aldrin into their lawns in the last few years. Either the laboratory equipment was contaminated from a previous run, or someone mixed aldrin into the soil samples."

"Could the lab have contaminated equipment?" Luke said.

"Sure, that's always a concern with gas chromatograph test equipment, because you might have contamination from the previous sample that went through the machine. However, labs always run a clean sample through the chromatograph after any prior testing. It's standard practice in the industry. I'll check the lab quality control report, but they would have rerun the tests if contamination showed up in the control sample," Beth said.

"What's your conclusion, Beth?" Luke asked.

She was silent for a minute. "I think the soil samples were diluted with soil from another location—a location contaminated with aldrin, not DDT. Aldrin was used, instead of DDT, as a pesticide in the LA basin." She met Luke's eyes. "Someone mixed soil from somewhere else with the residential yard soil samples."

The turkey sandwich churned in Luke's stomach.

"Where would that happen? At the lab? Do you think the lab did this?" Rudy asked.

Beth shrugged. "Why would a lab contaminate a soil sample unless they were paid big money? The lab would easily be found out and shut down immediately."

They all looked at each other for a long moment. "Someone wanted the DDT concentrations lower than before and diluted the soil samples," Beth said, in a hushed voice.

"Dilution is the solution," Rudy said, but no one laughed.

"Nobody says anything about this until we figure out what to do next. Beth, I'd like you to analyze the quality control reports from the lab. We need to confirm they ran a clean sample before they tested the soil," Luke said.

"Will do. That will take a phone call. I'll do it from my office," Beth said. She gathered up her computer and headed down the hall.

Luke shut the conference room door and looked at Rudy.

***

"What I'm about to say must stay in this room for now. Earl told me last week that while Chad was conducting the soil sampling, he thought Chad might have fiddled with the samples. Earl was too far away to see exactly what he was doing, but it's possible he was diluting the soil samples with soil from somewhere else."

Rudy shook his head. "That little prick. He gets paid well enough, has a good job, and then he does this shit. What was he thinking? Doesn't he know you can't fake out lab results? He must have gotten paid to do it. We have a serious problem, Luke. We should fire his ass right now."

"Hold on. Chad and his team are out doing the quarterly groundwater sampling today. They only have a week left, and I don't want to accuse him of anything unless we have more proof. At this point, let them finish the groundwater sampling. There's little to be gained by diluting groundwater samples in a routine quarterly event, so he'll do this correctly."

"I spoke to Antoine this morning, and the EPA wants the raw data files from the lab now. He's sending us a formal request. They'll figure it out just as fast as we did. We'll have to admit we made a mistake in the field and do the whole thing again. In the meantime, I will have to tell Nancy that we just spent $15,000 for nothing."

"That's why you get paid the big bucks. If Chad's responsible, he should take the fall. Nancy will understand."

Luke had spent enough time in the military and other leadership positions to know he couldn't blame unfortunate events on someone else when he was the guy in charge. He blamed himself for not pulling Chad from the site and ordering new sampling when he first talked with Earl, even though there was little proof of any wrongdoing. He walked down the hall to Nancy's office and knocked on the door.

"Hi, Luke. Please come in. What's up?"

"Nancy, we have a serious problem with the soil sampling in Torrance." He sat at her conference table, looking dejected, and told her about the sampling results and the conclusion Beth had presented.

Nancy frowned, then smiled at Luke. "Luke, you can only do so much if an employee wants to cheat or steal from you. Don't blame yourself, it's happened to me many times. The question is what to do about it now. Obviously, we'll need to resample. And, if this is all true, and if Chad did this, we'll need to let him go. Once we know for sure, you and I can let Guadalupe know that we will resample on our nickel. First, let's make sure we know it was Chad who did this. He's sampling groundwater this week, right? So, we have time to ensure we don't falsely accuse him."

Luke practically ran out of Nancy's office, closing his eyes for a moment as he walked down the hall toward the Coffee Nook. She was putting the blame on Chad and not him. He was still mad at himself for not suspecting Chad earlier, but there was nothing he could do now, except move forward.

***

The EPA's formal request for the laboratory's raw data went directly to Guadalupe later that afternoon, and Bob Burrows authorized Luke to send the lab results to the EPA. Luke forwarded the report to Antoine, knowing that the EPA would call him back in a day or two, after they'd reached Beth's conclusion about sample dilution. *We'll see how good the EPA lab guys really are.* Luke's next call was to Bob.

"Bob, how are you?"

"That's a rhetorical question, right? It's January in New Jersey. I'm tired of the snow, the cold, and the darkness. Everybody hates chemical companies, and I am at the epicenter of that hatred. Does that answer your fucking question?"

"I'll lead off with a different greeting next time," said Luke. "Just to make your day a little more irritating, let me tell you what happened with the DDT soil sampling." He informed Bob of the sample results and Webber's suspicion without mentioning Chad.

"I'm sorry, Bob. Of course, we'll pull new samples and rerun the tests at our cost."

Bob sighed. "There's not much else you could have done, Luke. What's most concerning to me is that someone in your company is willing to put everything on the line and risk getting caught. There must be more going on here, like blackmail or payoffs. Talk to Earl. He's your boots on the ground. Let's see what the EPA comes back with, and then we'll figure out what to do."

Luke exhaled a sigh of relief.

He made it home in time for Kara to head to the gym before dinner. He put the flowers he'd bought in a vase on the kitchen table, as a surprise when she returned. The kids were outside playing in the new snow with Columbo. Luke brought them into the house, wet and cold, and made hot chocolate, followed by spaghetti and meatballs with green beans as a vegetable.

"Hi, honey. Who are the flowers for?" Kara asked with a smile as she came into the house.

"The kids bought them for you since you are a great mother and a marathoner."

Luke sat and described the day's events to her as she gobbled her spaghetti.

"I would be careful of this Chad guy. Once you fire him, he may hold a grudge against you. And someone else convinced him to tamper with the samples. Do you know who that was?"

"I don't know who is bribing Chad, but I have an idea who it might be. Once Chad is gone, things should settle down."

***

The call from Antoine came the following day. "Luke, there is something wrong with the DDT soil sample results. Our chemists believe someone altered the samples in the field or in the lab. The DDT concentrations were unrealistically low, and our chemists identified other pesticides previously not present at the site. What did your chemists conclude?"

Luke was ready for the call, although he'd thought it would take the EPA a few more days to get back to him. "We came to the same conclusion, Antoine. We believe the samples were altered in the field and will repeat the sampling effort with much more oversight."

"I'm glad you see it like we do, Luke. Do you think someone on your sampling crew altered the samples? That's pretty serious. It may even be a criminal act under Superfund."

"I don't know. We're looking into it, but supposing it's true for a moment, I'm trying to understand why someone would alter the samples and take the risk of getting caught. It reeks of foul play by someone who doesn't want the soil removal to happen. We know there are homeowners who don't want to see the removal, and I suspect one of them is behind this," Luke said, attempting to move some of the blame to a homeowner and away from Webber.

"It's up to you guys to get your house in order. I'm mainly calling because the EPA has made an internal decision to move forward with the removal action under an Administrative Order, based on the previous soil sampling results," Antoine said. "We need to accelerate the soil removal, and there is no reason to expect that the DDT concentrations have changed significantly over the last two years. We're getting pressure from upstairs, and the state health department is starting to make its opinion known."

Luke was speechless. He was not expecting the EPA to move forward with a removal without more sampling. "Okay, so you won't be asking for another sampling effort. Has the EPA notified Guadalupe of this decision, or are you going to make me do it, so that Bob Burrows can rip my head off first?" Luke said.

"I'll get the Administrative Order approved and out next week. As to who notifies Bob, it's your choice whether you want to tell Bob ahead of the order or not. We won't talk to anyone at Guadalupe until the order is signed."

Now I have important information that I am keeping from my client. Do I keep it that way or brave the lion's den?

"So, how many homeowner yards are you planning to excavate?" Luke asked.

"We don't have a final number yet, but it may be as many as twenty," said Antoine. "I anticipate that we'll start in about three months. As you can imagine, we have a lot of work to do getting contractors lined up and arranging temporary housing for the displaced homeowners. Oh, one last thing, Luke, under the order, Guadalupe can participate in the removal action with the EPA or do it themselves. You know the personalities better than I do, but I doubt Guadalupe will agree to either. Anyway, I have to ask the question."

Luke grabbed another cup of coffee at the Coffee Nook and wandered around the office for a few minutes, dreading the call to Bob. He continued procrastinating and called Simone first.

"Simone, it's Luke. How are you?"

"I'm doing great. How are you?"

"I'm unsure how to answer that question without being accused of colluding with the EPA. You aren't recording this call, are you?" Luke said.

Simone laughed. "I'm a 1099 contractor to the EPA, not an employee, and you're a consultant to Guadalupe, so there are multiple degrees of separation for both of us. Does that make you feel any better?"

"Now that you say it like that, it does make me feel a little better, knowing we can still talk without our friendship being Exhibit A. So, back to business. I just talked with Antoine, and he told me of the EPA's plan to file an Administrative Order and initiate the soil removal action. Are you comfortable moving ahead with soil removal and using the DDT soil sample data from two years ago? That sounds like something Antoine is pushing so he can meet an internal schedule."

"Actually, it was my idea to move ahead with the removal action. The past levels were high enough that another round of data will most likely not change anything, and it will lead to another year of worthless debate. It's better for everyone to get this over and done with."

"I don't agree with you on this one. We'll probably end up excavating more yards than we need to. We'll waste a lot of Guadalupe's money and time for nothing, not to mention disrupting the homeowners' lives."

"Oh, Luke. Usually, you're the smartest man in the room, but I've been in this business longer than you have, and I can show you the statistical analysis and reasons for what we recommend. You'd come to the same conclusion. Trust me on this. The sooner we're done with this, the better."

Luke recognized an immovable object when he saw one. "Okay. I still think you're wrong, but at least I can tell Bob and Caroline that I argued for another round of sampling in an attempt to save money. Since we disagree, we can say we're not colluding, right?"

They both laughed and said goodbye. Feeling like he was on a roll, he took a deep breath and dialed Bob. Less than a minute later, he regretted the decision.

***

"They can kiss my big ass! There's no way in the world we're going to help EPA with the removal. This is their baby, and they'll be the ones the locals hate at the end of the day, not Guadalupe. That TV channel lady will be all over them and forget about us. We need to stay out of this completely. I mean it! If someone asks you about it, you raise your hands and say, 'I don't have a clue what's going on. It's not my business. Call the EPA!'"

Bob paused for a moment to catch his breath, then began again. "Regarding the sampling screw up by your field crew, and the fact that the EPA doesn't want to sample again, that doesn't matter to me, other than Webber paying the bill. We were taking the risk that DDT would be detected in yards previously considered clean, increasing the removal volume. It will probably reflect negatively on Guadalupe, the longer it's in the press. Let's just get it done. The removal action is perfect for our defense in the EF&J lawsuit. We can say the EPA is proposing unnecessary tasks and delaying the cleanup, not Guadalupe."

Luke finally exhaled.

Thanks, Simone. You do understand this process better than me.

14

"**J**immy! It's Chad. How you doing, man? In your neighborhood today, collecting quarterly ground-water samples. You got time for a beer? We have some things to talk about, if you know what I mean."

Chad turned up the volume on his phone so he could hear Jimmy over the noise of his milling machine. Obviously, Jimmy was on a job taking a layer of old asphalt off a parking lot. "I heard you were out here. Let's meet at Charlie's at six o'clock. I should be done by then. Beers are on me tonight."

The smell of kitchen grease hit Chad as he walked into Charlie's bar a second or two before six. Popcorn and peanut shells crunched underfoot as he made his way to a corner booth. Looking around, he decided it all added up to a working-class joint. Burgers and fries were the main staples, March Madness on the TV, and grungy baseball caps on men and women. Chad was excited to meet with Jimmy and collect his second payment. Chad took advantage of happy hour and ordered two Budweisers. They came together in frosted mugs, and he opened a tab. He replayed the soil sample dilution process and how easy it had been to taint them. *Was this a regular practice at other Superfund sites?*

Jimmy arrived fifteen minutes late. He still wore his reflective safety vest and removed a pair of smudged safety glasses only after he sat down.

"That goddamn asphalt milling machine of mine keeps breaking down and requiring my attention because nobody else can fix it. It's about forty years old, you know. One of these days, I will have to bite the bullet and buy a new one. Sorry, Chad, for bothering you with the details. How did the DDT soil sampling go?"

Chad leaned in and spoke in a quiet voice. "I added the dirt that you gave me to every sample jar. I haven't seen the lab results yet, but I'm sure the DDT concentrations are about half of what they were before, unless you gave me some dirt with DDT. I think you owe me my second payment."

"Good work, Chad," Jimmy said. "That dirt I brought you was from a paving job I did at Disneyland. I figured Disneyland has to have the cleanest dirt around."

Chad chuckled, and then again asked for his second payment, this time in a more serious tone.

"Yeah. About that," Jimmy said. "An acquaintance of mine told me there's something odd about the soil sample results, and the EPA might not accept them. Maybe because the concentration dropped so much, I don't know for sure. I need to be confident the results are in our favor before I can settle up with you."

"Whoa!" Chad said, raising his voice. "You never said my payment depended on the results. I did what you asked. Now I'm getting screwed? You can't hold me responsible for what the EPA is or isn't going to do. Besides, how do you know this for sure? Do you have a mole inside the EPA?"

"I have a lot of friends, Chad. When you get to be as old

as I am, and work with new people every day, you make lots of friends and acquaintances."

"Maybe your acquaintance is wrong."

Jimmy shook his head. "Look, I already paid you half, and it's not just my money, by the way, there are a few other contributors to the effort, and we want this stupid, goddamn removal action to go away. Find out what you can from your sources at Webber, and make something happen, okay?" Jimmy shifted in his chair and took a gulp of his beer. "Also, tell Luke to get on the right side of this removal action and do something to stop it. I don't think he gives a shit about us homeowners. He needs to be replaced with someone who will stand up to the EPA and their stupidity!"

"How am I supposed to make that happen? I can't talk to the EPA, let alone convince them to do something different," Chad said.

"I don't know!" Jimmy said, throwing his arms in the air. "That's why we're paying you. You're the one who understands this sampling stuff better than anyone else. Make something happen. Let me know if you're not up for the task, and I'll find someone else."

Chad sipped his beer and watched the basketball game for a few minutes. "I'll make something happen, Jimmy, but if the EPA believes I've done something to the samples, it's just a matter of time before Webber and Guadalupe think so. Then, I'm going to be looking for a job. Or worse."

***

"Okay, it sounds like everything we discussed a few days ago about another round of soil sampling is now off the table," Nancy said to Luke and Rudy after calling an emergency meeting to discuss the EPA's decision.

"I talked with Antoine and Simone, and they both think we are just wasting time with another round of soil sampling, and the homeowners are getting more and more agitated," Luke said. "So, in their opinion, it's better just to complete the removal action."

"What's Guadalupe think of this? Bob must be beside himself," Nancy said.

"Surprisingly, Bob seems somewhat indifferent to this latest twist. I called him earlier, thinking I was going to get an ass chewing, but he kinda liked the idea of not sampling anymore and risking a broader problem. He just wants to make sure we, that is us and Guadalupe, have nothing to do with the removal."

"What about Chad?" Nancy asked.

Rudy spoke up, "I talked with Chad this morning about the quarterly groundwater sampling effort, and he never mentioned the soil sampling. I left a few openings in the conversation for him to ask about the soil sample results, but he never did. I'm not sure if he knows we have the results yet, or he knows there is a problem, and he's delaying the inevitable."

"I've thought about this for a few days now, and I can't see any other way the sample results could be so dramatically different from previous years' testing. I hate to say it, but I think it was an inside job, and the only one with opportunity was Chad. He must have diluted the samples with soil from another location. The fact that Earl saw him doing some questionable things with the sampling bottles only makes him look more guilty." Nancy paused to jot down a quick note in her personal organizer. "We've never before detected aldrin at the site. I worked on a project years ago, when an employee tried to get his boss fired. We figured it out, fired the tech, and refused to pay him his last check so we could cover the lab costs. We had to hire a security guard for a month, because everyone in the office was concerned about what the guy might do." She looked at Luke and Rudy in turn. "Do you have any concerns about Chad becoming violent?"

Luke gathered his thoughts and spoke first. "He's always struck me as being hard working, and wanting to fit in with everyone. I don't see violent tendencies in him, but you could say that about most mass murderers too."

"I agree with Luke, except for the mass murderer part," Rudy said.

Nancy nodded, but didn't laugh at their attempt at humor.

"Okay, then. I'll talk with Sally in Human Resources, and we'll terminate him first thing on Monday morning when he's back in the office."

***

Luke and Kara took the kids and Columbo to the park on Saturday, all of them sporting shorts and pale skin that hadn't seen the sun in several months. Spring had started to creep into the air in early March, and youth soccer season was nearing. Luke volunteered to help coach Nathan's team, and they were determined to take advantage of the nice day and practice.

"That's too bad about Chad," Kara said as they watched the kids play on the playground. "I can't believe someone would alter samples like that. It seems so easy to get caught. Is he a vengeful type?"

"He usually doesn't talk much about his personal life, other than fun things he does on the weekend. He's a nice guy, pretty well-liked."

"Sometimes the nice guys are the guys you need to worry about," Kara said. "Is he married?"

"No."

"Does he ever talk about his family?"

"I know his dad was in the Air Force."

Kara reached down and scratched Columbo's ears. "Do you know what he does when he's not working?"

"Not really. Rudy says he does small plane maintenance for extra money. I guess I really don't know what to expect when he gets fired."

***

Luke arrived early Monday morning at his office and went directly to the Coffee Nook for his first coffee. He anxiously watched as the coffee machine moaned and groaned and slowly brewed his Americano. *Hurry up, I don't want to run into Chad right now.*

"Hey, Luke. Still drinking the same old Americano? This machine makes an awesome latte," Chad said, with his usual big smile.

Luke was speechless for a moment as their eyes met. "There's nothing like good old black coffee. You must have finished the groundwater sampling. How did it go?"

"No problems, as usual. Chuck and I finished a day early. We aim to please and make Guadalupe happy."

"Good job. Hey, I have to go and get on an early call," Luke said, abruptly turning away and walking calmly to his office. He closed his door and picked up his desk phone, holding it to his ear and listening to the dial tone while he checked email.

An hour later, he almost fell out of his chair when Nancy knocked on his door. "It's time, Luke."

Chad walked into Nancy's office and was noticeably surprised to see Luke and Rudy at the conference table, as well as Sally, Webber's HR director. His smile disappeared instantly as he quickly glanced around the room. Nancy removed a stack of draft reports from the table and asked him to have a seat. The conference table was uncomfortably small, so Nancy sat behind her desk to give the others more room. Luke was glad to have Nancy and Sally in the room, since he had been involved in only one employee termination before this one.

"Chad, let me cut to the chase," Nancy said. "The DDT soil sample results from the lab indicate the samples were tampered with, and we believe someone diluted the samples in the field. The DDT concentrations decreased more than is scientifically possible, and other pesticides that had never been detected prior were detected, including aldrin. We have never detected aldrin at the site. It is clear to all who reviewed the results that someone diluted the Torrance soil with soil from another location. Are you aware of any dilution or contamination during sampling and chain of custody?"

"It sounds like you are accusing me," Chad said.

Luke watched him pause, perhaps waiting for a reaction, but there was none.

"I took samples, filled the jars with soil according to protocol, and sent them to the lab. That's all I did." Chad's tone was defensive. "Did you check the lab quality control and see if they cleaned the equipment before the sample run? I bet they didn't clean the chromatograph properly, and they're trying to put the blame on me."

"We did all of that," Nancy said. "We have no choice but to assume that you diluted the samples since you and Chuck were the only two people conducting the sampling, and Chuck never handles samples. I'm asking one last time. Chad, did you dilute the samples in the field?"

Chad paused for a long moment, his eyes darting from person to person. "I followed protocol. I don't know why the sample results came out like they did."

"Okay then. You leave us no choice. We have to conclude you contaminated the samples, which warrants immediate termination of your employment. Sally will escort you back to your desk and give you your final check. I'm sorry that it had to come to this. Working with you over the years has been a pleasure, but this behavior cannot be tolerated."

Chad leaned in, closer to Luke, across the small table. "If you had done your job and told EPA to put this soil removal action bullshit to rest, none of this would have happened. All of this is a result of your incompetence!"

Luke had never seen Chad react with such hostility before. He kept his mouth shut and glared back at Chad until Nancy and Sally stood up, signaling the end of the meeting.

Chad got halfway to the door before he turned around. "All of you can go to hell. If it weren't for me, your precious little groundwater treatment facility wouldn't even run. For all my hard work on it and the extra time I put in, you never once even said, 'thanks.'"

Sally escorted Chad out of the office.

"We'll get through this, Luke," Nancy said. "All we can do is get back to work and move on."

15

After Luke returned to his office and closed the door, he called Kara at work— which he didn't do unless it was an emergency—and vented for a few minutes.

"He sounds pretty upset. Keep looking over your shoulder until he cools off," she said.

Luke stared out the office window at the mountains. Despite the recent warm weather, there was still a good amount of snow on the peaks. "I don't think he's dangerous. But who knows? I'll keep my eyes open. Thanks for listening, babe."

His next call was to Earl. He wanted to tell the older man what had happened before he heard it from someone else.

"Hey Earl, how are you?" Luke could hear the pumps running the treatment facility in the background and assumed Earl was performing his daily maintenance routine.

"It's a good day when the wind blows from the north because the smell of the coffee brewing company comes across the street. Normally, it's just the same old chemical smell from the other direction. I think I know why you are calling, but please, go ahead."

"Earl, I wanted you to hear it directly from me. We fired Chad this morning because we believe he diluted the soil samples in the field in a poor attempt to show lower DDT concentrations in the neighborhood. There is no denying that he did it."

"Chad left me a voicemail just before you called, Luke. He was clearly upset, vindictive, and mad at everyone in the Denver office. He still looks to me as a friend and wanted to blow off some steam. I think he knows he screwed up but doesn't want to admit it. I'll give him a call back and calm him down. Maybe I can get him focused on moving forward with his life. I think he's lucky you guys aren't pressing charges."

Luke was still puzzling over why Chad would take such a risk in the first place. "Somebody must be paying him off. Why else would he compromise an entire sampling round and risk his job and reputation?"

"Yeah, I agree with you; someone must have paid him a lot of money."

"Who do you think it was?"

"The usual suspects. We've got a few hotheads in town. But I can't prove anything."

"We'll find out eventually. My concern is that someone is willing to pay lots of money to stop this removal action."

"I'll keep my ear close to the ground, see if I can learn more about who is behind this. Please don't let anyone else know we've talked about this. If people around here figure out I'm passing on information, they'll never talk to me again," Earl said.

Chad's comment that Luke could have done more to convince the EPA to disregard the soil removal action still stung. "You know as well as I do, the EPA is driving the train. There is nothing else I can do to stop the removal action."

"I know that, Luke. You've done all you can. Don't feel bad. The only thing that might stop the EPA is a big lawsuit by the homeowners, or Guadalupe. But even then, lawsuits usually just result in expensive delay tactics."

Luke had barely hung up with Earl when his phone rang.

"Luke, it's Angelo downstairs in IT. Hey, I finally got into Chad's computer. Sorry, I was busy this morning. I'll give you access to last year's emails on the file server. There's a lot here, man. He must have spent his whole day writing emails. Have fun."

Angelo gave Luke over five thousand of Chad's emails from last year. Only a few in "trash" had been permanently deleted in the last ninety days. Luke was happy to see that Chad rarely deleted an email. Most were personal and not business-related, which Luke suspected was typical for most employees.

He sorted the emails by sender and scanned the list. There was the usual back and forth with Debbie about the construction and startup of the groundwater treatment facility, but it was all business. He was relieved that nothing appeared out of the ordinary with Debbie. Then, he played a hunch and searched for Jimmy Mendoza's name. Hundreds of emails popped up between the two. He began scanning them one at a time, looking for incriminating language.

It was apparent that Jimmy had legal experience and chose his words carefully. Luke formulated an image of Jimmy as a sort of mob boss, careful about what he put into writing. Phone calls would be Jimmy's preferred method of communicating. Fortunately, Chad's responses were more uninhibited. Several of his phrases stood out to Luke.

I sure am looking forward to a new truck, if you know what I mean.

I'll send Chuck to the hardware store in the morning to get sampling supplies. Stop by between 9 and 10?

I'll meet you at Sylvia's diner. Look forward to hearing your business proposal.

The emails and phrases confirmed Chad's tampering with the soil sampling, and incriminated Jimmy to a degree, but were not as conclusive as Luke wanted to see. For now, he would go forward believing that Jimmy was involved with Chad in the fraudulent sampling effort. He assumed Jimmy would be very disappointed when the EPA announced its decision to proceed with the soil removal action. The big question was, would Jimmy try and take revenge on someone?

***

"Luke, I'm at the treatment facility. We have a problem. You better get Debbie in your office right now, so I only have to say this once." Earl sounded slightly out of breath, and Luke wasted no time racing down the hall to Debbie's office. Earl rarely called, and never at 7:30 a.m. Pacific time.

"It's Earl," Luke said, shutting her office door. He put the phone on Debbie's desk and hit the speaker button.

"There's groundwater running from the site into the street. It's flooding all the way down to the elementary school, where we had our public meeting."

Debbie's face paled. "Has the treatment facility been shut down?" she asked.

"Water was still flowing when the fire department called me. I told them to cut the lock on the gate and pull the breaker, 'cause I was twenty minutes away. It's off now. I confirmed it was shut down as soon as I got here."

Luke jumped into the conversation. "So, treated groundwater

is running down the street and into the storm sewer. We normally discharge treated groundwater into that same storm sewer underground, right? Why is this a problem, and why is the fire department even there?"

"No, no, Luke, you're not understanding me. The water running down the street is untreated. The piping broke right where it comes out of the ground, before it goes through the treatment process," Earl said. "This is concentrated chlorobenzene and DDT, not treated groundwater!"

Luke looked at Debbie with a mixture of disbelief and horror. This was the worst situation imaginable. The treatment facility design had several automatic safety shutdowns. Any of these automatic shutdowns would turn off the groundwater pump, immediately stopping a spill at the surface. A water sensor in the containment berm surrounding the treatment facility was the most reliable of the automatic shutdowns. Leaking groundwater should have filled the area within the berm and triggered a shutdown of the groundwater pump. It was inconceivable that it had failed.

"Do you know what failed, Earl? It sounds like there was a leak right at the surface, above the groundwater pump. Did the pipe break?"

"I'm standing here looking at the pipe coupling. It definitely came loose. Sometimes vibrations can cause things to come loose, you know, but that seems unlikely to me. The containment berm overflowed. The water sensor must have failed too."

"How did the groundwater flow down the street to the elementary school? There are several storm drains along the curbs in the street that should have drained the water," Luke said.

"Good question, Luke. We always thought that was a good safety measure, but the hazmat guys said the drains have been blocked by construction sandbags. One of the guys told me there's supposed to be some asphalt paving work happening soon."

Earl's tone deepened and took on an edge of urgency. "I need to tell you what's going on right now. We can talk about the reasons for the leak later. There are puddles of water in the street. I'm using the term 'water,' but we all know what it really is. Some kids were riding their bikes through the puddles, making big splashes and fantails, having a good time on their way to school. They stunk pretty bad when they got to school, and one complained about his skin burning and itching. That's when a teacher called the fire department, who brought in the hazmat crew."

"A hazmat crew?" Fear rose in Luke's voice. "Is the kid okay? What did they do with him?"

"They took him in the bathroom, put him in the shower, and then sent him to the hospital. I told them that's just what we used to do at the plant when someone got contaminated with acid or DDT. I'm sure he'll be fine, but his parents could freak out, you know. You two should probably get on the next plane and get here ASAP. I'm not sure I can handle all of this by myself. Plus, it's probably not long before your girlfriend from KKAT gets out here, Luke."

Debbie cracked a small smile, while Luke gave the phone an annoyed look.

Luke's military training took over, and he started giving orders. "Just give her the facts, Earl. No speculation. I'll let Bob and Caroline know what's happening, and we'll head your way as soon as we can get to the airport. Call me at least every hour and leave a message with an update," Luke said.

"Let's go right now, Debbie. We can buy clothes and toothbrushes when we get there. Ask Cindy to find us some flights and a rental car, please? I'll call Guadalupe. We could be there a few days."

16

L uke called Kara on the way to DIA.

"We've got kids riding their bikes through puddles of water with chlorobenzene and DDT. They're being sent to the hospital by the hazmat crew. I need to be there as soon as possible to help manage the situation. I should be back in a day or two."

"Oh my god, are those kids going to be okay?" Kara asked.

"As long as they didn't get any contamination in their eyes or mouth, they should be fine, but I'm sure we've got some freaked-out parents and money-hungry lawyers ready to file lawsuits. I can't believe the treatment facility failed. We have to review our design today and make sure we don't have another spill. Bob and Caroline are going to be pissed!"

"You're not going to lose your job, are you?"

"I don't think so," he said, after a long beat. In the midst of all the chaos, the thought hadn't occurred to him. First, Chad's betrayal; now, the treatment facility fails. How he handled the response activities in the next few days would be critical for his reputation and his job.

"You've always said the treatment facility is super safe, yet two weeks after Chad gets fired, there's a toxic spill in the middle of the night. Hmm," Kara said.

"When you put it like that… Do you think he flew all the way out to Torrance and sabotaged the treatment facility to get revenge?" It sounded far-fetched. "He probably has another job by now and has forgotten about us."

"Just saying, Luke. Seems suspicious to me."

The next few hours passed in a blur. Luke and Debbie arrived at the treatment facility shortly after 3:00 in the afternoon. The main gate was open, and a bright red hazmat semi-truck, with hoses, pumps, and emergency lights, was parked next to the guard shack. Earl and the hazmat incident commander were still wearing their partially unzipped Tyvek suits and speculating on the cause of the spill. Luke put forward his hand and introduced himself to the commander. Debbie suited up and went straight to the treatment facility to make her assessment and determine what went wrong.

The commander recounted how he and his team had responded in accordance with the Spill Prevention, Control, and Countermeasure plan required by the state of California. Fire trucks had hosed down the streets, and the residual contamination was vacuumed up by "vac" trucks. Knowing that the spill was contained, Luke focused his attention on the condition of the two exposed kids.

"Where are they now? Are they still in the hospital, or were they released?" Luke asked.

"They were discharged around noon and sent home with a parent for observation. I'm sure their parents are asking them how they feel about every two minutes. In fact, it wouldn't surprise me if their parents take them back to the hospital," the commander said.

Luke wouldn't blame them a bit.

"Your girlfriend from KKAT was here earlier, looking for an

interview. I made myself scarce and let the commander here make a statement. He's better at this stuff than I am," Earl said. "But Haewon's coming back later, before the evening news, to get an update from you."

"Oh boy, I can't wait. Does she know that two kids went to the hospital from chlorobenzene and DDT exposure?"

"We are required to disclose if people require hospital treatment, so yes, she knows. However, we've withheld their names because they're minors," the commander said.

Debbie walked up with a pensive look on her face. "Luke, can you and Earl come to the guard shack for a minute? I have something I want to show you."

"Good time for me to go. I need to get back to the station to do my paperwork," the commander said as he packed up and walked away. Luke and Earl followed Debbie across the parking lot to the guard shack.

The shack was mounted on steel skids and sat about fifty feet from the treatment facility. It was a small, metal shed about ten feet by eight feet, with a steel door and a wall mounted air conditioner. The walls were neatly organized with hard hats, Tyvek suits, gloves, and face shields for personal protection. Empty containers and measuring equipment for soil and groundwater sampling were stacked on the wooden shelves. A few old chairs sat beside a banged-up metal desk covered with a computer, printer, and telephone.

Debbie had insisted that the groundwater treatment facility design include three wireless security cameras and several pole-mounted overhead lights with motion detector operation during the night. The computer would send a pre-recorded alert phone call to Debbie and Earl's phones in the event of a motion detection after regular business hours. The former plant site was in an industrial part of Torrance, and theft was not uncommon at adjacent facilities. The chain-link fence surrounding the thirteen-acre site included three strands of barbed wire and was a significant physical barrier. However, a determined person could find a way through. The fence had been cut several times before by skateboarders who found the raised asphalt areas perfect for performing tricks.

"Remember when I put in those security cameras last year? The ones I couldn't get to work for the longest time?" Debbie asked.

Both Luke and Earl nodded.

"Well, I got them to work the last time I was here, and we have a recording of last night on the computer."

Debbie clicked the play button, and the computer screen jumped to life. She fast-forwarded to 2:07 a.m., when an intruder ran from left to right across the screen and disappeared. The overhead lights had come on when motion was detected and illuminated the person briefly. The intruder was fully clothed, gloved, and wearing a face mask while looking away from the security camera. The intruder's height and gait were the only distinguishing characteristics on the video recording.

All three watched it at regular speed and slow motion, looking for details to identify the intruder. Nothing was obvious, including the intruder's gender, race, or identifying features. They concluded the culprit was either familiar with the treatment facility, or had a good knowledge of industrial equipment.

"Why didn't we get an alarm call-out when the motion detector was activated?" Luke asked, frowning. "I thought the system was supposed to call you and Earl when that happened."

Earl stepped in to answer Luke's question. "We had so many nuisance alert phone calls in the middle of the night, triggered by animals, birds, and light reflections, we turned it off until we could come up with a better solution."

"Where did the leak occur?" Luke asked, changing the subject.

"It's over here where the pipe comes out of the ground from the submersible pump," Debbie said.

"It's pretty obvious to me the pipe was intentionally loosened and didn't come apart on its own," Earl said. "Pipe fittings like this don't just come undone by themselves."

"You all should see this too," Debbie said, as she pointed to the water sensor float in the containment berm. "The float is clogged with debris, so it wasn't activated when the berm area overflowed. In light of the video, I think somebody stuffed some sticks and leaves in there so the sensor would not shut down the groundwater pump."

Earl broke his silence with a chuckle. "Well, this sure makes things interesting, doesn't it? I want the record to show that I had nothing to do with this sabotage. Y'all saw how fast the bad guy ran across the camera. I haven't run that fast in years or been that skinny."

Luke gave the man a grin. "We believe you, Earl. We have enough evidence to conclude this was an intentional and planned act. Take a lot of pictures, Debbie, and I'll call Guadalupe and the EPA and explain what we found."

"We should file a police report too," Earl said. "We don't need everyone blaming us. I doubt they'll ever catch anybody, but at least the son of a bitch that did this will know we're looking for him."

"Or her," Debbie said.

"I'll go check on the status of the two kids and talk to the parents. I know one of the families, and that would be a good place to start," Earl said.

"I agree," Luke said. "The fact you are still alive and in good health at age sixty-seven, after working at the DDT plant for your entire career, will be reassuring."

Luke called the EPA and Guadalupe and waited for Haewon. He looked forward to letting her run with the sabotage story on the evening news.

***

Haewon, with her cameraman in tow, hunted Luke down about forty-five minutes later. He'd been going over some soundbites in his head and felt ready for the interview.

"Thanks for giving me some time, Mr. Graham. I want to ask you a few questions about the massive toxic chemical spill this morning and its traumatic impact on the neighborhood and the elementary school kids."

Her presumptive statement agitated Luke, who'd been hoping they could avoid a verbal sparring match. "You must be talking about something that happened elsewhere in the LA basin, something that I am unaware of. If you want to talk about the sabotage of our treatment facility and the damage to my client's reputation, I am more than happy to discuss that," Luke said.

Haewon ignored his comment. "Mr. Graham, can you tell our viewers what happened here early this morning?"

"First, I want to thank the hazmat team for its response to the groundwater spill we had this morning on the former plant site. The hazmat team response was excellent and worked according to the plan and training we all went through here at the site. What's concerning to us—and should be concerning to all citizens in this area—is that we have reason to believe the spill resulted from an intentional act of sabotage."

"Why are you so sure this is sabotage? Could it have been a simple operator error, or poor design?"

"We have video images of an intruder entering the facility after cutting a hole in the chain link fence right over there. You can see it from here," Luke said, pointing toward the hole. "We also have indisputable evidence of his or her subsequent damage to the treatment facility. We're asking that anybody who has information about this crime bring it to the attention of the Torrance Police Department."

"Mr. Graham, we understand that several elementary school children were injured and sent to the hospital. Is this true?"

"You'll have to ask someone else about that. I don't have any first-hand knowledge of children going to the hospital. Now, if you'll excuse me, I need to get back to making repairs so we can continue our cleanup effort."

Luke turned and entered the guard shack before Haewon could ask more questions. Debbie was working away at the computer. They watched the live security camera feed as Haewon and her cameraman drove away in the TV van.

"That was a good interview, Luke. You didn't say much of anything. I hope it gets shown on TV tonight. We'll have neighbors looking at neighbors. Someone's going to squeal."

***

The next day, Antoine arrived. Luke greeted him in the parking lot.

"Luke, I want you to note that I have an economy rental car. I'm saving the American taxpayer some money."

"Well, it's good of you to show up the day after everything went to hell. Although, as I think about it now, having the

EPA show up yesterday would have made things look worse than they were."

"You're exactly right. This spill is a local hazmat problem and not an EPA problem. When I show up and the people find out I am EPA, things can get a little crazy. I'm more interested in what happened and whether we need to call in the DOJ."

"I'd say yes to the DOJ. Let me show you the surveillance tape." Luke led Antoine into the shack.

Luke watched as Antoine and Debbie shook hands. He had to give them credit. Nothing in their mannerisms hinted they shared anything but a professional relationship. And, in fairness, Luke didn't know that they didn't.

After watching the video countless times, Antoine said, "I can't tell who it is by watching the video, but I suspect that it's Chad, based on what you have told me."

"I'm placing my bet on Jimmy Mendoza," Luke said. "I can't believe that Chad would go to the effort and spend the money to come out here and do this. What do you think, Debbie?"

Debbie leaned back in the old chair, parting her brunette hair to one side, "I'm going to hold back judgment until I get more information."

Luke and Antoine smiled at her.

"Would the EPA seriously consider bringing in the DOJ and investigating this?" Luke asked. He wasn't sure that would play well with Caroline and Bob.

"Yes and no. Some people within the agency want to chase down criminals who commit crimes like this and throw the book at them. However, we're federal, so I doubt anything will happen anytime soon, and crimes like this tend to blow over in a few weeks, if nothing else happens."

"Well, if it makes you feel better, Debbie is going to make this place look like Fort Knox," Luke said. "We'll have a security guard every night and twenty-four-hour lighting until we get the automatic alarm call-out working better. Why don't you show Antoine the treatment facility and the hole in the perimeter fence? I need to make some phone calls."

Debbie took Antoine outside and began the extended tour she had given others many times. Luke didn't expect them to walk the entire site perimeter, but it gave him time to gather his thoughts on the day's events.

17

As Antoine had projected, a month passed, and homeowner concerns regarding the spill at the treatment facility subsided. However, Luke knew the consensus of the neighborhood was that Guadalupe, and he and Debbie in particular, were to blame for the failure of the groundwater treatment facility and the subsequent spill. This didn't surprise him. Even though they technically worked for Webber, the public had grown used to seeing their faces. Luke's explanation of sabotage was soon forgotten.

Luke gathered the team in the Longs Peak conference room to brief them on the upcoming activities. "The soil removal action will begin in a few days, and the temporary displacement of several homeowners at local hotel suites offering long-term accommodations has already started. Guadalupe assigned us to be their eyes on the ground and represent Guadalupe if necessary. The EPA selected a contractor to complete the soil removal and arranged for field oversight of the contractor using Ryan and Associates, a consulting company whose primary business is to support the EPA in cleanups on the West Coast. Since the EPA will demand cost reimbursement from Guadalupe, we will observe activities on behalf of Guadalupe."

"Must be nice to have your rent paid by the government. Maybe there is DDT in my apartment common area," Beth said, her eyes widening.

Luke continued. "Our objective is twofold. First, we need to make sure the contractor doesn't keep finding ways to add to the scope of work and charge the EPA for unnecessary work. We all know how contractors like change orders. Those cost overruns will probably come back to Guadalupe."

"Oh, yeah, I understand cost overruns. My kitchen remodel cost twice the quoted amount because of contractor change orders," Rudy said. "This-and-that type of stuff. The guy admitted that he knew the proposal wasn't enough when he bid the job, but he never would have won if he had added the extra costs into the proposal. I hope the EPA knows what it's doing, or we'll be arguing about change orders every day."

"I don't get it. What does this Ryan and Associates company do?" Beth said.

"They are EPA's representative in the field," said Luke. "Ryan has a lot of construction management type people that are good at watching over contractors. Guys like Antoine stay in San Francisco and let Ryan and Associates oversee fieldwork.

"We need to take copious notes of the contractor's daily activities in the field in fifteen-minute increments," Luke said. "When the job's done, we'll argue with the contractor and the EPA about whether any additional work was justified. Don't expect the contractor to be your friend, either."

"You know what will happen when this is all done?" Rudy asked. He went on, answering his own question. "Guadalupe will refuse to pay for any of the soil removal costs because the entire removal action is unnecessary, according to Bob and Caroline, and ultimately, there will be a hotly contested settlement between the EPA, Guadalupe, and their insurance company."

"That's a bit cynical, don't you think?"

"Don't be naive, Luke. Guadalupe has no intention of paying for any of this soil removal if they can avoid it. I've seen how Guadalupe acted on previous projects, before you were hired. They'll pay as little as they can. I mean, would you pay for this if you didn't think it was necessary?"

Luke glanced around the room and then continued. "Our second objective is to improve Webber's reputation in the area. Right or wrong, the locals blame us for the botched sampling effort, which some feel might have shown the removal action was unnecessary. Then, there's the spill that many consider was caused by a design problem on our end. Mainly, people are mad and want to blame someone. It just happens they're blaming us. They don't understand that we have minimal influence on the EPA's actions in this case. We need to communicate our message to the homeowners and defend ourselves, every chance we get," Luke said.

Debbie wore a stoic expression and shook her head as he spoke. He knew she'd been agonizing over the spill and was slowly beginning to accept that some residents would never fully accept that Webber wasn't responsible.

"I'll be there all of next week, when the removal action kicks off," Luke said. "Let me know who wants to go the following week. You'll be on *per diem*, so if you want to live cheap and earn extra cash, this is your opportunity."

Luke returned to his office and was surprised to have a new voicemail from Earl.

"Never a dull moment around here anymore. Jimmy called an emergency city council meeting last night, and about fifty people showed up. I'm on the email list, so I made it there just as it started. I had to walk through people in the parking lot who were carrying signs opposing the soil removal. They were banging on drums and making a ruckus. Jimmy just kept egging them on. He sure knows how to whip up a crowd. There was a smaller group that supported the removal. They kept yelling about their home values. Then Jimmy's friend, Ralph, the one with an IQ of about seventy on a good day, started arguing with a lady who I don't know, and she slapped him across the face. Ralph pushed her backward, and she fell over a chair and sprawled out on the floor, legs in the air, screaming. That's when all hell broke loose, and somebody called the police. Jimmy never got a chance to vote on anything or say what the council would do. Whew! Call me back when you get a chance."

Luke walked down the hall for a refill at the Coffee Nook, gathering his thoughts, and then went to Rudy's office, where he replayed Earl's voicemail. After a fifteen-minute call with Earl, replaying the previous night's events, Luke agreed to call Antoine and Bob and share the information.

"I suggest you play like Switzerland and keep your distance. Let the EPA take the heat. Like Bob said, this is the EPA's removal action, not ours," Rudy said.

"I don't think it is that simple. Whether we like it or not, we're in the middle of this whole thing. I'm more inclined to go on the offensive. I think Jimmy Mendoza is the instigator and an asshole who needs to be put in his place. I'll get with Earl as soon as I get there, and we'll go talk to Jimmy."

"Good luck. Watch out for hot asphalt. I don't want to name a street after you," Rudy said.

Luke thought about the intelligence that he had received

from Van about Jimmy's former business partner's mysterious death.

Maybe I should ask Van to come to California with me.

***

Luke called Van before the end of the day. "Russo, it's Luke. Hey, I'm flying the plane to California on Monday for a week. Do you want to come with me? We'll be back in time for Kara's marathon the following Sunday."

"I thought you would never ask. What's the situation on the ground these days?" Van said.

"There's a lot of tension between homeowners who want the soil removal and those who don't. It's starting to get physical."

"Sounds like you want me to be an innocent bystander of some sort, but pack heat just in case," Van said.

"I'm not worried. Well, not much, anyway. Jimmy Mendoza, the self-appointed leader of the homeowners, seems to be the one who's all worked up. But, as you know from your research, he's one of those guys who is always worked up about something," Luke said. "All we need to do is observe the soil removal contractor and take notes. Should be pretty easy duty, and I can show you the project site and explain everything. Can you work remotely for a week?"

"I'm good for a week as long as I can get a secure satellite connection and board my cat. There are some things going on in the world that I can share with you that I am sure you'll find most interesting," Van replied.

"Sounds good. Let's plan on meeting at 0600 and wheels up at 0700 on Monday, even though the wheels don't retract on the Cirrus. If we leave early, we'll get over the mountains and into Long Beach while the air is smooth. I'll call you over the weekend and make plans for the week," Luke said.

Next, he called Kara, promising to be home the following Sunday for her marathon. Knowing the importance of the event, he gave himself an extra day on the return flight, to allow for bad weather.

"Hey, I talked to Bill Samuelson and he said he wants to come and watch you run. He was all over it and decided to make T-shirts for all of us that say, 'Remember Angela,' with her picture on the back. He knows a guy who can get them made this week. Plus, I thought he could go with your parents and the kids. Never hurts to have another adult like him there."

"That would be great and give me some extra inspiration. I think I can beat four hours and thirty minutes. I'm feeling good, and nothing hurts," Kara said.

She was in her last week of training, and he had encouraged her to recruit her parents so that they could spend a few nights in the house and help take care of Nathan and Kaylie. Kara's parents rarely made the two-hour drive to visit. He didn't understand why. Maybe it was the drive, or they were uncomfortable around him and the house. Luke would be in California for the week, so if that was the case, they should be willing to stay with Kara.

"I'll be there, babe, unless we have a mechanical or weather problem. If we do, I'll fly back commercial. Pilots who 'gotta get there' often make really bad decisions and never get there."

***

Luke and Van arrived at the Arapahoe County airport hangar an hour before takeoff to go through the pre-flight checklist and plan the flight. Luke owned the single-engine Cirrus SR20 plane with three other pilots, and they all shared equally in the cost and maintenance. He'd booked the plane for the entire week and hoped to get additional flight time in the LA basin and over the coast, if his work allowed it. They pulled the Cirrus from the hangar onto the apron and loaded their luggage.

"Looks like about four hours of flight time today, Russo. We'll make a stop in Page, Arizona, by Lake Powell, for fuel and to stretch. There's not much headwind up high today, so we can put on our oxygen masks for a while and cruise up to seventeen thousand feet. We'll get really good groundspeed at that altitude for the same reason jets like to fly at high altitudes."

"What happens if we run out of oxygen, Rattler?" Van asked.

"We just go to sleep and wake up when we get to a lower altitude. Hopefully, before we hit the ground."

"This isn't the time for smart-ass humor. You know I get uneasy about flying in small planes."

"Okay, bad joke. To answer your question, if we run out of oxygen, we'll fly at a lower altitude, like twelve thousand feet. We've climbed fourteeners before, so we'll be fine at that altitude. If your fingernails turn blue, we'll drop down even lower."

They climbed into the low-wing plane, and Luke took a few minutes to familiarize Van with the controls and instruments. Luke was in his element, while Van bit his fingernails and stared at all the instruments. Luke yelled, "Clear," out the window and turned the ignition key to start the turbocharged, 215-horsepower engine, as a rush of wind burst by the open window. The plane was sleek and fast, compared to other general aviation aircraft, capable of cruising at two hundred miles per hour.

"So, Russo, we'll go to the run-up area on the taxiway and check out the engine before we take off. It's standard practice, and you can read the checklist to me." Luke knew the checklist by memory, but it was good practice to step through it, and it would be a calming exercise for Van.

As Van read through the checklist of fuel settings, oil pressure, flight controls, and radio frequencies, Luke revved the engine to 1800 rpm. "First, we'll optimize our mixture, the fuel-to-air ratio that gets the best engine performance and doesn't waste fuel. Then we'll test our magnetos, to make sure they are working normally," Luke said.

"What the hell is a magneto, Rattler?" Van asked.

"Great question, Russo. A magneto is simply a rotating magnet turned by the propellor shaft that generates electricity for the spark plug. It's like pulling the cord on a lawn mower. Once this engine starts running, it will keep running until it runs out of fuel. It doesn't require a battery or an alternator to run. It's a really simple machine, compared to a car."

"I'm not sure if that's comforting," Van said.

"Maybe this will help. Each of the six cylinders has two spark plugs. The left magneto feeds one spark plug in each cylinder, and the right magneto feeds the other spark plug. So, if you lose one magneto, you still have one that works, and the engine can run almost as well as with two magnetos. It's a safety feature, but that's what you want with an airplane engine."

Van nodded but didn't appear to relax at all. Luke had always been curious about his friend's dislike for flying. It was at odds with the rest of Van's tough-guy persona. If he could get Van to fly with him a few more times, he could convince Van it really was the safest way to travel.

Luke taxied the Cirrus to the runway ramp and called the tower. "Arapahoe Tower, Cirrus 3-4-5-Tango-Charlie ready for takeoff, Runway 1-7 Left, for a southwest departure."

"Five-Tango-Charlie cleared for takeoff, Runway 1-7 Left, depart straight out; I'll call your turn," the tower controller said.

"Okay, Russo, here we go. It's going to be beautiful up there. You're gonna love it today." He eased the throttle forward, and the Cirrus accelerated quickly in the cool morning air, gaining altitude and turning toward California.

Luke eased the Cirrus off the runway to the airplane parking area in Long Beach after a smooth and uneventful flight. The view of the Rocky Mountains and the Grand Canyon had been spectacular. Van seemed to relax after Luke described the Cirrus Airframe parachute system, which would allow the plane to slowly descend to the ground when activated in an in-flight emergency.

With Van's help, Luke secured the Cirrus to the tarmac anchors. The rental car he'd arranged to pick up from the FBO at the airport was ready, so they hopped in and headed to lunch with Earl. Luke had arranged the lunch to get the latest updates on the removal action and the homeowners and to introduce Earl to Van. Earl had suggested having lunch in Long Beach, away from the locals in Torrance, and safe from the chance of being overheard.

"Great to meet you in person, Van," Earl said. "Luke has told me a lot of good things about you and your security work. We finally meet in person."

"Any friend of Luke's is a friend of mine," Van said.

Luke started the conversation with a question for Earl. A question he should have already known the answer to. "Earl, are you from around here? I don't think you've ever told me where you grew up."

"I'm essentially a southern California native. I was born in the Oklahoma panhandle, but my parents moved to Santa

Ana when I was a baby and bought a small farm, back when there were farms around here."

"Must have been nice to grow up around here with the ocean and the beach. I was raised in south Chicago. We had a cold lake, but nothing like the ocean here," Van said, with a shallow sigh.

Earl continued to share more entertaining childhood stories of growing up in rural Santa Ana and the ups and downs of DDT over the years. Even Luke did more listening than talking and appreciated Earl's storytelling and historical perspective. Much to Luke's relief, the half-hour of getting to know one another flew by. Earl and Van were getting along.

The chatter in the restaurant had become louder as people sat for lunch, making the conversation less likely to be overheard by diners at adjacent tables.

Luke gestured to Van. "Do you want to give Earl a briefing?"

Van nodded once. "I'm sure I don't have to tell you that the success of security work is only as good as the information that goes into it. Right now, that information, and the quality of that information, is coming from you, since you have boots on the ground every day and are considered a 'local.' Jimmy Mendoza is a loose cannon, and we have to take his personal threats seriously. We also don't know the whereabouts of Chad or the two women from EF&J. They've all done bad things in the past and will likely do bad things again. People don't change. I know Luke is counting on you."

"I hear you loud and clear, Mr. Russo." Earl gave Van a brief salute. "Let me give you the latest intel."

Luke smiled at Earl's use of military jargon. The older man looked directly at him and said, "Jimmy has made it clear that he wants you replaced with someone who will stand up to the EPA and support the homeowners. He's only seen Bob and

Caroline once and doesn't understand their positions and authority. He thinks you are the face of Guadalupe, and you make the decisions. He has insinuated that he will do whatever is necessary to get you out of here. I don't know if this is just bluster on Jimmy's part or not. He packs a lot of hot air, as you know."

"Jimmy doesn't scare—"

"Luke," Van broke in. "You need to listen to Earl. These are serious allegations, and your life could be in danger. I know that sounds extreme, but you've got to start thinking that way. Don't be naive. Jimmy's got a history of violence."

"Jimmy is planning a protest later this week when soil removal is scheduled to begin," said Earl. "I heard this from Alberto, the construction superintendent. He's a no-bullshit kind of guy, just like Jimmy, but he has a job to do, and he has the permits and federal authority to move in, so it could get ugly. Several families are moving to the Residence Inn until the soil removal is completed. Alberto thinks it will take several weeks, since he has to remove the soil from all the yards and replace it with clean fill. Then, it's just a landscaping job of replanting and sprinklers. Of course, the removal has to be done in Tyvek suits, with dust control measures." Earl flashed a grin. "A lot of overkill if you ask me, but then, nobody asked me."

"What do you think Luke and I should focus on?" Van asked.

"Bob told me to observe the soil removal contractor and educate homeowners, when I can, about the minimal risk of exposure to DDT they have," Earl said. "I think we just remind the homeowners that, at the end of the day, they'll have a new, clean yard, and we can all quit talking about DDT contamination. I've been doing this over the last two weeks, but we should probably be a fair distance away when the protest happens."

"Makes sense to me," Van said. "Do you agree, Luke?"

"Unfortunately, I do," Luke said, shaking his head and grimacing. "I'd like to shut up that son of a bitch Mendoza. He gets away with saying anything he wants, and the homeowners believe him because he's loud and has a commanding presence."

"Maybe so, but this isn't the time to take him on," Van said.

18

Luke picked up the lunch tab and he and Van drove to Van Kirk Elementary School to meet Alberto, after promising Van and Earl that he would make every reasonable attempt to avoid Jimmy Mendoza. Luke knew a good working relationship with the construction superintendent was critical to completing a project on budget. Alberto's office was a skid-mounted trailer that leaned slightly on the uneven pavement. It was located in the back of the elementary school parking lot and served as the construction company's onsite headquarters. An electrical extension cord led into the school, and a port-o-potty was nearby. The two contractors with hard hats and reflective vests looked up at him from a table with a plan-view drawing of the houses. The air was cloudy with cigarette smoke.

"Hi, I'm Luke Graham, representing Guadalupe Chemical, and this is my coworker, Van Russo. Is Alberto here?"

A calendar with pictures of Bobcat Skid Steers hung over a small aluminum sink. It was the equipment of choice for a job like this. The small window air conditioner hummed and kept the office reasonably comfortable.

Luke felt one of the men sizing him up, staring at him with dark brown eyes. "Well, if it ain't Mister Graham himself. I'm Alberto."

Luke didn't hide a surprised look.

Alberto laughed. "I've heard a lot about you. It's good to finally meet a Guadalupe man."

"You do realize that I am not a Guadalupe employee. I work for Webber Environmental. I'm just a consultant to Guadalupe and have nothing, I repeat absolutely nothing, to do with this soil removal project, other than observing and answering questions from homeowners, if they ever come up," Luke said, taking a deep breath. "You should be talking to Ryan and Associates about the removal activities. They're the ones that work for the EPA."

"Okay, amigo. I get it now. Everything's good," Alberto said, raising his hands. "Jimmy Mendoza was here looking for you a while ago. I told him I ain't never met you, but he started to get kinda huffy with me like I was hiding you in the closet or something. You two got something going here that I need to know about?" Alberto asked.

Luke knew better than to air his differences with Jimmy before Alberto. Still, he understood that the experienced construction superintendent could see a potential problem before it became one. He chose his words carefully.

"Jimmy opposes the soil removal, as you may have figured out. So does Guadalupe by the way, but the EPA decided to move ahead anyway. Hopefully, Jimmy will come around and see the positives of having a clean community," Luke said. He decided not to mention Earl's knowledge of a protest in the morning. He didn't want to start a rumor if the protest didn't happen.

A timely call from Debbie provided a good excuse for Luke and Van to avoid further discussion with Alberto. Luke stepped outside to take the call.

"Hey, Luke. Can you check on the security alarm at the groundwater treatment facility? I think it's working, but I'm a little nervous after the spill."

"Will do." Luke knew Van wanted to see the facility and the security alarms, and this was a good opportunity for a tour. But after that, given their non-stop day, drinks and dinner in Manhattan Beach were next on the agenda.

***

Luke and Van checked into the third floor of the Manhattan Beach Super Lodge after dinner. Cindy had made room reservations for Luke the previous week and requested adjoining rooms so they could talk. The hotel's special room rate was less than Luke's *per diem* hotel rate, allowing for a bottle of Crown Royal Canadian whiskey to be purchased for nightcaps. Luke joined Van in his room, and they toasted their drinks in plastic hotel cups while discussing the day's events and planning for the next day.

They hadn't been at it long before Luke realized the time. Kara was expecting his call before it was too late, so he left the adjoining room door slightly ajar and slipped into his room. He sat at his desk, gazing out at the west coast.

"Hey, babe, did you get a training run in today? Do you feel ready?

"I did ten miles today. I'll do two more runs, then start walking and eating pasta, to load up on carbs. They say that is what you need to do."

"How are your parents doing?"

"Fine."

"Are they starting to drive you crazy?"

"Yep."

"Are they in the room with you now?"

"Yep."

Luke could envision the kitchen, and his in-laws taking control of the meal preparation while lecturing Kara on her pre-race diet. At the same time, Nathan, Kaylie, and Columbo were probably demolishing the basement. A few easy days and nights in the hotel with Van sounded good. Nathan and Kaylie gave him their day's highlights, and he signed off.

He pulled up his email on his VPN account and went directly to the one from Bob Burrows. Luke hadn't thought much about the EF&J lawsuit in the last few weeks. He expected it would raise its head when he least wanted to deal with it.

Luke, EF&J's attorneys want to depose Lenny in two weeks in Long Beach and ask him about his salvage operations over the years. I'll be there in person, of course. If you plan to be in Torrance, you can join me.

Trips to Torrance were getting in the way of Luke attending Nathan's soccer games, but he had soil removal oversight responsibility. The billable hours were always good too.

I can probably be in Long Beach with you, Bob. Let's talk tomorrow.

Luke heard a metallic click at the door behind him while answering the next email. It sounded like the door opening. Were the walls really that thin in this hotel? He turned. A man stood a few feet from him, wearing nice slacks and a long-sleeved dress shirt. He had a ski mask over his face and pointed a 9mm Smith & Wesson at Luke's face.

It took Luke a few seconds before he realized that a man was actually in his room pointing a pistol at his head. The memory of his ten-year-old childhood friend aiming his dad's loaded pistol at him, just for fun, flashed into his mind.

Luke raised his hands slowly, staring at the pistol, and spoke in a loud voice. "Hey, it's cool. What do you want from me? Are you sure you're in the right room?"

"Listen to me, Luke. You need to get the hell out of town and quit fucking up our lives. This dirt removal and all this talk about DDT causing cancer is bullshit, and you know it. You can put an end to this, so go do it."

Luke wasn't sure if the man was finished or if there was more to come, but he was encouraged that the intruder spoke of the future. His voice was unfamiliar, with no particular accent or distinguishing inflections. His eyes were brown and glaring.

Out of the corner of his eye, Luke saw Van at the connecting door.

"I hear what you're saying, man. I'm just a working stiff trying to do my job," Luke said, hoping to keep the masked man's attention, but the man caught sight of Van in the big wall mirror. He started turning around when Van hit him with a right hook to the lower jaw.

Van grabbed the pistol muzzle with his left hand, rotating it down and out of the man's grip as he fell backward. The back of his head connected with the corner of Luke's desk, and he was unconscious before he hit the floor.

The fight was over in less than three seconds.

Luke bent over and examined the unconscious man. "Wow, that had to hurt. Do you think he's dead?"

"He'll be okay. The jaw will take a few months to heal, though." Van shook his punching hand, then reached for the man's ski cap. Before he pulled it off, he glanced at Luke.

"Do you want to bet on who it is?" Van asked, with a smile on his face.

"I think it's Mendoza," Luke said, "but he didn't sound like Mendoza. Maybe the ski mask distorted his voice."

"I think it's one of Mendoza's goons," Van said, removing the mask. The man had short, dark hair and was clean-shaven. His slack jaw sported a red mark and was already beginning to swell. Blood ran from the corner of his mouth and from a gash on the back of his head.

"You win again, Van. Who the hell is this guy?" Luke picked up then dropped the man's arm, noting the well-pressed shirt. "He looks like he just got off work."

Van searched the man's pockets but found nothing.

"We've got a gun with a serial number, and we'll see where he goes when he wakes up. I'll figure out who he is," Van said. "Grab your stuff and throw it into my room before he wakes up. I don't think he saw me until I was well into the room. He won't suspect I'm next door. Let's keep this quiet for now."

Luke did as Van asked in record time. Van locked both sides of the connecting door.

"We should call the police," Luke said, as he sank down on Van's bed and reaction set in. His legs, all of a sudden, had turned to jelly.

"I think we'll get farther if we let this guy run back home. I think he was here for shock value, not to do any real harm." Van slipped on a light jacket. "I'm going to stake out the parking lot. You stay here." He nodded toward the pistol he'd set on the bedside table. "You have the legal right to shoot someone if they break into your room. This room is legally your home."

"I may have the right, but I don't want to shoot anybody," Luke said.

"Goddamn it, Luke! That guy just put a gun to your head. This is war." Van turned and left the room.

Luke flipped off the lights, put his ear to the adjoining door, and waited. It was a long ten minutes until he heard the sink run and the intruder leaving the room. He was relieved that the man was alive. He crossed carefully to the window in the dark room and peeked into the parking lot. The man walked across the parking lot, holding a washcloth to the back of his head, and slipped into the passenger side of a blue minivan.

A minute later, Van re-entered the room. "I've got his number. California tags."

"Who the hell drives a minivan as a getaway car?"

"Maybe she'll tell us. Soccer moms don't usually hold up very well when interrogated."

"There was a woman at the wheel?"

"Yep."

Van pulled out his laptop and connected it to his portable Yagi antenna. "I'm glad we are on the north side of the hotel, Luke. I have to point this baby toward the north star. Did you get us a room on this side intentionally?"

"I did. I knew all of this was going to happen, so I asked Cindy specifically to get us a room on this side," Luke said, keeping a straight face.

Van laughed. "You're full of shit, but sometimes it helps to be lucky in this business. Give me a minute, and I'll find out who's about to get their jaw wired shut for six weeks. By the way, if you ever get in a fight, keep your teeth clenched together. You won't get a broken jaw that way."

Luke decided that information deserved another round of Crown Royal. This whole situation had become surreal. He turned on the weather channel for distraction while Van worked on identifying the man. He contemplated calling Kara. However, she would worry. What about Bob and Caroline?

"Got him!" Van said. "Mr. Ross C. Jennings. Lives in Fresno. Looks like he's in agriculture. The minivan belongs to him and his wife, Jane."

"What the hell is he doing down here in Torrance, threatening me? He must have some hatred of Guadalupe or the EPA."

"Maybe he knows our friends Jimmy or Chad. Doesn't matter, because he's out of commission for a while." Van paused and looked directly at Luke. "Don't believe for a moment that he's our only threat."

***

The following day, Simone flashed her contractor's badge to the security guard in the lobby of the EPA office in San Francisco. Her guest cubicle was on the sixth floor. After being terminated in the latest EPA right-sizing effort, she was no longer required to be in the office throughout the week. Instead, she traveled to the office twice weekly, which was more than enough given her contractor status. Her cubicle was small and stark, with a few pictures of her six-year-old daughter, Alison, and her husband, Mark. The human health and ecological risk assessment reports she'd authored were stacked neatly on the small bookshelf. She made herself a cup of herbal tea and walked through the sea of other cubicles, stopping to chat with a few of her office mates on her way to Antoine's office for their 9:00 a.m. status meeting. She missed the camaraderie of working in the office but didn't miss the daily commute. Part-time office work allowed her to work from home and spend more time with Alison.

After the usual discussion about transients and pets on the Bay Area Rapid Transit (BART) train under the East Bay, Antoine gave Simone an update on the soil removal action. "I talked with Ryan and Associates this morning, and they said a picket line was obstructing their access to the first yard to be excavated. Instead of fighting it, they went a few doors down the street, to a more sympathetic homeowner. They don't know if the protesters are leaving or what. They said that Mr. Mendoza was out there leading the effort. There are a lot of people with anti-EPA and anti-Guadalupe signs. He even saw a sign that said, 'I'll eat my yard before I let you take it away.'"

They both laughed for a moment and then Antoine continued. "We're trying to help homeowners, increase their home value, all expenses paid, and they would rather fight us. I don't get it."

Simone was also puzzled by the reaction from many of the homeowners. Why wouldn't they appreciate a clean yard with no risk from DDT exposure or property devaluation in the future? The inconvenience was minimal, and the EPA was putting homeowners up in nice places during the soil removal. *Sort of an all-expenses-paid staycation.* She thought there must be another reason for the antagonistic reaction from homeowners.

"Do you think that Mr. Mendoza is just a very effective organizer?" Simone asked, before answering her own question. "I think there is more behind all this than just Mr. Mendoza and a few yards contaminated with DDT." She paused for a moment, looking out the window at the Golden Gate Bridge and the wine-producing Napa Valley. "DDT must have been used in the Napa Valley on the vineyards at some time. For that matter, we know DDT was used throughout California in the fifties and sixties. Hell, it was used on our farm. It has to be in the soil everywhere, but at what concentration, and is it a risk to human health after so many years? If it is a risk to homeowners in Torrance, it could be a risk anywhere." Simone paused, and then cut off Antoine as he attempted to reply.

"How many DDT-contaminated sites are out there that will be affected by the lower cleanup standard, Antoine?"

"I'm working on a few sites right now that will probably be affected, but none of them are as far along as we are with the Guadalupe site. You're right, there are DDT-contaminated sites all around us, especially in California's agricultural regions, that we don't know about and probably never will. Some will be discovered in a property transaction investigation or historical uncovering. But, to answer your question, a lower cleanup standard for DDT will obviously affect many more properties. No doubt about that. Don't blame yourself for all of this, if that's what you're doing; a lot of science went into lowering the cleanup standard. You followed a scientific process and did what was right."

Simone thought about Luke out there overseeing the soil removal and wished she could talk with him, just to say "hi" and get his take on the protests, but she had to honor their agreement not to speak while the EF&J lawsuit progressed. A subpoena could arrive any day.

At 4:00 p.m., she packed her briefcase and prepared to leave the office for the day when she noticed a voicemail on her personal cell phone. She didn't recognize the 1-800 number but decided to listen to the message anyway as she walked down the stairs to the lobby. It was probably a junk call. The voice was garbled and monotone, like the messenger was speaking underwater.

"Simone, I know who you are and what you do for the EPA. Your crack science about DDT is garbage, and you know it!

Why do you keep recommending these stupid DDT cleanups? You need to face reality. I would hate for something to happen to you or that beautiful little girl of yours, but if you don't stop this nonsense about DDT causing cancer in everybody, we might have to do something ugly."

Simone stopped on the second-floor landing, holding the railing to keep her balance. She took a few deep breaths to calm herself and stop shaking. *How did someone get my personal cell phone number? Do they know Alison? Do they know where she goes to school?*

She rushed back upstairs to Antoine's office, closing the door behind her.

"What's up, Simone? Are you okay?" Antoine asked.

She raised one finger as she sat down, taking another few deep breaths to regain her composure. Antoine noticed and waited, a concerned look on his face. After a long minute, she replayed the voicemail on speaker.

"What should I do?"

He immediately called Carol, Director of Security, and she came to Antoine's office within minutes. Carol had served in the Army Military Police and had worked at the EPA for over twenty years. As she listened to the phone call, a disgusted look crossed her face.

"First of all, this isn't my first rodeo. I say that to give you a measure of confidence. You are not the only person in the EPA to get a death threat. We have a few every week across the country, and the number is increasing with the easy access to burner phones and the inability to trace these calls. The threats very rarely amount to anything, but we do take them seriously." Carol recorded the message onto her own phone. "I'll report this to the police, but don't expect them to do much investigative work because they don't have time. And, like I said, these are usually just people venting. I want you to keep your eyes open and be aware of the people around you and your family. If you notice anyone new, think you're being followed or watched, let me know immediately." Carol fished a business card out of the black backpack she had with her. "My home number is at the bottom. Call me any time, day or night. Things will calm down after this project is completed." She unzipped another pocket in the backpack and pulled out a small spray canister. "In the meantime, I want you to carry this mace, just in case. Get familiar with it, and don't be afraid to use it."

Carol's no-nonsense attitude calmed Simone's jangling nerves. She slipped the mace into her purse, hoping she wouldn't have to use it.

"I'll go with you on BART to the East Bay and make sure you get to your car," said Antoine. "Have you called Mark yet?"

Simone shook her head. "You don't have to follow me home, Antoine. It's so far out of your way."

"I've got time. You won't even know I'm in the same train car as you. Don't look for me, but know I am nearby if some looney shows up. You can work solely from home for now, if you want."

Simone stepped into a vacant office to call Mark. The call went to voicemail. *Damn it. Why doesn't he ever answer?* She was momentarily alarmed, then remembered that he was with Alison at a friend's birthday party. She decided to wait until she got home and tell him after their daughter was in bed.

Luke was her next call. He picked up on the second ring.

"Hey Simone, how are you? You're missing all of the fun out here. You should come down to Torrance and join us."

"Luke, listen, I only have a minute, and then I need to catch the BART. I just received a death threat on my cell phone. I'll forward the message to you when we hang up. The EPA security people know about it and are doing their typical thing, which isn't much, other than telling me to be careful and look over my shoulder. Oh, and to spray a bad guy with mace. I'm going to work from home for a while. We have a good home security system and a big dog. Mark will probably enjoy walking around with his pistol on his hip too," Simone said, with a weak smile. She took a deep breath and stopped shaking.

"Okay. Call me tomorrow, when you have more time. It's going to be all right. It's just an attempt to intimidate you. If somebody wanted to kill you, they wouldn't warn you first, you know?" Luke said.

"Thanks, Luke. I'm not sure that makes me feel better, but anyway, I appreciate your concern."

She put on her sunglasses and walked out of the lobby toward the BART station, observing everyone around her. Never had she noticed so many different people walking in all directions, some coming toward her and some walking away. *How am I supposed to know who the bad guy is, or if there is even a bad guy out here?*

Antoine followed about fifty feet behind her and got on the same train car. As usual, it was crowded at this time, and Simone held onto the spray can of mace in her coat pocket. Riders began to exit the train as it progressed from station to station along the East Bay. Concord was near the end of the line, and only half a dozen riders, including Antoine, still reading his newspaper, remained as they neared the station. The absence of the crowded train now felt less secure in an odd way. Finally, they arrived. She walked directly to her car, locking herself inside. Antoine appeared to be reading the BART system map, but she could see him watching her out of the corner of his eye.

She drove away from the parking lot, constantly looking in her rearview mirror and making numerous unnecessary turns. She pulled into a crowded parking lot and called Mark, convinced she wasn't being followed. He answered, and Simone could hear Alison in the backseat, talking non-stop about the birthday party. Hearing their voices drained her of what little energy she had left.

"We'll see you at home, honey," Mark said. She agreed and hung up, finally turning the car toward home.

How can a person live in fear like this every day?

19

The next day, Luke sat in the rental car with Van in the back corner of the Van Kirk Elementary School parking lot. They were facing away from the construction activity, observing it in the rearview mirrors only, at Van's insistence. It made Luke feel a little like a secret agent. All the same, he jumped when his phone rang.

"Simone, great to hear your voice. Any more threats last night?"

"Nothing new, Luke. Mark and I talked it through for a couple of hours last night and convinced ourselves that we don't need to be that concerned. Mark is happy to be walking around the house like an armed bodyguard, and I'm not convinced that someone actually wants to kill me."

"I agree with all the advice you're getting. We should all stay alert for the time being, and try not to let these lowlifes control our lives," Luke said.

They talked for a few more minutes about the death threats and reassured each other that everything would be okay. He didn't want to tell Simone about his hotel room invasion. It could wait until she was less distracted. He hadn't told Kara either, not wanting to alarm her and her parents right before the weekend marathon. It was the kind of news that would be less alarming face to face.

Alberto was unloading the excavation equipment and preparing for the soil removal, which would begin the following day. The number of protesters had dwindled to a dozen after lunch, once Jimmy Mendoza left to complete an asphalt paving job. Even the KKAT television crew had moved on to cover a semi-trailer truck crash which had closed down the 405 during the afternoon rush hour.

Luke repeatedly played Simone's voicemail to Van, so they could listen for clues about who it was and possibly determine whether it was a real threat or just a scare tactic. A threat against an EPA toxicologist he was close to was both concerning and intriguing. How many people even knew what a toxicologist did?

Van ran the voicemail through his voice recognition software, but nothing more specific than "white male from California, Oregon, or Washington" was revealed.

"One thing is for sure, Luke. This is not Ross Jennings. His jaw is wired shut by now, and he's drinking liquid food through a straw. Someone else is involved, but whether they're working with Ross is anybody's guess."

"You know, it sounds like this guy knows Simone personally. The way he talks about her 'crack science' implies he has some knowledge about DDT cleanup levels and, interestingly, he doesn't talk about his yard or make any reference to soil removal in Torrance. Also, I think we can rule out anybody from EF&J, because it doesn't make sense that they would make threats over lowering the levels. Maybe it's a friend of this Ross guy."

"I think the EPA woke up the entire farming community. There are a lot of farmers out there who used DDT at one time. Can you imagine? It would cost a fortune to dig up and replace the top three inches of soil at an almond orchard—or any small farm. The financial liability would bankrupt most farmers, as would the bad publicity. Who would want to eat almonds from a contaminated orchard? Put that on the side of the package, 'Grown with DDT, no insects on our almonds!'"

"You're not funny, Russo, and besides, the DDT doesn't get taken up by the trees and reside in the almonds, although a lot of people probably think it does."

"Exactly. Let's meet with Earl in the morning and see if we can come up with some new ideas," Van said, around a yawn. "I need to sleep on it, and I still have work to do tonight."

"Good idea. Let me see if Earl can make it in the morning," Luke said, punching Earl's number. "Hey Earl, can you meet Van and me for breakfast at the Ocean View Motel in Torrance in the morning? We have some new information that I'm sure you will find very interesting," Luke said, with a smirk.

"I thought you were at the Manhattan Beach Super Lodge. Now, the Ocean View Motel in Torrance? You're going in the wrong direction, son. There isn't a view of the ocean anywhere in Torrance. You must be desperate to save money on hotel expenses, Luke."

"We had a little trouble with the hotel security system. I'll fill you in tomorrow, 6:30. When you arrive, ask the desk to put your breakfast on Van Russo's room, number 212. I don't exist at this place," Luke said.

***

Earl arrived in his Ford Bronco at the Ocean View at precisely 6:30 on Friday to meet Luke and Van for breakfast. They were sitting in the corner with their backs to the wall looking into the parking lot, reading the *LA Times*. Earl's flannel shirt and Wranglers were starched and ironed.

"You're looking dapper this morning, Earl," Luke said.

"I have a feeling I might be on the KKAT evening news one of these days. Well, boys, I can't wait to hear how you ended up at this hotel. It's gotta be a good story. I know it's not that the scrambled eggs are any better," the older man said.

"You're right, Earl. It's not about the eggs, but get some anyway and pull up a chair," Luke said.

Earl went to the buffet and filled his plate to overflowing with eggs and bacon before he sat down.

"We changed hotels because a guy put a 9mm in my face on Tuesday night and started lecturing me about my job performance."

Earl whistled. "Did he have any good suggestions?"

"He didn't get the chance," Van said. "His mouth is wired shut for six weeks, and we have a new 9mm."

Earl grinned. "Good for you."

"Do you know a Ross Jennings?" Van asked.

"Never heard of him. Is he a homeowner?

"No, and based on what he said to Luke, he doesn't seem interested in the soil removal. We think he lives in Fresno, in the Central Valley. Why would someone like that be threatening Luke?"

Earl added cream and sugar to the weak motel coffee while he pondered the question. "You guys need to appreciate that Guadalupe sold DDT to about every farmer and co-op in California. DDT would probably be detected in any soil sample in California's ag land. I'd guess there are a lot of farmers who might get worried when the EPA says DDT is more dangerous than we previously thought."

"I think you're right," said Van. " I suspect there are all sorts of Ross Jennings out there. However, they're in the clear unless the EPA has a reason to sample their land and actually finds something. That leads me to believe these threats are not serious but just pissed off farmers who don't like the EPA."

"I can sort of see why someone would threaten Simone, since she's EPA, or as good as, but why me?" Luke said. "My only connection is through Guadalupe, and I want to see higher cleanup standards, not lower. It doesn't make sense why I would be a target."

"Luke, nobody around here really knows much about you. Some think you are on EPA's side. Some think you are on Guadalupe's side. They blame you for Guadalupe's contamination and the soil removal inconvenience because they don't know any better. It doesn't help that Jimmy Mendoza blames you for just about everything, every chance he gets. People have to have someone to blame, and I hate to say it, but you are it," Earl said.

Luke was speechless for a moment, considering what Earl had said. "This asshole Mendoza is playing offense, and I'm losing. It's time to turn the tables on him. What do you think, Van?"

"I knew this a week ago, Luke, but you needed to come to the same conclusion on your own."

"Okay. One more scoop of scrambled eggs, and then we'll go see what's happening at the elementary school," Luke said, raising his fists in the air.

***

Luke and Van parked next to Earl's Ford Bronco near Alberto's construction trailer at the elementary school. Picketers were already lined up in front of a homeowner's yard across the street. It was only 8:00 in the morning.

Jimmy Mendoza had a bullhorn and led a denigrating chant: "EPA, stay away! Quit destroying our neighborhood!"

"Van, my client, Bob Burrows, told me just to observe the removal activity. This is the EPA's project, and we have nothing to do with it. So, do you think I am violating my client's orders if KKAT requests an interview from me and I throw Jimmy Mendoza under the bus?"

Van frowned for a moment. "This is how I see it. If you go and ask for an interview, you violate your client's request. But if they ask you for an interview, you'll have no other choice. If you're interviewed, don't name Mendoza. First of all, I'm sure the reporter already has him on her radar. And, secondly, the less attention you give him, the less ammunition you give him."

The protestors continued to walk in circles while Luke and Van watched from the car. "If they walk any slower, Van, they're going to fall over like dominoes. That guy in the yellow shirt has only made ten laps in the last hour. I counted."

Luke watched as several of Alberto's crew tried to get a skid-steer to start. One of the men ran his finger around the gas cap and made a face. "Sugar!" he shouted.

Alberto threw his hands in the air and stormed back to the construction trailer, cursing in both Spanish and English. He was shaking his head so violently that his hard hat fell from his head and bounced on the asphalt.

Luke lowered his car window slightly and listened as Alberto ranted. "*Hijo de puta*! Somebody put sugar in the skid-steer gas tank. Now I have to drain the entire fuel tank and clean the injectors. I don't have time for this shit. Someone needs to get that Mendoza asshole off my job site, and if they won't, I will. You know he's responsible for this. I'm calling the police."

Van moved to the backseat of the car, where the windows were tinted, and scrutinized the protestors through his binoculars. "This looks like a school pep rally. Some moms have their small kids out there who are half asleep, and others are just standing around gossiping. A couple of the men look angry and start yelling whenever Mendoza says something in his bullhorn."

"Oh man, wait til you see this," Van said. "There's that guy that bumped into you last night at the restaurant and glared at you. I thought that was quite odd. You probably didn't see me give him the hairy eyeball back. I'd love to go bump into him right now and knock his ass to the street."

The KKAT news truck pulled into the parking lot and set up its broadcasting antennae. Haewon Lee and her cameraman stepped out of the truck with their KKAT hats and shirts and did a recording check. She wasted no time and immediately began looking around, likely searching for somebody to interview. She headed toward a protestor with a sign that read, "I can live with DDT—Not the EPA."

"Nature calls," Luke said, opening the car door. "Don't let anybody take my seat." He climbed out of the car and headed toward the port-a-potty by way of the KKAT news truck.

He made eye contact with Haewon and waited. She wrapped up her interview with the protestor and quickly approached him. "Mr. Graham, it's good to see you here representing Guadalupe. I have a few questions for you. Our viewers need to hear from Guadalupe about this soil removal effort."

"Sure, I have a few minutes," he said. Haewon turned on her microphone, and the cameraman zoomed in on Luke's face.

"Today, we are speaking with Luke Graham, a representative of Guadalupe Chemical Corporation and the person responsible for the cleanup of the former DDT manufacturing site. Mr. Graham, what is Guadalupe's position regarding the soil removal project? Is Guadalupe in favor of the project or not?"

Luke had already decided he wouldn't try to explain his consulting relationship with Guadalupe–nobody seemed to understand that. Spreading his arms wide, he responded to Haewon. "This is all a result of the EPA changing its DDT cleanup levels in people's yards. We, that is, Guadalupe Chemical and me, a consultant to Guadalupe, have nothing to do with this soil removal project. This is totally an EPA effort, and I am here just to observe and answer questions when I can. We don't believe the soil removal is necessary, and at the end of the day, we believe it won't make any difference in the health and safety of the people living in the neighborhood."

"If that is the case, why hasn't Guadalupe done more to stop this project?"

Luke could feel his adrenaline pumping and anger growing as he responded to Haewon's leading questions. He started to manually control his breathing to keep from losing control.

From the corner of his eye, he saw Van and Earl saunter up. *Good. They have my back and know when I've gone too far.*

"We made our case to the EPA, but they are the regulatory agency here. They have the right, by law, to do what they deem necessary based on their interpretation of the science. Again. Let me make this clear. If Guadalupe could stop this soil removal, they would. Guadalupe believes that the removal is unnecessary."

"What do you say to these protestors, Mr. Graham?"

Luke took another deep breath. "It's not my position to tell the protestors what to do. I told you what Guadalupe thinks about all this. I will say Guadalupe supports peaceful protest as a basic American right. However, we don't want to see people like Jimmy Mendoza, the guy with the bullhorn, get everybody riled up by spreading lies and misinformation. That's when people get hurt. Does Mr. Mendoza have his own interests in mind? Something he hasn't shared?" Luke shrugged. "I don't know. Maybe he simply doesn't want the EPA to touch his yard, or maybe he has some other motivation. And he's willing to threaten people to get what he wants."

"What do you mean by 'threaten people'? Did Mr. Mendoza threaten you, Mr. Graham?"

"I mean like death threats and violence. He should be arrested and questioned for..."

Van raised his mobile phone to his ear as though he was on a call, grabbed Luke by the shoulder, and pulled him away. "Sorry, we have an emergency that Mr. Graham needs to attend to," he said to Haewon.

Luke was nearly airborne as Van pulled him around. "That's enough," he whispered into Luke's ear. "She is taking you down a path where you will say something stupid and get attacked or, at a minimum, lose your job. Get control of yourself, Rattler."

"I had to dig into Mendoza and create some suspicion," Luke said.

"Yes, you did, if I might say so, but you can't afford to go too far. It's not worth losing your job over or getting shot."

Earl gave them a salute and headed off toward the construction trailer. Luke and Van walked back to the rental car, Van pretending to talk on his mobile phone throughout. When they reached the car, Van directed Luke into the back. Luke grudgingly did as he was told. His friend was right. This was not worth losing his job over. He'd stay in the backseat where he could watch, unobserved.

For the moment, he kept his eyes on Haewon. She was threading her way through the crowd of protestors and construction workers, apparently looking for more interviews.

"I wonder what Jimmy will say tonight when he watches the news," Luke said.

"I'm more concerned about how he will react in the next thirty minutes, when your TV friend asks him who he has been threatening. We'll probably learn something just based on his reaction," Van said.

Luke swore under his breath. "You'd think my years in the military would have taught me to hold my temper better. Let's grab Earl and go check on the groundwater treatment facility. Maybe we can find something productive to do over there."

Van got behind the wheel and drove as Luke put a call into Kara. "Hey babe, how's it going?"

"I'm as ready as I will ever be, and the weather is supposed to be good, so I'm actually looking forward to it. The best parts are that my parents will leave as soon as it is over, and I get to eat lots of pasta between now and Sunday," she said, laughing. "You are still planning to fly back tomorrow, right?"

"Yep, we're still good for Saturday morning. I'm ready to head back. It's kinda boring out here just watching these contractors do their thing. I did another TV interview. I'm starting to get better at this TV stuff."

Van smiled at Luke in the rearview mirror.

"I'll bring you completely up to date once I get home."

Kara gave him a quick report on the kids before hanging up. Luke smiled as he pocketed his phone.

"My updates with Kara are always short and sweet."

Van nodded. "You handled it well. As we agreed, Kara

doesn't need to know all the details yet. Fortunately, she won't see KKAT in Denver."

Alberto was loading his skid-steers on trailers when Luke and Van returned to the elementary school in the late afternoon.

"I wouldn't have to haul these away every night if I could trust these people not to sabotage my gas tanks," said Alberto. "That still pisses me off, and it will cost the EPA a lot more money to do the job. I still think that asshole, Mendoza, or one of his knuckleheads, did it. By the way, he was wandering around here all morning looking for you."

"Did he say why?"

"He just wanted to know where you were. Garth, here, asked him if he might have some spare sugar for my coffee, and he walked out and never came back," Alberto said, with a smile that showed his gold front tooth. "You met Garth yet?"

A tall man with a round face and scraggly beard stood up to shake Luke's hand. He leaned forward to avoid hitting his head on the trailer ceiling. The buttons on his shirt were about to pop loose and expose his ample belly. Luke reluctantly stuck out his soft, small hand, knowing it would be overwhelmed by Garth's handshake. *Maybe if I squeeze a stress ball every day, I can build some callouses.*

"Good to meet you, Garth. I'll never admit that I said this, but keep up the intimidation. Maybe Mendoza will return to minding his own business," Luke said.

20

"**G**randma, I'm hungry. My stomach made a funny noise. When are we going to eat dinner?" Nathan asked.

"We'll eat as soon as your mother returns from her run, honey. We're having chicken with macaroni and cheese tonight," Shawna said.

"Mom is always running, Grandma."

"Her marathon is in two days, and then she will take a break from running, so I'm told. Why don't you take Columbo outside? He's been in the house for a long time."

Nathan went out the front door and walked Columbo down the street while Shawna continued cooking. The phone rang and she answered. "Hello?"

"I want to speak to Kara," the caller said.

"I'm sorry, I can't hear you very well. Can you speak up, please?" Shawna said.

"Don't play games with me, Kara. I know it's you, and you need to listen carefully. That husband of yours is sticking his nose in places he has no business. He got a lucky break in the hotel room the other night. He might have had a bullet between the eyes if that friend of his wasn't there. I'd hate to see something happen to you or your beautiful kids because of your stupid husband. Good luck in the marathon."

Then, a dial tone. Shawna stared at the receiver and tried to comprehend what she heard. *A bullet between the eyes.* What did that mean? *The beautiful kids.* She ran to the front door with the phone still in her hands.

"Nathan! Nathan!" No answer. *Where is he?* She ran out of the house and looked up and down the street. *Why did I let him go out when it was getting dark, and where is Kara?* She called again, but there was still no response from Nathan. Which direction should she go? She turned to the right, toward Nathan's best friend's house, and started speed walking. Her heart was racing.

Finally, Columbo ran toward her with his leash trailing on the ground. She ran toward Columbo and picked him up. "Nathan!" She still had the phone in her shaking hand, weighing a call to call 911, when Nathan came out of the dark, walking her way.

"Columbo got away from me, Grandma. I couldn't find him." Tears welled up in his eyes as a car came slowly up the street behind him.

"Hurry up, Nathan. I have food on the stove. We need to get home before it burns," Shawna said.

She ran toward Nathan as the car pulled to the curb and stopped. "Is everything okay?" the driver asked.

"We're okay, Mr. Walton. We found Columbo," Nathan said.

"Let's go eat, Nathan." Shawna looked away and tried to catch her breath. "Mom should be home by now."

***

When Shawna arrived with Nathan, Frank Burgess was in the

kitchen taking the chicken out of the oven, which was starting to burn. Frank and Shawna had met in Taiwan while Frank was on leave during service in Vietnam in 1966. They married a year later after Frank was discharged and moved to Berkeley, where Frank studied civil engineering on the GI bill. Kara was born a year later, and they moved to Denver for his new job.

"Shawna, where have you been, girl? This chicken's about to burn." There was a brief pause as the kitchen became crowded with Nathan, Kaylie, and Columbo. Frank looked at Shawna and said, "You look like you just saw a ghost. Are you feeling okay?"

"I'll be fine, honey, but we must talk as soon as Kara gets home."

"What do we need to talk about?" Kara asked, as she came into the kitchen from her training run.

Shawna stepped up and gave Kara a long hug.

"Wow, Mom, you haven't hugged me like that in a long time. What's the occasion?"

"I'm hungry," Nathan said.

Shawna turned away. After preparing plates for the kids, she pulled Kara and Frank aside. "I just received a phone call from a guy that thought I was you, and he proceeded to threaten me, I mean you, because of something about what Luke is involved with. He said that Luke almost got shot between the eyes in the hotel earlier this week, and then he wished you well in the marathon. I've never fully understood what Luke does for a living, but I never thought it was dangerous!"

***

Kara ignored her mother's comment about Luke. She had

heard it before. "What do you mean, shot between the eyes?" Kara asked.

"I don't know, that's all he said, and then he talked about the kids and how we need to look out for them and not let them get in trouble. It was like a threat targeting the kids."

"What did he sound like? Did he have an accent?" Frank asked.

"I don't know. Look, I was caught off guard. I wasn't expecting a death threat when I picked up the phone. He only talked for about fifteen seconds. His voice was sort of muffled, probably with a handkerchief or something like they do in the movies."

"I'm going upstairs and calling Luke. He has some explaining to do," Kara said.

"I'm locking the doors and shutting the curtains. I can't believe Luke is out there telling everybody that DDT is bad and we're all going to die from it. This isn't Agent Orange, for God's sake. He needs to keep his mouth shut," Frank said with a tense jaw.

"Luke, I'm upstairs by myself. My mom just got a threatening phone call from somebody, thinking it was me. The person said you need to quit doing whatever it is you are doing with DDT and that you were lucky that you didn't get shot between the eyes. What the hell are you involved in? Did somebody really point a gun in your face?" She paused to breathe. "This caller also wished me luck in the marathon. How would somebody know I'm running a marathon?" Kara said, her voice rising again.

Luke had planned to tell Kara about the hotel room threat after Kara's marathon when her parents were gone, but now it was out. Who knew about the hotel intruder and also knew that Kara was running a marathon?

"I was going to tell you about the hotel room threat when I got back, and you were done with your marathon. I'm so sorry this happened and I don't think there's any real danger. I'll be home as soon as I can wrap everything up here... It's no big deal, Babe. It's just some homeowner out here who is mad about their lawn being replaced. It will calm down soon. Several lawns have already been replaced and everything is going smoothly."

"What do you mean, it's no big deal? Somebody stuck a gun in your face and threatened to blow your head off. In my book, that's a very big deal! You have a family! If I didn't know you so well, I'd think you were running drugs or something."

"No. This is about DDT in people's yards. That's it. I don't know why somebody would threaten me over something like this. Maybe all of these farmers have an underground network where they talk every morning over coffee and get all freaked out about cleaning up DDT, and I'm the boogeyman this week."

"Is Van with you? Are you two in the same hotel room?"

"We are. We moved to a cheap motel under Van's name. We're pretty certain the guy who came into my room is Ross Jennings from Fresno. Get this: he came to the hotel with his wife in their minivan! Van made sure he would be out of commission for a month or so. I'm not worried."

"Don't tell me anymore. Did you call the police and report the break-in?"

"No. We decided not to draw any more attention to us or the threat. We still might."

There was a long silence before Kara finally spoke. "I'll turn on the security system tonight, so it calls the police if a door or window is opened. We pay a lot for that service, so we should use it. That should calm Mom down; she seems pretty freaked out. Are you and Van still flying back tomorrow?" Kara said.

"That's the plan, assuming we don't get shot down."

"Real funny. You'd better get here because I am running this fricking marathon regardless. Also, Mom and Dad want me to file a police report tonight, so I plan to do that."

"You know that whomever you write down as a suspect on the report may get a call from the police, so I wouldn't put anyone down as a suspect. You may create more problems than we want," Luke said.

They hung up, and Kara went back downstairs. Frank and Shawna were eating macaroni and cheese and discussing school with Nathan and Kaylie.

"Hey, Mom, Grandma says we're going to stay with her for two weeks while our house gets painted. That will be a blast."

"Is that right, Grandma?" Kara said, glaring at Shawna. "I didn't know we were getting our house painted. What color did you choose?"

"Just for two weeks, Kara. Things should calm down by then, if there is nothing to worry about," Frank said.

"We'll talk about it when Dad gets home, Nathan."

"Did Grandma tell you we almost lost Columbo? He pulled the leash out of my hands. It was getting dark, and I couldn't find him, but he ran to Grandma."

"Oh really? When did that happen, Grandma? I just keep getting surprised, don't I?" Kara said.

"It was right before you got home, Kara. It was no big deal. Nathan was a good boy and helped us find the dog."

***

"Van, Kara just got a death threat on the phone. Unfortunately, I'm hearing it third-hand, because her mother took the call and tried to explain it to Kara, who tried to explain it to me," Luke said, shaking his head. "It sounds like the same bastard who threatened Simone."

Van didn't respond to Luke for several minutes as the sun set over the Pacific Ocean in Manhattan Beach. The onshore ocean breeze and seagulls were music to Van's ears. "Did you hear me, Russo?"

"I heard you. You know it's sacrilegious to talk while the sun sets over the ocean for the last few minutes?"

"Since when did you become a religious man, Van? Actually, I'm a little worried about Kara and the kids right now."

"Okay. What else did the caller have to say?" Van asked.

"He made a reference to me. He also knew about Kara running a marathon."

The sun dropped below the surface of the ocean. "Luke, it's time to take the offensive and turn the tables. We did it with Ross Jennings; we need to do the same to a few others, whoever they are."

"Let's meet with Earl again tomorrow before we leave and discuss the latest threat," Luke said.

"You know you're trusting Earl more than you should."

"What? You don't trust *Earl*? You think he's a double agent or something?"

"Luke, I don't know him very well, and neither do you. He seems legit, but maybe he shares information with the other side and doesn't even realize it. After all, Jimmy seems to know a lot about what you and I are doing. I can test Earl in the morning," Van said.

"What does that mean, 'test Earl'? Are you going to make

him eat dirt with DDT? I guarantee that won't make him talk," Luke said, with a grin.

***

Luke and Van were in the elementary school parking lot in the rental car at 6:45 on a beautiful southern California Saturday morning, watching Alberto get his crews lined out and equipment started. A food truck arrived and started selling coffee and breakfast burritos to the protesters, many of whom had been there the last few days. They seemed to be waiting for Jimmy Mendoza to arrive and direct the protest. If the day followed the previous days' pattern, Jimmy would send the protesters to the houses where yards were scheduled to be removed that morning.

"Everybody seems a little more jovial today, Luke. Do you think it's because it's Saturday, or are they starting to burn out on this protesting stuff and realize their yards will disappear no matter what they do?"

"I think it's the latter, Van. You don't want to die on the sword because your lawn is getting replaced with clean soil, even if Jimmy Mendoza says it warrants a protest. I'll call Earl and have him stop by so you can talk to him."

Earl drove up in his Ford Bronco an hour later and found Luke and Van in the rental car with the windows up eating breakfast burritos. "These are pretty good, Earl, you should get one," Luke said.

"I ate my breakfast hours ago, boys. What's the latest?"

"My wife received a death threat last night in Colorado. Sounds like the same guy who threatened Simone, from what we heard. I'm getting tired of this. My goal is simply to clean up this mess. That's what I'm paid to do, and that's what I want to do. I don't need these distractions, and I don't need to be Enemy Number One when it comes to DDT."

"Earl, we need to get some answers from Jimmy Mendoza about who is behind these threats. Maybe it's Jimmy by himself, but I think there are more people, and I want to know who they are. If you can get me some names, I'll do the research," Van said.

"Sounds like you want me to buy Jimmy a burrito," Earl said.

"You should probably do that right now before he leaves," Van said.

Luke moved to the back seat of the rental car as Earl headed to the protest site, a block away. Luke closed his eyes and drummed his fingers on the armrest, trying to decipher the clues. He should call Kara and check on the family or maybe call Simone. He couldn't decide what to do, so he reached for his logbook and filled in the day's construction events. Bob and Caroline were still unaware of the threats, as were Nancy and Rudy. He had Debbie scheduled to be on-site next week to replace him. If threats were made against her, he would have to come clean about threats to himself and Kara, and then it would be a question of why he hadn't alerted others about the threats. Luke concluded that Ross Jennings wouldn't be threatening anybody in the near future, and if Jimmy started to calm down, it wouldn't be necessary to alarm everyone on the project team.

It was close to an hour before Earl walked around the corner of the elementary school. Luke opened the back door of the rental car for him. The elementary school parking lot was empty except for Alberto walking to and from his construction trailer.

"What did Jimmy have to say?" Van asked.

"First of all, if I am going to keep being a spy, I'll need to get some darker sunglasses and one of those FBI-style hats. To answer your question, though, we spent a lot of time talking about the EPA lowering the cleanup level for DDT and Guadalupe's lack of action to stop EPA's soil removal, which was mostly targeted at you, Luke. Sorry to say. He did mention a friend of his named Ross, who is leading a group of pissed-off farmers in the Central Valley. Sounds like they're worried the Feds will condemn their land. I wasn't sure what that has to do with yards getting cleaned up in Torrance, but he kept harping on the farmers."

"What else did he say about this Ross guy?" Van asked.

"Not much, although I had the impression that they seemed to know each other from somewhere in the past. I asked him about Chad, and he said they got together about two weeks ago."

"Where did they get together?"

"I didn't ask, and he didn't say, but something in the conversation made me think it was out here instead of Colorado."

"I wonder why he and Chad would be getting together," Luke said.

"Jimmy didn't elaborate, and I didn't want to be too inquisitive and ask more questions," Earl said. "However, he did say that several of the homeowners who were so pissed off several weeks ago have come to terms with the soil removal and accepted it. That's pretty much it."

"Thanks, Earl, for talking to him. Did he suspect that you are spying for me?" Luke said, with a grin.

Earl shook his head. "He seemed pretty open with me about people and their involvement, but he's a vindictive SOB, and you seem to be at the top of his list for some reason."

"You should know that I have Debbie coming out here next week to oversee Alberto and his crew like I'm doing this week. I haven't told her anything about death threats because

I don't want to get everyone alarmed, and I don't think they will focus on her, but I could be wrong."

"I'll hang out with her the first couple of days and see how it's going with Jimmy. If he threatens her, I'm calling the police, but Jimmy never mentioned her name, so I tend to agree with you that he will leave her alone."

They said their goodbyes, and Earl drove away in his old Bronco. Luke took a deep breath and smiled. He turned to Van and said, "Do you still think Earl is a double agent?"

"The thing about double agents, Luke, is that you never know someone is a double agent until it is too late. Whether he is or not, we just got more information than we gave away, and what we gave away was kind of meaningless. By the way, we never told Earl about Ross Jennings, so he must have heard that from Jimmy."

Luke and Van drove to the Long Beach airport to return to Denver. Luke returned the rental car to the Fixed Base Operator (FBO) and asked for the plane's fuel tanks to be filled while he and Van did a pre-flight inspection of the plane. Luke unlocked the pilot side door and reached for the passenger door lock to let in Van when Van opened the door.

"I never locked the passenger door?" Luke asked, with concern in his voice.

"It doesn't appear that you did. Did you leave the keys with the FBO?"

"No, I had them the whole time. I'd better not do that again."

21

Frank was the first to get out of bed and let Columbo into the backyard. This time, he watched Columbo do his business and surveyed the backyard. It was Saturday morning and quiet in the neighborhood with a beautiful, calming sunrise. Frank brewed his favorite black coffee and opened the window shades on all the first-floor windows. Shawna had insisted the window shades be closed the night before. No sooner had Frank sat down with the *Rocky Mountain News* and begun reading the Sports section when he heard Nathan's footsteps coming down the stairs.

"Hi, Grandpa. Whatcha doing?"

"Just trying to do a little reading, Nathan. You know it's Saturday. You don't have to get up early today if you still want to sleep in."

"That's okay, I'm wide awake now. Do you want to watch *SpongeBob* with me?

"Sure, turn it on, and I'll be there in a minute, okay?"

Next came Kaylie, and then Shawna, and finally Kara.

"When is Dad coming home, Mom?" Kaylie asked.

"He should be here after lunch. He just called and said he was refueling the plane."

"It always scares me when he is flying in that small plane," Shawna said to Kara.

"Mom, he was in the Navy and has thousands of flying hours. In fact, he has more hours than most commercial pilots his age. How many times do I have to say it? We're more likely to get killed driving in Denver traffic."

"I don't want you raising two kids on your own," Shawna said, seeming to ignore her daughter's comment.

"Are you ready for the marathon tomorrow, honey?" Frank asked.

"As ready as I will ever be. I am actually looking forward to it and being done with it at the same time. I'm glad I have the two of you, and Luke, and Van cheering me on. That makes me feel better. I'll be watching everybody on the sidelines as I run by wondering, 'Is he a bad guy? Maybe it's him. No, it's him.' I guess it will keep my mind busy instead of thinking about running the entire time."

***

Luke walked in the door from the garage with a bag over his shoulder and a big smile on his face. Nathan and Kaylie jumped on him, and Kara gave him a longer-than-usual hug. Frank shook his hand, and even Shawna smiled at him.

They went to the park, and Frank and Kara threw the soccer ball to the kids while Luke and Shawna sat on a park bench together.

Luke could sense Shawna's uneasiness and waited for her to speak. "Whatever you are doing, Luke, scares me to death, and I am worried about my only daughter and grandkids. What is it that you do that would cause somebody to threaten you and your family?" Shawna asked, shaking her head.

"Don't worry about it, it's nothing. It will blow over in a few days."

"It's nothing? Having a gun put between your eyes is nothing? Having your family threatened is nothing?"

"They're just trying to scare us. Nobody is going to commit first-degree murder to get rid of me. I'm just an environmental consultant doing my job. It's all a game. There are probably one or two guys trying to scare us so that I will quit my job and quit talking about soil removal and DDT. If someone wants to get rid of me, they should have taken me out months ago, not now; it's too late. The EPA is running the show now, and there is nothing I can do to stop it. There is no need to worry."

"I want to believe you, Luke, but I don't. I've never known anyone who has gotten a death threat. Frank already has his concealed carry permit and carries once in a while. I'm sure he will do it more now around Kara and the grandkids."

Luke shook his head. "Carrying a pistol is just a feel-good thing, Shawna, and not a good thing to do around little kids. What would you do if you wanted to threaten someone? Would you run them off the road? No. You would spray paint their house. You would steal the kid's bike. Do you get what I am saying? Whoever it is already has you scared, which means he accomplished what he wanted to accomplish without ever leaving his house. People who make these threats are cowards, Shawna, cowards." Luke became more assertive as he spoke, repeating what Van said about death threats and those who make them. "Tomorrow, I want you and Frank to hang out with the kids at the twelve-mile mark and the finish, and Van and I will look after Kara at various points on the run. We've already figured out how to cover her while she runs."

***

Luke was awakened by the alarm clock early Sunday morning. Kara was already downstairs in the kitchen. He wondered if it was the anxiety of the marathon, the fear of a death threat, or both that woke her up so early. He went downstairs and joined her as she ate a hard-boiled egg, a piece of toast, and a glass of orange juice. He held her closely and explained where he and Van would be throughout the race.

Luke and Kara went upstairs to wake Nathan and Kaylie before heading to the marathon starting area. "Nathan, I'll be wearing number 7275. I want you and your sister to look for me as I run by and wave and yell as loud as you can. That will probably be about eleven o'clock. I'll wave as I run by. There are about twenty thousand runners in this marathon, so look out for your sister and stay close to your grandparents. Okay?"

Nathan nodded, still half asleep.

"We'll look for you, Mom."

"Love you, Nathan. Dad and I need to go and get checked in. We'll see you at mile 16 and after the race. Don't forget to wear your 'Remember Angela' T-shirt," Kara said, as she leaned over and kissed Nathan on the forehead.

Downstairs, Luke grabbed her bib in one hand and a video camera in the other. He saw a wave of confidence sweep over her face and knew the months of training were about to pay off.

They drove down to the marathon starting area where Luke planned to drop off Kara. He gave her another hug with words of encouragement. She had an ear-to-ear smile on her face and was bouncing on her toes, stretching her legs.

"I'll see you at the finish," she said, waving to Luke as she walked into the mass of runners wearing numbers between 7,000 and 8,000.

Luke called Van. "Where are you?"

"I'm at Glen Creighton Park, halfway between mile 15 and 16. Just like we thought, this is the first place where the runners will be close to the crowd while they make the long right-hand turn. It's the perfect place to assault a runner if you want to. The spectators are mostly on one side of the road. I'm on the other side where I can see all the spectators. It's only a guess, but something tells me this is where an assault will happen, if it's going to happen. After she runs by, I'll go over to the turn at mile 20."

"Sounds good, Russo. I'll head to my position near the finish line, between mile 24 and 25, as soon as Kara starts running. Call me when she runs by you," Luke said.

"You got it, Rattler."

Boom! The race began, and the fastest runners immediately jockeyed for position. Luke watched Kara waiting impatiently as seven thousand runners before her started running. An RFID chip in her bib would activate and log her start time to the one-hundredth of a second when she crossed the starting gate. Finally, Kara was running.

***

There was an air of excitement as the lead runners neared mile 15. Spectators crowded beside each other against the ropes, waving and yelling at the runners as they passed. The bib numbers increased, 2,000, 3,000... 6,000. Van called Luke. "I think she's getting close. I just saw number 7070." Van watched as spectators held out their arms and gave high fives. Van spotted Kara and watched as she rounded the corner at Creighton

Park. She was on the other side of the street, but she looked good and seemed to be running with confidence.

Van attempted to thread his way closer to the ropes when a man wearing a blue sweatshirt and sunglasses gave her a high-five but appeared to grab her hand and yank on it, spinning Kara sidewise. She tripped and fell to the asphalt hard, her Colorado Avs ball cap and sunglasses coming off. She rolled over once but bounded back to her feet, gathering her sunglasses and ball cap—a move Van guessed she had mastered during years of playing soccer. Looking stunned, with blood dripping from her knee, elbow, and forehead, she walked for a hundred yards before she began jogging, then running again.

"Luke, Kara just hit the ground, hard, and I think this guy pulled her down intentionally. I'm after him," Van said, yelling into his phone. "Good news is Kara's back up and running. She looks okay to me." Van didn't hesitate as he crossed under the rope and ran toward the man in the blue sweatshirt. The man looked over his shoulder, and their eyes met. Van was still fifty feet away when the man dipped into the crowd. Van merged with runners, his phone to his ear as he looked for the blue sweatshirt. "I see him, Luke. He's speed walking across the supermarket parking lot. Shit, the light just turned green. I have to wait a minute." When the light turned red, Van crossed the street and went into a full run, around cars and shopping carts, in the parking lot.

"Get out of my way! I'm security. Get out of my way." He ran to where he had last seen his quarry, taking deep breaths and cursing himself for not being in better shape. He climbed on a large truck bumper and began scanning the parking lot. A man in blue was nearby, getting into a car. Van ran to the car and grabbed the door before the man could shut it. Groceries spilled from the shopping bag he tossed into the car. The man was clearly older than the suspect, and looked at Van with eyes wide open, holding his hands up.

"I'll give you my money. Don't hurt me; I'm just buying groceries, for Pete's sake."

Van looked in all directions for the man who had assaulted Kara. He was nowhere to be seen.

Van dug into his pocket and pulled out his wallet. He handed the guy a twenty. "Sorry. I thought you were someone else," he said, before continuing his search of the parking lot.

After a few more minutes, Van phoned Luke again. "Damn it. The son of a bitch got away."

"What did he look like?"

"Probably six-foot, white male, brown hair with a blue sweatshirt, sunglasses, and a dark blue baseball cap. I didn't get a good look. He was across the street, and it happened fast."

Van wasn't going to give up searching. He walked around the parking lot and went to the second-floor balcony of a nearby apartment complex to gain a better view of the crowd. He cursed again and made another call.

"I lost the guy, Luke. I'm not sure if he was running from me, or if he just walked away. It might have been an accident, and maybe he felt bad that his high-five made Kara fall to the ground. Let's see what she has to say about it."

"He did it intentionally, Russo! Don't be so damn naive. He looked her up on the webpage, got her bib number, and waited for her to run by. It could have been some crazy farmer dude, or that son of a bitch Chad. He still lives in Denver, you know, and he is linked to Jimmy and probably the Californian farmers. I'm not waiting anymore for things to happen to me. I'm taking the offensive and going after these bastards who are threatening my family. I'm going to pay Chad a visit and interrogate him."

"I think you mean 'we,' Luke. You're not doing anything by yourself. Kara told me to look after you, and that's what I will do," Van said as he listened to Luke rant.

***

Shawna and Frank were at mile 18 with Nathan, Kaylie, and Bill Samuelson, cheering and waving as a few runners in the 7,000's approached. Kaylie was on Frank's shoulders, a few feet above the crowd, with the best view of the runners, when bib number 7275 came down the street. Kara instantly saw Kaylie and began waving to her. She heard Nathan and Frank starting to yell and cheer her on. The cheers were encouraging, and she felt a new burst of energy. She waved at her mom as she ran by but could tell her mother was focused on her bloody knee and the trail of dried blood that ran down her calf and into her shoe. Kara knew her bloody elbow had rubbed against her bib.

"Oh my god, are you all right?" her mother screamed over the noise of the crowd.

Kara slowed as she ran by her family. "I'm okay. I took a fall a few miles back. I'll be alright. See you at the finish."

Nathan yelled, "Go, Mom, go."

Kara smiled. He was either oblivious to the blood or thought it made her look cool.

***

Luke was waiting helplessly at the finish line when Kara crossed. He pulled her over to the side and held her up while she caught her breath and started to recover from running 26.2 miles. He gave her some electrolytes, and they sat down on the curb. "You did it, babe, and you're still alive."

"Damn, that was a long way."

Kara looked like she had played three tournament soccer matches.

"I didn't think running a marathon was a contact sport. You're a little bloodier than I thought you would be. Are you okay?" Luke asked.

"I'll probably be a little sore tomorrow. I was giving high-fives, but some guy grabbed my wrist and spun me sideways. When he let go, I went flying to the ground. Fortunately, I rolled out of it and only scraped myself. It looks worse than it is. Don't tell my mother about this, or she will call the police and take the kids away. I'm only half joking. I saw a guy get tripped up and fall. It's not that uncommon."

"Did you see the guy who grabbed you?" Luke asked.

"I have an image of a guy in a blue sweatshirt with sunglasses and a hat. That's all, and then I kept running. It seemed intentional, but I can't be sure. What was my time, by the way? I passed more runners than passed me."

"We'll see when we look it up on the website, but most of the 7,000's were behind you," Luke replied. "This probably isn't the time to ask, but are you going to do this again?"

"Buy me a milkshake on the way home and give me a massage tonight, and we'll talk about it tomorrow."

The family gathered at home after the race and decided to have a celebratory lunch at the family's favorite restaurant. They sat in a six-person, round booth with Nathan and Kaylie in the middle.

"Mom, you look funny with that bandage on your head. That's a kid's bandage," Nathan said, giggling.

"I know, Nathan. So is the one on my elbow. See?" Kara said.

Luke made a mental note to buy another box. Kara leaned on him with a carefree smile on her face. The thought of a death threat seemed to be the last thing on her mind. They all ordered drinks, and Kara replayed the marathon mile by mile.

"Then it got all bunched up, and the guy in front of me slowed down, and I stumbled over him and went to the ground. He never even saw me fall down, but a few nice runners behind me helped me up, and I walked it off. I probably lost a few minutes because of that fall," Kara said.

Luke smiled and said, "We'll put an asterisk by your time." He knew it was a lie but was impressed that Kara delivered it well. *Does she lie to me more often than I realize?*

Shawna, Frank, and the kids seemed to quickly forget about Kara's fall.

"That was an impressive race, Kara," said Frank. "I didn't know you could do something like that."

"I've always been able to do it, Dad. I just never had the confidence, and I was never encouraged to try something like this until Luke came along," she said, smiling at him.

The criticism hung in the air momentarily before Frank began to talk about his busy work schedule the next day.

***

The early Monday commuter traffic was heavier than usual when Luke punched out a call to Van. "Russo, Monday morning is my favorite time of the week. The in-laws are gone, and we kept the kids. Kara's mom was pretty upset with the death threat. She's panicked and ready to hire a bodyguard."

"How's Kara taking it?"

"She doesn't seem too worried about it, even after getting thrown to the ground by that guy in the blue sweatshirt. Any more ideas on who it might be?"

"I have to say, I'm not totally convinced it was an intentional act. There was a lot of high-fiving going on, and with the corner in the turn, you couldn't see a particular runner until they were fifty feet from you, or less. Most of the runners wore hats and sunglasses and could be unrecognizable. I guess if someone knew her bib number and roughly when she would be running by, they could be ready, but still, it's a long shot that somebody could identify Kara and grab her that quickly."

"If the person knew what she looked like, that would help. The only person I can think of who lives in Denver, has seen her before, and might grab her like that is Chad. I'll see if people in the office know where he is today and what he is doing. I'm also going to tell my boss and Bob and Caroline at Guadalupe about each of the death threats. I'll leave out the hotel details for now. I don't want to freak out everyone in the office, but it's time to go public."

He went straight to the Coffee Nook and made a double espresso. The taste of an espresso on Monday morning instantly made him smile for a few minutes as the caffeine kicked in. Friday afternoon beers did not come close to Monday morning coffee. Nancy was another early morning person in the office, and Luke headed straight to her office.

"Hey Luke, good to see you. How was California?" she asked.

"Other than some equipment sabotage and a few death threats, it was business as usual, and a dozen yards have been removed and replaced."

"Did the contractor get a death threat from a homeowner? I've heard of that happening before."

"Actually, *I* got a death threat, and so did Simone at the EPA, and so did my wife."

Nancy's smile abruptly ended, and she stared at Luke, obviously waiting for more details.

"First, someone called Simone on her personal cell phone and left a message threatening her family. The guy said it was because she was responsible for lowering the cleanup standard for DDT. Then someone threatened me at the hotel. He said it was because I should be doing more to stand up to the EPA and all of its nonsense related to DDT cleanup. Then Kara was threatened on our home phone. Unfortunately, her mother took the call instead of Kara."

"Oh boy, that probably added to the excitement," Nancy said.

"That's an understatement," Luke said, with a laugh. "We're pretty convinced the threats came from at least two different people. I say 'we' because I have a friend I served with in Iraq who's in the DOD security business, who is looking out for us."

"How's Kara taking this?"

"We adhere to the belief that if you want to kill me or my family, you wouldn't warn us ahead of time. So, Kara isn't too concerned, and by the way, she finished her first marathon yesterday."

"That's awesome. I understand she trained hard for a long time. Is someone else doing contractor oversight this week?"

"Yes. Debbie flew out last night and is there today."

"Did you tell her about the death threats?

"No. I decided not to, but I asked Earl to watch over her all week. He knows about the threats. But, I don't think she is in the spotlight like I am, so I'm not worried."

Nancy paused. "It's great that you aren't worried, Luke, but you need to call Debbie as soon as we're done here and let her decide if she wants to stay out there. If something happens to her and we know there was a threat and didn't let her know, that would haunt all of us."

When Nancy and Luke finished meeting, he went to his office and called Debbie. It was 6:30 a.m. in California, and she was having breakfast with Earl.

"I was wondering when you were going to call, Luke."

I should have told her over the weekend. Nancy is right, as usual. Earl must have told her about the threats.

"I assume Earl has filled you in on some of the events from last week. Are you okay with what is going on?" Luke said.

"I'm fine with it, Luke. I actually kind of hope I get a death threat. It will add to my résumé and make for a good story to tell at the next party."

Luke took a deep breath. "Good. I've learned in the last week that people have very different responses to threats like this. Stay close to Earl and get to know Alberto and his sidekick, Garth. You want Garth to be your friend while you are there. Nobody is going to mess with you when you're with Garth."

Next, he called Bob and explained the soil removal protests and death threats in detail. He held back on the hotel details.

"Aw, hell, Luke. Caroline and I have been threatened so many times, I can't count that high. None of these threats have ever amounted to a hill of beans. We've asked the police and FBI to track down a few of them. Most were from enviro activists, like EF&J, but we never pressed charges. Those wackos. I don't pay attention to them anymore."

"Did anyone ever put a gun to your face and threaten you?"

Bob paused, "I can't say that ever happened to me, Luke, but it sounds like someone did that to you. Am I hearing you correctly?"

Half joking, Luke said, "From this point forward, I consider you my personal attorney, and everything I say is protected under attorney-client privilege."

Bob laughed. "Don't you want to know my rate before you spill your guts?"

"Listen, some guy with a mask put a 9mm in my face, with his finger on the trigger, and threatened me and my family. He told me to take charge of the EPA and put an end to this DDT cleanup stuff, or else I would be sorry. I tried to explain that I couldn't control the EPA when my friend in the next room took him down and rearranged his face. We did some digging and found out his name. He appears to be a farmer in the Central Valley who's afraid that he will need to clean up his farm someday because they used DDT in the past. By the way, the gun wasn't loaded."

"Okay, this is also between you and me. In fact, I will deny this call ever happened if I'm ever asked. You're a former military guy. Make sure this guy knows that if he ever threatens you and your family again, you will respond accordingly. These kinds of people should not be free to roam in our society. You have the greatest legal defense there is: Someone threatened you with death. I suggest you take advantage of it."

Luke looked at the mountains out of his window and took a deep breath. "Bob, I think guys like him are just emotionally driven. I don't think he's dangerous. That said, I understand what you're saying, and I will protect myself if necessary. Do I get hazardous duty pay from Guadalupe?" he asked.

"No. Sorry to say, but you should look at this as a bonus from Guadalupe because you get the opportunity to legitimately settle a score. That's so much better than hazard pay."

Another cup of coffee from the Coffee Nook, and then Luke

went to his weekly project meeting. Rudy and Beth sat next to each other at the conference table, laughing and discussing the weekend. Rudy was sipping coffee from a large white mug with the saying: "Chemist in Training."

He held up the mug. "Beth here is teaching me about chemistry. I have to admit, you don't learn much about chemistry when you're getting a PhD in hydrogeology."

"Just because you are a doctor doesn't mean you can't learn more," Beth said, nodding.

"Umm, it's great to see that you are expanding your horizons, Rudy," Luke said, raising an eyebrow.

He sat down and gave a brief, sanitized summary of the soil removal and the death threats. "I'd rather you hear it from me than someone else," he added.

"Holy shit. I've never known anyone who got a death threat. Did you call the police?" Rudy asked.

"No. I've been told they don't, or can't, do much in these cases, and we didn't want the attention. Earl and I spent a lot of time thinking this through, and that was our decision."

"Based on what you're telling me, I'm not going out there for a long time. Do you think it was Chad?" Rudy asked.

"I have no idea." Luke didn't want to start rumors. "Do you all know what Chad is doing these days?"

"I heard he's still looking for a new job, and it's not going well, but that was from a friend of a friend," Beth said. None of the others answered.

Luke went back to his office and listened to a voicemail from Kara.

"Honey, I think I have seen that guy who grabbed my hand before. He looks familiar from somewhere. I can't place him, but I know I have seen him."

22

The nagging question surrounding Kara's high-five fall was still in Luke's mind a few days later. Was it accidental, or had it been done on purpose, as some kind of a warning? Luke's opinion seemed to change every five minutes. Even Van, who'd witnessed the attack, wasn't convinced it was intentional. Luke itched to go over it again with his friend, but Van was out of touch on a "special assignment," somewhere unknown.

Luke assumed the soil removal action in California was going as scheduled since he hadn't heard from Debbie or Earl in the last twenty-four hours. Assuming anything bothered him. He dialed Debbie.

"Debbie, how's it going out there? Any threats? Are there still protests in the streets?"

"Everything is going fine, and Alberto is on schedule. I've gotten to know him and Garth. They are like an odd comedy team when they get going. It's entertaining being around them. Earl and I have been hanging out together, too, and spent some time at the groundwater treatment system checking on everything and taking some monthly samples. No death threats for me, darn it."

"Have you seen Jimmy Mendoza?"

"I did see him yesterday at the protest. There were only five people. Pretty lame, if you ask me. Jimmy saw me and gave me a dirty look, like he didn't want me around, but he didn't say anything to me, and I didn't say anything to him. Do you think that counts as a death threat? I was hoping for something more tangible."

"Debbie, you can put a death threat on your résumé. I'll vouch for you," Luke said.

"Awesome!"

Two more calls and then Luke could get back to work without being interrupted. "Bob, it's Luke. Do you have a few minutes for an update?"

"I do, but let me go first, in case I get this call back I've been waiting for and I have to cut you off. First, the good news. EF&J decided to drop the collusion lawsuit against us and the EPA. I think they realized they might piss off the EPA, and that would work against them in some other cases. However, they made their point about Guadalupe and got a bunch of publicity and probably a lot of fundraising. I hate these god-damn money-sucking leeches. They serve no purpose except to create their nice-paying jobs and flatter each other with a job well done. They'll do something stupid one of these days and lose credibility. Just watch."

"That's great they closed the collusion case, Bob. One less thing we have to worry about, and we can get back to doing what we are supposed to do, like cleaning up the site."

"I wish I had your idealistic enthusiasm, Luke. You know it's going to take forever to clean up this site, and all we can do for now is contain the problem, so it doesn't cause more problems. At least we get paid well during the process. I shouldn't be telling you this, but by now, you've probably come to the same conclusion."

Luke tilted his head and weighed Bob's comment. He refused to take the bait and disclose his feelings to Bob about the site cleanup and EF&J. It seemed too personal, and Bob was his client. Luke wanted to be friends, but not friendly.

"That's kind of a cynical view of the cleanup, Bob."

"I know it is, and I shouldn't say things like this. I'll work on my attitude," said Bob, with a snort. "The other thing I wanted you to know is that Lenny and Earl have depositions on Friday next week, in Long Beach, regarding the offshore contamination case. You need to be there with me. Come in the night before and leave the next day. I'm still somewhat surprised they've never deposed you. Maybe they believe you don't have the historical knowledge. Oh well, lucky break for you. We'll meet them for breakfast down by the pier, and I will coach them some more. Then, we'll go to downtown for the deposition. Wear a nice suit. You don't need to prepare, but I want you to hear the questioning. We'll talk about it. Hey, I have to take this call. I'll call you back."

Luke knew that Bob wouldn't call back anytime soon, since he'd conveyed the necessary points in his message. He called Cindy, asked her to arrange flights, and then called Kara. "Hey, babe. I just talked with Bob, and we have to give depositions next week in Long Beach. I'm planning to fly out next Thursday evening and come back late on Friday."

"What? I just got our company's Avalanche playoff tickets for Friday against St. Louis. You do know if we win tonight, we'll be in the Western Conference finals, and we're favored to win our second Stanley Cup. Will you be back in time for the game?"

Luke could hear the disappointment in Kara's voice. "I'm not supposed to land until 8:05, so it's unlikely I'll make it to the game. Can you find a client to go with you?"

"I'm sure I can, but this will be a lot of fun. It could be a once-in-a-lifetime opportunity," Kara said.

"I'll talk to Bob again and see when he expects the depositions to be done and I can leave. Maybe I can catch an earlier flight. Don't ask anyone until I find out."

His next call was to Simone. He shut his office door, and she answered on the second ring. "Hey Simone, I just heard from Bob that EF&J retracted their lawsuit about us colluding with the EPA. That means we can talk to one another without worrying about what we say."

"Okay. Is there something you want to tell me?" Simone said.

"Umm, nothing in particular. Just wanted to see if you've had any more death threats and ask you a question about the offshore contamination."

"I haven't had any more threats, but I take a different way home each time I go to the San Francisco office and try to stay in crowded BART trains. We're in a new routine of not being in a routine, if that makes sense. How about you?"

Luke realized that in all the activity over the weekend, he hadn't shared the hotel threat or the phone call to his house with Simone. He decided that she didn't need to know about the hotel threat, but she needed to hear about his threat at home. Whatever he told her would likely get to Antoine, and anything that Debbie knew would probably get to Antoine, since they now talked more than the job required. Luke went into ten minutes of storytelling with Simone until they started laughing about death threats.

Then, he changed the subject to the offshore contamination lawsuit. "My question is simply this, how long does DDT last on the ocean floor before it breaks down into carbon and hydrogen?

My client believes that after thirty or forty years, the DDT will naturally disappear, and if this lawsuit drags on long enough, there will be no evidence left on the ocean floor."

"That's not necessarily a bad strategy, Luke. Nature has a way of cleaning things up over time. The problem is, when DDT breaks down, it creates DDT daughter products, and it takes years for those to break down further. We know of at least forty-five DDT-related daughter products in the blubber of dead dolphins on the shores in the Palos Verdes area. The breakdown of DDT will continue for at least one hundred years, if not even longer. Of course, we have yet to determine how long this will ultimately take, and we don't know how bad these breakdown products are for humans or the environment. Labs don't even manufacture these DDT byproducts, so I can't test them for risk to human health and the environment. Our understanding of all these byproducts is pathetic."

"Why are we so worried about contaminated groundwater contained under the site where nobody comes in contact with it, and not the floor of the ocean outside our backyard, where fish that we eat live?" Luke said, shaking his head in his hands.

"The EPA moves forward one step at a time based on what we know today. The EPA knew the groundwater and soil at the site were contaminated, so we started there. We're just now looking at the offshore contamination, and I assure you, it is becoming a greater effort now than ever before," Simone said.

She concluded the call by telling Luke she'd missed talking to him. He told her the same, then leaned back in his chair, again taking in the snow-capped mountain view that helped him clear his mind. He had a lot of irons in the fire, but nothing was urgent, so he finally had time to start drafting the groundwater remediation plan for the site. After all, it was his primary consulting assignment for Guadalupe. Surely, it wouldn't take centuries to clean up the site. He knew he could do better than that. The soil removal action had been a lengthy distraction, and the EF&J lawsuits were interesting, but none of this was meaningful to the overall site cleanup. Knowing that his work priorities could change at any minute, Luke took advantage of the quiet lull and began writing.

***

Luke landed at LAX on Thursday and picked up his rental car when rush hour was winding down. It was his preferred flight schedule whenever he flew commercial. Cindy knew that and routinely booked for him. He drove directly to Manhattan Beach, found a parking spot where he changed into shorts and a T-shirt in the passenger seat, and began walking on the beach in his sandals. The sun was close to setting. Perfect timing.

He laced his fingers behind his head as he walked on the soft sand. There was a cool onshore breeze and the pleasing sound of seagulls crooning in the air. Little kids ran in the sand, chased by the water as it raced onto the beach. Thinking of his family, he called Kara. They talked until dark while he walked on the beach.

Bob and Luke had agreed to meet for drinks after Bob arrived later that night from Boston. It was almost 11:00 when Bob called and said he was at the hotel bar. He told Luke he was already on his second bourbon when Luke joined him.

"Sorry I'm so late. The plane was delayed five hours because of some mechanical problem," Bob said, his eyes red and watery. "You know they never tell you why. It always makes you wonder what the mechanical problem is, doesn't it? Is it just a burned-out light bulb, or is the landing gear broken?"

"There's a lot of redundancy in these big planes. As long as the engines have fuel and the controls work, it's all good. So, what's the schedule for tomorrow?"

"We'll meet Lenny and Earl for breakfast here at the hotel, go through some dos and don'ts about giving depositions, and then go meet the EF&J lawyers. Maybe Brooke will be there, and I can wink at her. That will get under her skin."

Bob's phone rang and he immediately answered it. "Lenny, what's going on? …No way… Really? Where are you now? We'll come over and see if we can help. See you in about fifteen minutes."

"What's up?"

"Lenny's boat is on fire. Something exploded. Let's hop in my car and get over to the pier."

Bob raced straight to the Port of Long Beach entrance and Lenny's salvage boat without missing a turn. Luke was impressed with the man's sense of direction despite a few drinks. Several fire trucks and Port Authority police cars were near the salvage boat. Flashing lights filled the night sky, and firefighters rolled up fire hoses. Debris from the boat's pilot house littered the boat and the pier. It looked like it had been hit by a tornado. The smell of diesel exhaust from the fire truck engines was heavy in the cool night air. Bob parked the rental car outside the police tape, and he and Luke looked for Lenny.

"Sorry, gentlemen, you aren't allowed in the restricted area," a police officer said, walking aggressively toward them and shining his flashlight in Bob's face.

"I'm Lenny Donahue's attorney, and I need to speak to him right now," Bob said, presenting his driver's license. Luke hoped the smell of diesel in the air was more potent than the smell of bourbon on Bob's breath.

"Okay, go ahead. Don't touch anything or step on anything. We're still collecting evidence," the officer said.

A fireman moved, and they spotted Lenny.

"Hey Bob, can you believe this? My pilot house burned to a crisp. I don't know what would have exploded. I didn't keep anything explosive in my office. Even the heaters are electric, but my entire fucking office is gone, all my records and everything!" Lenny said, waving his arms and yelling.

"It's okay, Lenny, we'll help you get to the bottom of this," Bob said, lighting a cigarette. "If I had to guess, it's those goddamn environmental activists at EF&J. They're probably seeking retribution against you and hoping to get publicity about the offshore dumping at the same time."

"I haven't dumped anything offshore since 1973. I'm just a salvage company," Lenny said, as the blue and red emergency vehicle lights flashed across his face.

"Sorry, gentlemen, I need you to back up behind the yellow tape. This is now a crime scene. We found a body in the pilot house," the police officer said.

"You what?" Lenny stumbled back a pace, and Luke grabbed his arm.

"That's right, sir. You heard me. There appears to be a dead female in the pilot house," the police officer said. "Do you know who it might be?"

Lenny, Bob, and Luke stiffened and stared at the police officer in disbelief.

"Hell. I don't know who she is. No one should be in there at this hour. All my employees are men. Do you know who she is?" Lenny asked.

"She doesn't appear to have any ID on her, so it could take a day or two to figure it out. I don't know any more than that.

The investigator just showed up, so all of you will need to talk with him before you leave."

The investigator was an expressionless and monotone man in his early forties, wearing a blazer and jeans. Luke thought of Van in the desert, interrogating Iraqi soldiers. He'd never asked his friend how he'd made them talk.

A few hours ago, I was walking on the beach enjoying the peace and tranquility of the sunset, and now I'm being questioned at 1:00 in the morning by someone who enjoys questioning people at 1:00 in the morning.

"I need names, contact information, and purpose for being here," the investigator said. He started with Lenny. Bob was last.

"Okay, first question. Do any of you have any idea why this may have happened?"

Lenny spoke first. "I used to dump waste offshore, back when it was legal, and I have a lot of people today who don't like me for what I did."

"What about your business today? Are you in debt, or have some disgruntled employees who might want to do this?"

"I have two employees who have been with me for over ten years. We're like family, and I own the boat outright. I don't have any debt."

"How about you, Mr. Burrows? Remind me, are you Mr. Donahue's attorney, or are you here for some other reason?" the investigator asked.

"Lenny and the company I work for, Guadalupe Chemical, are being sued by an environmental activist company named Environmental Freedom & Justice. They have done things like this in the past. Lenny is supposed to be deposed tomorrow, I mean today, in Long Beach. My hunch is that the dead woman is with EF&J and that she accidentally blew herself up with dynamite. Serves her right."

The investigator stared coldly at Bob and asked, "Who might the dead female be, Mr. Burrows?"

"I have no idea who she could be," Bob said, curtly.

Luke could see it on Bob's face. He'd realized he was talking too loosely and needed to answer questions without elaborating or inserting his opinions. Maybe it was the two bourbons. The investigator was serious, and Bob's comments would lead to more questions.

"We don't know if the bomb was made from dynamite, do we, Mr. Burrows? It could have been RDX, or nitro, or TNT. These are all common explosives these days," the investigator said.

"It sure smells like dynamite," Bob said.

"It sounds like you have experience with explosives, Mr. Burrows."

"I was involved with blasting many years ago, when I did road construction work. I remember the smell," Bob said.

"Hmm. When explosives kill people, evidence gets strewn all over the place. There is usually a lot of evidence, like bomb parts, body parts, fingerprints..." the investigator said then turned to Luke. "What about you, Mr. Graham? What are you doing here tonight?"

"I flew in from Denver earlier this afternoon. I went for a walk on the beach before meeting Bob at the hotel. We were catching up when Bob's phone rang, and Lenny said his boat was on fire. We rushed over here right away," Luke said.

"Okay. We'll know more in a day or two. I suggest you all stay close by. Is there anything else I should know that you haven't told me?" asked the investigator. He handed out his business card. "If something comes to mind, you can call me directly."

They all shook their heads in agreement. Luke thought about his death threats but didn't see any relevance to this explosion. He felt terrible for Lenny but was bone tired and wanted to go to bed.

***

Luke awoke at 6:00 a.m., his phone ringing after three hours of fitful sleep. He didn't wake in time to answer Bob's call and waited for his voicemail. Bob had decided, before they'd left the pier, to postpone the depositions. Lenny would be at his salvage boat most of the day talking to the investigator and negotiating with insurance companies.

"Luke," Bob's voice boomed from the phone. "I'm at LAX. I got an early flight back to Boston. I'm not going to sit on my ass all day waiting for that arrogant investigator to call me. He can find me in Boston. Whoever the dead girl is, she should have known better than to play with explosives. You can get yourself killed. Let me know if you learn anything else today, and be careful what you say to the investigator. You don't want to become a suspect."

Luke decided to stay in Torrance until his scheduled flight that afternoon, and to check on the soil removal action and meet with Earl to update him on last night's commotion. He also had time to call Van, who had returned from his mysterious assignment.

"Van, you will never believe what happened last night."

"I might. Make it fast. I have a meeting in a few minutes."

"There was an explosion on Lenny's boat last night, and a woman who was in the pilot house died in the explosion. They are still trying to identify her, but everyone seems to think she accidentally blew herself up. The investigator is asking a lot of questions. I feel like he is accusing Bob, or Lenny, or me."

"That's what investigators do, Luke. They make you feel guilty when you are innocent, and then they see who does something out of the ordinary, or says something they shouldn't, because the silence makes them talk. Be very careful about what you say to anyone and hire an attorney if it goes further. Try to get more information before you leave town, and I'll do some research. I gotta go," Van said and hung up.

Luke stared at his phone. Was someone trying to kill Lenny or just scare him? EF&J was suing Lenny; why would they want to kill him? It didn't make sense.

The phone rang. It was Earl.

"This job gets more interesting every day. I never thought I would hear about a boat explosion and death threats. Sounds like some gal blew herself up. Do they know who did it?" Earl asked.

"I'm probably not the first person they will call when they figure it out," said Luke. "We should go to the pier after lunch and get an update. If you go with me, Earl, the investigator will probably want to ask you some questions."

"Fine with me. I know nothing and have nothing to hide," Earl said.

Earl picked Luke up and drove to the pier, parking the Bronco outside the area surrounded by yellow police tape. The fire hoses were gone, and the location had been cleared of most of the larger debris. The remaining frame of the charred pilot house still stood, albeit at an angle, surrounding the metal desk and file cabinet. The remains of the sofa and chairs were in black piles on the boat's deck. Lab technicians were sifting through the ash with plastic bags, labelling pieces of evidence.

Luke found Lenny sitting in his car, talking on his mobile

phone. As he approached, Lenny abruptly hung up his phone and waved.

"Have you been here all night?" Luke asked.

"I have. I dozed off a few hours while waiting for the lab technicians, but I want to make sure I don't miss anything. The investigator is supposed to show up in a few minutes, and we'll see if he has any new information about the woman who got killed. The fire completely destroyed my file cabinets and all of my records. He said one of the drawers was open when the explosion occurred, which is odd because I always close the drawers so I don't run into them. Maybe the explosion opened it. I also forgot to tell the fire department I had a two-gallon gas can under my desk that I used for that stupid leaf blower. The gas can must have ignited and helped the fire. Otherwise, there wouldn't have been much to burn."

"What was in the file cabinets, Lenny?" Luke asked.

"That pilot house was my office, Luke. Going back to the fifties, when Dad ran things, all my records were in there. Bob said I would have to make copies of the files when this lawsuit enters the discovery phase. So much for that, huh?"

"You can't make up a better excuse, Lenny. It's kind of ironic that EF&J could be responsible for destroying the documents they want to see."

Luke returned to the Bronco and sat with Earl while Lenny called his insurance agent again.

"I hope Lenny has good insurance coverage on this. It will take months to get this salvage boat back in service. He also said all of his business records were destroyed in the fire," Luke said.

"See that police officer over there? He and my son went to high school together. My son, John, and Robert played football together for four years. I watched every game, and so did Robert's parents. We became good friends and still see each other occasionally. Robert and I had a moment to catch up on life and family while you talked to Lenny. Just between you and me, the woman who was killed has been positively identified as Amy Nunez, the woman with EF&J whom we met at the public meeting. A police report will be completed next week, and I'll get a copy of it."

"How do they know it was Amy? Are they sure?" Luke said.

"The police found her arm about ten feet from the pilot house and took fingerprints. Her arm wasn't burned like the rest of her body," said Earl. "Robert said they will also use dental records to confirm her identity. He said that everything points to Amy setting a time bomb under Lenny's desk, and accidentally blowing herself up. The police don't know if Amy was trying to kill Lenny or just trying to blow up the pilot house when no one was in it," Earl said.

"I can think of one person the investigators are definitely going to want to talk to," Luke said.

"Who's that?"

"Brooke Burr."

23

Ten minutes before the puck dropped, Luke picked up his ticket at will call and found his seat next to Kara at the Colorado Avalanche playoff hockey game. She beamed at him, wearing her well-fitted Joe Sakic #19 jersey and favorite white Avs cap. As they hugged and kissed, thoughts of the salvage boat explosion and images of Amy's arm on the ground drifted away.

However, the respite was short-lived. When Luke returned to his office on Monday, he found himself repeating the explosion story over and over again. The story changed each time someone questioned him about it, gaining more details and exaggeration. Nancy and Rudy met with Luke in private and asked more specific questions.

"You're starting to live a pretty exciting life for an environmental consultant. Are you at all concerned that something like this could happen to one of our staff, including yourself?" Nancy asked. "After all, there have been death threats."

"We haven't had any more death threats in several weeks, and the soil removal work is nearing an end. So, I'm hoping we're done with that stuff. The explosion appears to have been a targeted effort on Lenny and the salvage company, and the person who did it is dead, so we don't need to worry about her anymore," Luke said, with a slight grin.

"Is Guadalupe worried they may be the next target of a violent attack?" Rudy asked.

"I talked with Bob this morning, and he's adamant that Guadalupe has no involvement in the explosion whatsoever, as a target or otherwise," Luke said.

"We should have a security guard with us during the next groundwater sampling round. We'll have employees on the site and in the neighborhoods, taking samples," Rudy said.

"That's a good idea. It will provide additional protection and reduce our potential liability. See if you can get Guadalupe to approve that in the budget. At least for this next round of quarterly sampling," Nancy asked.

Luke left the meeting and stopped by the Coffee Nook for a third cup where he ran into Beth.

"Wow, Luke, I just heard about the explosion on the salvage boat. That's pretty exciting and scary, Beth said.

Luke filled her in on some of the details.

"Do you want some creamer in your coffee?" Beth asked, pouring a tablespoon of powdered creamer into her cup.

Luke grinned. "No, thanks. You never know what chemicals are in there."

Beth smiled back. "It's mostly powdered dairy milk. I'm not worried about it, but it's good to see you're paying attention to chemistry and what you are putting into your body. By the way, did they take any chemical residue samples from the explosion area? I'd love to see the analyses if they did. Chemical residue can tell you a lot about a crime scene," Beth said.

"I'm sure they did. I'll see if Earl can get you a copy of the report. He knows the head investigator." Luke wondered why he hadn't thought of testing the chemical residue. It seemed so obvious now that Beth brought it up.

He returned to his office to find an email from Earl with a draft police report attached.

"Speak of the devil," he said. The email subject was titled *Confidential* and there was no text in the body of the email. Luke kept his reply equally cryptic. *Received*, he typed back. Then he downloaded the report to an external drive, moved the email exchange to his electronic trash, and emptied it. He'd meant what he'd said to Nancy. Hopefully, this whole nightmare was wrapping up, but it didn't hurt to be careful. He shut his office door and called Van.

"Hey, Russo, I just got a copy of the police report from Earl. I'll come by after work, and we can print it out and analyze it at your house."

"Great. Make sure you delete the report from your email and empty your trash."

"Already done," Luke said, with a satisfied smile. He glanced at the doorway before pulling up the report on his computer and paging through it to the Conclusion section.

At approximately 10:32 p.m. on the night of May 10, 2001, an explosion occurred in the pilot house of the salvage boat Croaker II, *owned by Lenny Roger Donahue. The explosion and subsequent fire, enhanced by two gallons of stored gasoline in the pilot house, destroyed the majority of contents and resulted in the death of a female who was in the pilot house at the time of the explosion. The female was identified through forensic testing as Amy Gloria Nunez of San Jose, California.... video cameras owned and operated by the Port of Long Beach showed a woman similar in build and stature to Ms. Nunez break into the front door window of the* Croaker *pilot house at 10:04 p.m., with a backpack on her back. She was not seen leaving the pilot house prior to the explosion...*

Luke called Kara. "Hey, babe, sorry to bother you at work, but you're going to love this. I got a copy of the police report on the explosion. It reads just like one of your old *Columbo* movie episodes. I'm going to stop by Van's house on the way home and discuss it with him for a few minutes. He'll have some thoughts, I'm sure."

"Just remember, honey, the criminal has to have a motive. What was Amy's motive? I'll talk to you when you get home," Kara said.

Luke returned to the report.

...debris from the explosion was strewn predominantly in a westerly direction toward the dock, indicating that the explosive device was against the west side of the heavy metal desk when it exploded. Pieces of a commercially available detonator timer were found in the debris. A file cabinet was located in the primary blast zone and one drawer of the file cabinet appeared to be fully extended at the time of the explosion. The materials in the file cabinet were destroyed by the ensuing fire, with the exception of the one fully extended drawer, which was blown free of the fire. This is where the lower arm of the murdered suspect was retrieved. ...Ms. Nunez has been arrested on two previous occasions for civil disobedience and investigated by the FBI for possession of the military explosive C4... In conclusion, Ms. Nunez had the motive and necessary skills and expertise to detonate a homemade bomb in the pilot house of the Croaker II, *destroying the pilot house for political purposes.*

The police report was convincing, but Luke kept thinking about Amy's motive. "Political purposes." It was a nice, vague term. But what real benefit did Amy's causes gain from the explosion? The offshore dumping occurred half a century ago. He knew little about Amy's background and why she was committed to the environmental activist cause. Maybe she had lost a loved one to chemical contamination and cancer, or perhaps she was driven by an intense anti-dumping hatred. Luke could only guess without having more information.

***

Van opened his front door before Luke could knock and stuck his hand out. Luke dropped the thumb drive into Van's hand.

"Get yourself something to drink and ignore the mess. I've been out of town," Van said, disappearing into his office.

Luke knew Van had returned a week ago but chose not to distract him with a smart-ass comment. Van returned in a few minutes with two copies of the police report. Even though Luke had already read the report once, Van finished in half the time.

"I know this is a draft report, but it's incomplete and lacking in several ways," Van said. "For example, from the position of Amy's body, it doesn't sound like she was standing next to the bomb when it exploded as the report says. It's more likely she was standing by the file cabinet. Her body was found in one piece, with the exception of her arm, which was protected by the metal of the cabinet. If she had been holding the bomb when it exploded, that wouldn't be the case."

He must have noticed Luke's surprise. "I saw a lot of this kind of thing in the desert," he said, with a shrug.

"Maybe she set the timer incorrectly, and the bomb went off before it was supposed to," Luke said.

Van raised an eyebrow. "Let me ask you this. Would you set a bomb and then go look through a file cabinet while the timer was ticking? Or would you look through the file cabinet first, then set the timer, right before you left the scene?"

***

It was Tuesday, Simone's day to take the BART to her office in downtown San Francisco. Attempting to disguise her daily routine, she walked to a small coffee shop she had never been to. The coffee was less than desirable, and the service was mediocre. She could check it off her list of coffee shops to visit. As she had a million times before, she told herself that the death threat was just a scare, but she was enjoying her random routine as a fun way to break up the monotony of daily work.

Antoine stepped into her office and shut the door before she could sit down and turn on her computer.

"I just heard from Carol in Security that there was an explosion on Lenny Donahue's salvage boat and that it killed a gal from EF&J."

"You mean Brooke Burr?" Simone said, as her mouth fell open.

"No, it was that other woman. The one who didn't say much at the public meeting and acted kind of strange."

"You're thinking of Amy Nunez," Simone said.

"That's her. They're saying she blew herself up with a bomb by accident, and maybe it had something to do with the lawsuit between EF&J and Guadalupe."

Simone immediately went to the EF&J website, where she and Antoine read the latest news from Brooke Burr on the front page.

Environmental Freedom & Justice mourns the death of long-time, dedicated employee and activist, Amy Nunez, who died last week in a mysterious explosion in Long Beach while investigating the epic DDT contamination off the Palos Verdes shelf in southern California. Amy's efforts to uncover the truth about offshore dumping of DDT, both legally and illegally over decades, may have cost her life. Amy was attempting to locate missing records regarding the decades of dumping DDT into the ocean. Many of these records appear to have been intentionally destroyed. Click here to see more...

"That's a different explanation of the explosion than what Carol told me in our security briefing. I wonder if Brooke Burr knows something we don't, or is she just trying to use Amy's death as a fundraising opportunity?" Antoine said.

"What else did Carol say about this?" Simone said.

"She's ramping up security in the office and advising all of us who have anything to do with DDT to be on a higher level of awareness."

Simone leaned back in her chair and spoke directly to Antoine, "I have been thinking about these threats for some time, Antoine, and now with this explosion, I'm asking you if I can work remotely for a few months while things settle down. My daughter is just about out of school for the summer, and I'd like to stay with my cousin in Fresno for a few months. He has three kids, including a seven-year-old daughter, the same as Alison, and they get along well."

"Let me check with HR. I don't have a problem with it. It's not much different than our current arrangement, but let me see if there is a policy I don't know about," Antoine replied.

***

At 12:30 in the morning, Luke fumbled for his cell phone.

"Rattler, it's Van."

"I never would have guessed," Luke said, through a yawn.

"Are you already in bed? God save me from the life of the domesticated."

Luke crawled out of bed and slipped into the hallway. After smothering another yawn, he padded, barefoot, down the stairs. "What's up?"

"These investigators are all the same, Luke. They just want to solve the case as quickly as possible and move on to the next one, with a lot of time off in between. Like I said earlier, why would you set the bomb and then go looking through the file cabinet? It doesn't make sense, even for someone who has never used a bomb before."

"Right. That makes sense to me," Luke said, fighting the urge to close his eyes.

"Secondly, why would EF&J want to blow up the pilot house? They wanted Croaker's records. The report doesn't say whether or not Amy had any of their files in her backpack.

"Lastly, the investigator only looked at one hour's worth of footage from the dock camera video. I don't know if they have more video, but what happened two, three, or six hours before the explosion? Maybe it was just a coincidence that Amy was there when the bomb was set to explode. Perhaps someone else was there earlier. My point is, Rattler, maybe the bomb wasn't her bomb."

"Thanks, Russo. That's a lot to think about. Let's talk to-morrow," Luke said. He hung up and headed upstairs to go back to bed, but doubted he would get much more sleep. His mind was running wild.

24

"**N**athan, it's time to get up. The trout are calling. They're almost as big as you are," Luke said.

It was early Saturday morning, before the sun was up. Luke was taking Nathan and Van to Casper, Wyoming, in the single-engine Cirrus SR22. The seven miles of blue-ribbon trout fishing on the North Platte River, known as the "Miracle Mile," was one of the best in the country. Luke assembled enough fishing gear for the three of them the night before and loaded it into the cargo of the Cirrus along with their waders and overnight bags. It was one of Luke's favorite destinations. He and Van already had their Wyoming fishing licenses, and Nathan fished for free because of his young age.

It was a beautiful May morning with no storms in the area. There was no traffic, due to the early hour, and they made it to the Arapahoe County airport in record time. Luke had checked the weather and filed his flight plan to Casper before waking his son. Two days earlier, he had called the airport for Avgas, so the Cirrus was ready. Van was waiting for them in the parking lot. They opened the hangar and pulled out the plane.

"How fast are we going to go, Dad?" Nathan asked.

"We'll be flying a little over two hundred miles per hour, son. That's about three times as fast as you go in a car."

"Wow, that's fast."

They each put on their headsets and did a radio check. "Can you hear me, Nathan?" Luke asked.

"Loud and clear, Dad."

As a copilot, Van sat in the right seat and read the checklist, while Nathan watched and listened from the back seat. Either Van was feeling better about the flight today or doing a good job of faking it for Nathan's sake.

The takeoff was uneventful, and Luke turned the Cirrus due north, toward Wyoming. "Keep your eyes open, you two. There's always a lot of traffic over Denver, even at this time of day. Air traffic control has us on their radar, but it doesn't hurt to keep looking for other planes," Luke said, knowing it was good to give passengers something to do.

The air was smooth, and Luke climbed to eight thousand feet and leveled off just below DIA's airspace, where commercial jets flew. "Look to the right, Nathan," he said, pointing out the window toward a large baseball stadium. "That's Coors Field."

"Wow, that's awesome, Dad. I can see where we sat last time."

Van was looking down and admiring the view when Luke heard a slight lowering in the engine's pitch. Van and Nathan didn't seem to notice, but Luke's years in the cockpit made him subconsciously alert for any unusual sounds. He scanned the instruments and noticed a slight decrease in engine RPMs. As he checked the other instruments, the plane started to slowly lose altitude. He raised the nose of the aircraft to maintain his altitude. His first thought was a failed magneto, as he had discussed with Van a month ago. Instinctively, he turned the plane slightly toward the Broomfield airport, northwest of Denver, while he assessed the engine.

"Hey, guys, I'm going to test out our engine and make sure

everything is running okay. Don't be alarmed if it shuts off for a second."

Van looked at Luke with wide eyes but kept his mouth shut. Luke turned the ignition key and shut off the first magneto. Nothing happened. He turned the key and shut off the second magneto. The engine stopped. Luke turned the key back to its original position, and the engine immediately restarted.

"That's what happens when you lose a magneto, Russo. It's best to land and get it repaired rather than fly with just one. So, we'll land in Broomfield. They have a good shop there."

Luke dialed in the correct radio frequency for the Broomfield airport. "Broomfield, Cirrus 3-4-5-Tango-Charlie, we've lost a magneto and request straight in Runway 3-0."

"5-Tango-Charlie cleared to land Runway 30, maintain pattern altitude at seven thousand."

"Broomfield, 5-Tango Charlie, I'll stay at eight thousand just in case something else happens, and I need the altitude."

He glanced around at his passengers. Van still looked freaked, but Nathan's eyes shined with excitement. "Hey guys, we'll start a steep descent to the runway in another minute. Hopefully, this repair won't take too long," Luke said.

Just then, the engine stopped abruptly, and the propellor made slow revolutions as the aircraft began to lose serious altitude. Luke trimmed the Cirrus to make the most distance with the engine out and tried to restart the engine, to no avail.

"This can't be good," Van said, meeting Luke's eyes.

"We'll be okay," Luke said, giving his son a thumbs up before uttering the words no pilot ever wanted to speak. "Mayday, mayday, Broomfield Tower, 5 Tango Charlie, we have a total engine failure."

"5 Tango Charlie, do you think you will make the runway?"

"Not sure. We'll either make it or land short in the grass," Luke said.

"5 Tango Charlie, do you want emergency response personnel?"

Before Luke answered the Broomfield tower, he considered whether he would have to pay for the emergency response and file a report with the FAA. If he landed on the runway, nothing would come of the landing. If he landed in the grass, or shorter, he'd probably make the evening news.

"Broomfield tower, please deploy emergency response," Luke said. Better safe than sorry.

"They want the practice anyway, Rattler, and it might be needed, by the looks of how far the runway is," Van said, giving Nathan a comforting wink.

Luke lowered the flaps enough to extend their flight and pulled the nose up as the airspeed dropped and the propellor quit spinning. The stall warning started to blast as the plane neared the runway. Luke kept the aircraft just above the ground, stretching every bit of distance out of the powerless aircraft. Fifty feet, thirty feet, ten feet. The aircraft bounced to a stop on the runway with nine thousand feet of pavement in front of it.

"5 Tango Charlie, Broomfield. Congratulations, you just made the shortest runway landing in the airport's history."

Van removed his headset and microphone as a tow truck arrived to tow the aircraft off the runway for repairs. The emotion in his eyes was intense. "What's the likelihood of both magnetos failing at the same time?"

"About the same as the sun not coming up tomorrow," Luke replied.

***

Luke exited the repair shop with a sigh. "They say it'll be Monday before they get the parts and can install them."

"I'll rent a car. We're not letting this stop us from fishing. Right, Nathan?" Van said.

"Right, Mr. Van. You're the man," Nathan said, as he reached for a high-five.

Van was as good as his word, and they drove across the border into Wyoming a few hours later. Luke received a call from the Broomfield airport just before they reached the river.

"Mr. Graham, this is Wesley, in the maintenance shop."

"Thanks for calling back, Wesley," Luke said. "What did you find?"

"Well, I've worked on lots of magnetos over the years, Mr. Graham, but I ain't never seen nothing like this. Someone tried to make these fall apart on you. I can show you when you come back to get the plane. I'll put these old ones in a box for you."

Luke had met Wesley before they'd left Broomfield. The man looked more like a rancher than a mechanic, complete with a cowboy hat, boots, and a mouthful of dip. Often, ranchers and farmers made the best technicians because they'd worked around equipment since they were old enough to walk. "Thanks, Wesley. Could you do me a favor? Please tape the box shut, sign your name across the tape, and lock the box in the airplane. Keep the keys in your pocket until I get back there."

"You got it, Mr. Graham. I understand what you're saying," Wesley said.

Luke checked to make sure Nathan was still asleep in the backseat, then relayed the conversation to Van.

"There's only one explanation I can think of, Russo. Our suspect, Chad, is a part-time airplane mechanic with a motive. He could have found out that I was planning to use the Cirrus. Let's call the police on this one."

"I doubt they'll buy it. All we have are some broken parts and a mechanic's hunch that the parts were tampered with. Now, if you had crashed the plane short of the runway, we would have a better case."

"Damn. How stupid of me. Why didn't I crash land a million dollar airplane in the grass?" Luke said, slapping his forehead.

Van grinned. "Believe me, I'm thankful you found the runway. In fact, it looked like pretty skilled flying from where I was sitting. I'll tell Nathan when he is older. Don't worry. We'll put the evidence together, and remember, there are many ways to ensure justice is served."

Luke called Archie Valentine, the Maintenance Director of Blue Sky Flight Academy, where the Cirrus was regularly hangered.

"Hey Luke, I heard you went to Casper this morning. How was the flight?" Archie asked. The man's gruff voice and British accent never failed to take Luke by surprise.

Luke kept his response light. "Well, we lost a magneto over Denver, so I landed in Broomfield to get it repaired, and we rented a car to finish the trip. The maintenance guy said he can repair it in a few days. No big deal. I'll fly it back when it's fixed. Hey, I'm trying to locate an old coworker of mine who works on airplanes. His name is Chad Purcell. Do you know him?"

"I know who he is, but I haven't met the chap. He works

over at Winston Aviation. I think he's been there a month or so. Sorry about your trip. I'm glad it worked out okay. You made the right decision to land and get it fixed."

"While I have you, Archie, I left my headset in the Cirrus last night, and it was gone this morning. I think someone got into the plane and took it. I don't always lock the doors. Stupid me. Do you have security camera footage from last night? I'd like to see if someone got into the cockpit."

"We keep seven days of security camera video. I can pull it down and copy it to a disk for you," Archie said.

"Thanks, Archie. I don't want anyone else getting stuff stolen. It might be interesting to see what else happens around the planes in the middle of the night," Luke said, before saying his farewells and hanging up.

"That was good, Luke. I don't think he suspected you were trying to get information on Chad. But if someone swiped your headset, what were you using this morning?" Van asked.

"Pilots always have spares. Let's see what we get on the video and from the magnetos. That may be enough evidence to get Chad taken in for questioning. I consider this attempted murder," Luke said.

The Miracle Mile lived up to its expectations. Luke and Van caught several rainbow and cutthroat trout. Nathan, with Van's help, brought in the largest fish he had ever hooked. For a few hours, they forgot all about death threats and crashing planes and enjoyed camping on the North Platte River.

***

Luke stopped by Blue Sky Flight Academy after work on Monday and picked up a disk of the security camera video from Archie

Valentine. Archie was a large man whose clothes and hands were perpetually stained with oil and grease and a regular Band-Aid or two. His personality was more likable than his image.

"I haven't had a chance to look through the video, Luke, but you have seven days' worth of exciting viewing there. I hope you have a fast-forward button," Archie said, with a deep-throated chuckle.

Later that same day after work, Luke battled the rush hour traffic to drive the rental car back to the Broomfield airport. He parked it near the maintenance shop and went inside to pick up the Cirrus and the box of magnetos.

"I want you to look at this, Mr. Graham," Wesley said. He pulled out his knife and cut open the tape around the box with his signature. "You see the keyed shaft and the set screw here?" He pointed with a greasy finger. "That ain't normal. Either your last mechanic didn't know what the hell he was doing, or someone tried to make these magnetos fail and cause the engine to quit." Wesley went into excruciating detail about the magneto assembly while Luke took pictures.

"How do you know so much about airplane engines, Wesley?" Luke said, briefly imagining himself as a prosecuting attorney.

"My daddy was a crop duster out in eastern Colorado, where I come from. I learned to fly when I was fourteen, but Daddy did all the flying. Me and my brothers learned how to maintain the plane and load the pesticides. He died of cancer in his fifties, and we sold the business to a competitor and moved to Broomfield."

"Did you ever use DDT?" Luke asked.

"Sure. We used it in the sprayer truck around town and in the baseball park when the mosquitoes got bad. Mama didn't want us working around it when we was little. She thought it was bad for us. Based on everything I know today, I'd say she was right. I'd rather be working around engines."

Luke nodded. Wesley would make a credible witness in court when the time came.

He flew the Cirrus back to the Arapahoe County airport and pushed it into the hangar, then drove directly to Van's house with the security video.

"Let's start watching from when I requested to top off the tanks with fuel on Thursday afternoon. We can run through the video at five times the normal speed, and if we see some movement, we'll go back and look closer. This may take a while. How about a beer and some popcorn?"

Luke had just gotten comfortable in front of the TV when a figure appeared on the video. It moved next to the Cirrus engine cowling, carrying a cordless work light. The time was 10:33 p.m..

Van slowed, then stopped the video playback.

"Nothing like putting a good light on your face for the camera," Luke said. "What an idiot. That's the best picture of Chad I've seen since the Christmas party. Too bad he didn't do that on the groundwater treatment facility video, or we would have him for vandalism too."

25

uke made it home for dinner with Kara and the kids while Columbo sat on the floor, waiting for spillage and scraps. Nathan continued to tell his mother about the fish he caught. They got bigger with each retelling. As soon as the kids left the table, Luke filled in Kara about the magnetos and the security camera video. Her eyes were cold. Luke knew she was thinking what he was: An engine failure over Denver could have resulted in a deadly crash landing that left no survivors.

"What are you planning to do now? Are you going to call the police and press charges?" Kara asked.

"Not quite yet. I want to make sure we have enough evidence for a strong case when we go to the police. Van has a friend who is a private investigator that has offered to look at our evidence and give us some advice first."

Kara responded with an assertive tone. "Here is what I think you should do. Get Chad in a room with everyone at the flight academy and show him the damning evidence so that he confesses, just like in a *Columbo* episode. You could have Mr. Valentine call Chad over for a staff introduction meeting, then he walks into a conference room with you, Van, Valentine, and a police officer. Chad will panic as soon as he sees you. He'll either run or sit down. If he runs, you all will know he's guilty. If he sits down, you get him to confess."

"Can't I just talk to the police ahead of time and have him arrested?" Luke said.

"No, you want him to confess so he proves your case. Better yet, if you weren't in the room when he walks in, he'll think it's a normal introductory meeting because he won't know anybody else. Then you walk in, and he'll go apoplectic," Kara said, with a big grin and outstretched arms.

"Are you sure you weren't a *Columbo* writer?" Luke asked, They smiled and ate the rest of the meal in silence.

***

Luke went to see Archie Valentine when the flight academy opened the following day. He entered the office with a box of two broken magnetos and the disk with the security camera video. He smiled at Archie and shut the door behind himself. Luke had known Archie for several years. He and the other owners of the Cirrus hangered the aircraft next to the flight academy rental planes for a reasonable annual fee. Luke and Archie frequently crossed paths at the flight academy and had a friendly relationship. Luke decided he could trust Archie and displayed the magnetos on the table.

"Archie, I want to show you the magnetos from my Cirrus and get your opinion since you know this better than I do. I think they were tampered with," Luke said.

Archie looked them over for a long time, shining his pocket flashlight on the parts and feeling the metal edges with his grease-stained hands. "This doesn't appear to be a natural failure. It looks like the keyed shafts were filed down. It's pretty obvious to me that someone did this intentionally to make the magneto fail, and the fact that both were filed down is even more concerning," he said.

Luke put the security disk in the video player and forwarded it to where Chad was under the engine cowling with the cordless work light illuminating the engine and his face. "I can't tell what the person is doing, but he went to both sides of the engine cowling, near the magnetos. He is there long enough to file these keyed shafts down."

"That's a good picture of his face and his Winston Aviation overalls, but I don't know what Chad looks like," Archie said, showing his pride in his security cameras. "Whoa, you can even see his name on the overalls. What a drongo. I can't quite read it for certain, but it has four letters. I'll bet we can enhance the image and see who it is."

Archie stopped the video player and zoomed in on the nametag. The nametag became blurrier as he zoomed in, but it was still easy to read. "Well, I'll be damned. Will you look at that? Chad should have had enough sense to take off his nametag."

Luke could hardly contain the grin on his face while listening to Archie Valentine's assessment. He told Archie about the events in Torrance, California, at the groundwater treatment facility, winding up his summary by explaining how Chad falsified the soil samples and was fired from Webber Environmental.

"Chad blames me for his firing, and he definitely has a grudge against me. I also think there are more people involved," Luke said. He went on to explain in more detail the DDT soil sampling efforts and the protests by the neighbors.

"This chap doesn't seem too bright, Luke. It makes sense that someone else is whispering in his ear, telling him what to do," Archie said. "Why don't you let me call the police and we'll have a little meeting with Chad tomorrow."

"Sounds good, but let me suggest some ideas on how to make Chad confess during the meeting," Luke said.

After another half hour, Luke said goodbye to Archie and headed downtown. He went directly to Nancy's office and gave her the short version of events over the last week and a summary of the compelling evidence.

"I wanted you to hear about this from me, Nancy, because if Chad gets arrested tomorrow for attempted murder, it won't be long before everyone in the office knows about it. The meeting is scheduled for mid-morning tomorrow. If everything goes as planned, it won't last long. I'll give you a call when it's over."

Nancy leaned back in her chair and crossed her arms, staring at Luke. "I'm glad you and Nathan made it to the runway, Luke. I want to know if Chad is responsible for this."

Luke went to the Coffee Nook for his first cup of the day. He was dragging, being out of his usual routine.

"Hey Luke, have the police sent you a copy of the report on the explosion yet? Do they think that girl from EF&J blew herself up?" Rudy asked, coming up behind Luke.

"What explosion are you talking about?" Luke responded, trying not to spill hot coffee on his hand.

"The explosion in Long Beach, remember? Was there another explosion I don't know about?" Rudy asked, moving closer and speaking softly.

"Sorry, Rudy. I was thinking about something else. Actually, I still need the final police report. It's supposed to be completed in another week or two. The investigator may be questioning some more people," Luke said.

"I can't wait to read it, Luke. You're allowed to share it with me, yeah?"

***

Luke hid in the storage closet at the flight academy next to Archie's office. The door was ajar enough for him to see through Archie's office window. He listened as Alice, an instructor and manager at the school, greeted Chad at the front door. She treated him to a cup of fresh coffee and walked him down the skinny hall back to Archie's office. The office had a small conference table where others had gathered and one empty chair in the back of the room.

"Chad, I'm Archie Valentine, Maintenance Director here at Blue Sky. Good to finally meet you," Archie said, standing and shaking hands with Chad. "We like to introduce ourselves to the Winston Aviation team members, since we rely on you boys when our maintenance workload gets out of control."

"It's a pleasure to meet you, Archie," Chad said. He smiled big. His long blond hair flowed from under his Winston Aviation ball cap.

"I see you have met Alice. She's our Chief Flight Instructor and office manager, at least until she gets so tired of dealing with office minutia that we'll have to find someone else to take the role," Archie said.

Alice nodded her head. "You got that right."

"This young chap is Van Russo. He is our security consultant. We count on him to know everything about our airplanes, what they are being used for, and the hangars. No drug runners using our planes, you know."

Van stood and shook hands with Chad. "Good to meet you, Chad," Van said in a monotone voice. Chad returned the courtesy to Van. Luke had assured Van that Chad had never heard Van's name in conversation and would not know he and Van were close friends.

Luke listened as Archie continued to point at the people around the table. "This is Wesley Cartwright, the Maintenance Technician at the Broomfield airport. Since some of Blue Sky's planes are located in Broomfield, we rely on Wesley to fulfill a lot of the maintenance over there."

Wesley spit into a Dr. Pepper can before he stood up to shake hands with Chad. "How ya doing? Pleasure to meet you."

"Last but not least is Sergeant Hayson. She is the City of Centennial police officer responsible for airport operations. If you ever need law enforcement support, she's the one you want to talk to," Archie said.

Chad took off his ball cap and ran his hand through his hair while his gaze darted around the room, as if he was trying not to look at anyone in particular. He sat down and lowered the zipper on the front of his overalls. Archie paused for a moment while looking over his notes. This was Luke's signal to leave the storage room.

Luke entered the conference room with a cardboard box and dropped it on the table with a thud. "Sorry to barge in on your meeting, Archie, but I thought you should see these magnetos from my Cirrus. You know, they both failed me on Saturday, over Denver. I was lucky to make it to Broomfield before I had a total engine failure. Had my son and a friend in the plane and everything," Luke said, meeting Chad's gaze. "Well, I'll be damned, if it isn't Chad Purcell. I haven't seen you since you were fired from Webber Environmental for taking a bribe. I'm surprised you found a new job."

Chad remained speechless as the others in the small conference room stared at him for an uncomfortable moment.

"I was wondering, Archie, if Wesley could tell us what happened to these magnetos. He was kind enough to replace them over the weekend so I could fly the Cirrus back here," Luke said.

"Sounds like we all need to listen up on this one," Archie said.

Wesley spit into his can again and removed the damaged magnetos from the box. "These here are the two I removed from Luke's plane on Saturday. As you can see, they both completely failed..." Wesley went on to describe the damage to the magnetos in detail. He passed them around the room for everyone to observe while he continued to drone on with his analysis.

"So, you see, I don't think there's any way they both failed on their own. In my humble opinion, someone messed with them," Wesley said.

Chad ran his hands through his hair again with an uncertain expression on his face. Luke thought he was attempting to look like he had never seen the magnetos before and was interested in Wesley's analysis.

"Mr. Russo has some security footage of the airplane hangar from the night before I flew the plane. I'd like you to see it," Luke said, once again making eye contact with Chad. It might have been a trick of the lighting, but Chad seemed very pale. Luke couldn't resist a smile.

Van leaned forward. "The video is much clearer than you normally see from a security camera. Archie bought some really good equipment. Luke just happened to get lucky. The plane was tied down right under the camera," he said, addressing the table at large. "It's not clear what the person is doing under the engine cowling, but you can see that the person is dressed in blue overalls, much like the ones that Winston Aviation personnel wear. If I can zoom in on the name on the overalls, you can see that it says..." Van stopped speaking and squinted at the video, as if trying to make out the name on the overalls.

"I'll be damned. Ain't that your name, Chad?" Wesley said.

"You guys are trying to set me up," Chad said. "That's not me. Someone else took my overalls and did this."

"I'm afraid we've checked. You only have one pair of overalls and wear them home every night just like everyone else. That excuse doesn't add up, son," Archie said. He stood and stepped between Chad and the door, blocking it with his large frame. The room was quiet except for the humming of a distant plane idling its engine.

Chad shrunk back in his chair and began to speak with an apologetic tone in his voice. "I was forced to do this by Jimmy Mendoza. You all don't understand. He's crazy! He was going to *kill* me if I didn't do it. I didn't want to hurt anybody. He's the one who has it out for you, Luke, not me," Chad said, looking at the table. "I thought the magnetos would fail as soon as you started the engine. I didn't mean any harm."

Sergeant Hayson rose from her chair and pulled handcuffs from her belt. "Mr. Purcell, please put your hands behind your back. You're under arrest for the attempted murder of Luke Graham, Van Russo, and Nathan Graham."

"Attempted murder? What do you mean? I wasn't trying to kill anybody!"

"We'll let the court decide that." She read Chad his Miranda rights and escorted him toward the door.

"One last question, Chad," Luke asked. "Have you been to any marathons lately?"

"I don't run marathons, Luke," Chad said as he was led out of the conference room by Sergeant Hayson.

Raising his chin slightly, Archie said, "Fine job, team. Fine job."

26

“Hey, Luke, It's Simone. How's it going out there in Denver?”

“Doing good. Great to hear from you. Any more death threats?” Luke asked.

“No more threats. I still drive around like I'm lost and take strange routes in town. Don't tell anyone, but I have moved to Fresno for the summer with Alison and will work out of here. We have an old family farmhouse that we are staying in. My cousin, Carl, takes care of it and runs the farm as well. His daughter is Alison's age, so they have a lot of fun together. So, the primary reason for my call is to suggest we have the next Guadalupe update meeting in Fresno. Do you think Bob and Caroline would be open to the idea?”

“I don't see why not. San Francisco or Fresno, what's the difference flying from the East Coast? Bob likes a good steak, and Caroline probably won't come anyway,” Luke said.

“Okay then, let's plan on Fresno in two weeks for the next meeting,” Simone said.

“That sounds good. While I have you on the phone, I want you to know the latest scare that happened to me in Denver,” Luke said. He then detailed the emergency landing and Chad's confession.

"That's scary, but I always knew you were a good pilot, Luke. I remember the times we went flying together in Albuquerque and you taught me how to land an airplane. If you need me to testify, just let me know."

Luke finished the call with Simone and immediately dialed Van. "Russo, you are never going to believe this, but the EPA wants to have the next meeting in Fresno. It's perfect. We have a legitimate reason to go to Fresno and find our friend, Ross Jennings. Plus, Guadalupe is paying for my trip, so we can split your costs."

Van paused for an uncomfortably long time before responding. "Guadalupe should be paying for both of us to find Ross Jennings and pay him a visit after what he did to you just for doing your job as Guadalupe's consultant," Van said.

"You make a good point, but I'm not going there now. I'll take a free trip without anyone asking questions about why we are going and I'll split your airline ticket with you. By the way, what do you plan on doing to Ross Jennings after we find him?" Luke said.

"That's a good question, Luke. I'm not sure yet, but our response has to match his action of putting a gun to your head, albeit unloaded. We also know that he has some kind of relationship with Jimmy Mendoza and maybe others like Chad. I'm concerned he will keep being a threat to you, and we need to shut him down."

"How do we do that?"

"We'll introduce him to Oscar."

"Who's Oscar?"

***

Luke headed to DIA in mid-afternoon, direct from his office. Van was already at the gate, his usual three hours early. To the best of Luke's knowledge, Van had never missed a flight, even though flying was his least favorite mode of transportation. They'd decided to search out Ross Jennings the following morning before the EPA meeting. Van had an address for Ross and thought that a surprise appearance at his home or work might be a simple way to convince the man and his wife that what they did to Luke could have serious consequences and not to consider any possible future threats.

Simone had offered to take Luke and Van out for dinner since Bob, Rudy, and Debbie weren't arriving in Fresno until the following day. Simone had told Luke that she hadn't seen Van since they graduated from University of New Mexico, and it would be a chance for the three of them to catch up.

The restaurant was busy when Luke and Van arrived. They were seated across from each other at a booth for four and enjoying a beer when Luke saw Simone enter the front door. He waved her down, and she came to the table with a big smile on her face.

"It's so great to see you guys. Van, you look the same as you did in college. You haven't gained a pound. Oh, let me introduce you to my cousin, Carl Jennings. His wife, Jane, is watching my daughter Alison in return for me buying Carl a steak dinner. He lives here in Fresno and runs the old family farm," Simone said. All three of the men shook hands. Then, Simone sat beside Van, and Carl slid in next to Luke.

"I hope you don't mind that I invited my cousin; he hasn't had much solid food in a few months. Our horse kicked him while he was shoeing her and broke his jaw," Simone said.

Van stared at Carl and said, "That must have really hurt. It looks like you have a scar on your forehead as well. Is that from the horse?"

"I think the hammer bounced back in my face when she kicked it out of my hand," Carl said. "If you ever want to lose weight, just get your jaw wired shut. It sure makes it easier. But I'm making up for it now."

"I would rather go on a diet," Simone said.

Luke had only been half listening. Suddenly, he looked at Van, blinking his eyes.

"Are you all right, Luke? You look like you just saw a ghost," Simone said. "You probably need some food. We should order."

Van stared hard across the table, right at Carl. At that moment, Luke realized that Van, too, had recognized Carl and was trying to make the man uneasy. It took everything he had to refrain from smiling and let the game with Carl proceed slowly.

The conversations bounced from college stories to the history of the family farm that Carl operated. The small talk continued as the drinks and food arrived at the table, until Simone's cell phone rang.

"Oh, it's Antoine. He's my boss, Carl. I'd better step out and take the call. You guys keep talking. I'll be back in a few minutes."

Van glared across the table again. "It must suck to have your mouth wired shut. If I were you, I would have shot that horse right between the eyes with my 9mm," Van said. "Of course, you must have a 9mm to do that."

"So, Carl, are you related to Ross and Jane Jennings? There can't be that many Jennings around here. You must know them," Luke asked.

"Ross is my first name, but I have been going by my middle name, Carl, since I was a little boy. I'm surprised it took you smartasses so long to figure that out," Carl said.

"Wow, and here you are, eating dinner with your cousin, Simone, who obviously doesn't know about your extracurricular activities. She's part of the team responsible for lowering the DDT cleanup levels," Luke said, pointing out the irony of the situation. "Do the two of you talk about this kind of stuff?"

"We don't talk much about DDT and the EPA. It's a subject that is pretty much off-limits in the family. One of these days the EPA will be digging up our farm because we used DDT years ago. She doesn't seem to get it," Carl said.

"Let me get to the point, Carl, before Simone gets back," said Van. "We knew we would find you around here, and I wanted you to know more about us. I want to introduce you to a buddy of mine who lives in Madera. That's only like thirty minutes away, right?"

"That's right. It's good to know you can read a map," Carl said.

"That's one thing I learned in the Army Special Forces. My friend's name is Oscar. We served together in Desert Storm. I saved his life twice, and he'll never forget it. He's always willing to do me a favor if I ask," Van said.

"Is that the crazy guy you told me about, who killed more Iraqi military than anyone else in your unit?" Luke asked.

"That's him, Luke. You might say Oscar is somewhat deranged. He took pleasure in killing the enemy, unlike the rest of us. Honestly, I always worried about him being a serial killer or something like that when he got back to the States." Van squinted and shook his head, glancing back and forth between Luke and Carl. "Hopefully, he's more of a normal guy now. That's why we need to go see him, make sure he's stable before we introduce him to Carl."

"I don't need to meet him," Carl said, softly.

"I'm sorry. I didn't hear you. Can you say that again? It's kinda loud in here," Van said.

Carl spoke slowly and loudly, "I said, I don't need to meet him."

"Well, that's okay, your choice. I just want you to know that if something ever happens to me or my friend Luke here, Oscar will come looking for you," Van said. He leaned in closer to Carl. "I remember one night in boot camp. I woke up in the middle of the night, and Oscar was about three inches from my face, with beer on his breath and his bayonet under my chin. He just laughed, and I realized how easy it was to die when you go to sleep. I confess, I sleep a little lighter these days because of that night, and you probably should too," Van said.

"Sorry I took so long, but he's the boss," Simone said, walking back to the table. "I hope you guys have gotten to know each other better."

"We've covered a lot of topics, Simone. I think we know each other a lot better than we did before. Isn't that right, Carl?" Luke asked.

27

Luke admired how Antoine ran a meeting. He started on time and began wrapping up the meeting just before 4:00 p.m.. "I think we had a great meeting today. Simone and I appreciate you guys making the trip to beautiful Fresno to accommodate our budget-tightening efforts. I think we're all happy that the soil removal activities are complete, and we have residents back in their homes without any more death threats," Antoine said, to snickers in the room. "It's also good to hear the groundwater treatment facility is working well and that you and Luke are progressing with the feasibility study for full-scale cleanup," Antoine said, smiling at Debbie.

Luke figured everyone in the room knew the full-scale groundwater cleanup facility would cost tens of millions and take decades to clean up the groundwater, even if no one said as much. Luke took comfort in knowing the contaminated shallow groundwater underneath the site was not used for drinking water or commercial purposes and did not pose an immediate risk to people in the area. His greatest concern was the contamination would spread vertically into the deeper aquifers used for drinking water. Still, Rudy and his colleagues seemed to think that scenario was decades away, if ever.

He had high hopes for Debbie's full-scale cleanup facility. It utilized a new technique known as "air sparging," which required air to be injected into the groundwater and recovered, after it had captured volatile organic contaminants from the groundwater. The contaminants in the air, mostly chlorobenzene, would be captured with carbon. Without chlorobenzene in the groundwater, DDT would be immobilized in the soil indefinitely.

The group stood up and began to disperse. Debbie and Antoine were the first to leave. "Antoine is giving me a ride back to San Fran. I have an old friend there who wants me to go sailing this weekend," Debbie said, with a grin. The others in the room heckled her as she and Antoine left for the parking lot.

Rudy grabbed his bag and headed to the airport, while Simone organized her materials and waited to say goodbye to Luke. Luke pulled Bob aside before he could leave and asked him if he had heard more from the investigator about the salvage boat explosion.

"Nobody ever contacted me after we left the dock that night. I assume they are completing their report and will send it out soon," Bob said.

Van joined them.

"Bob, let me introduce you to my friend, Van. We served in Desert Storm together, and we're going to see an old Army friend up in Madera tonight," Luke said.

Bob and Van shook hands. "I have to assume that Luke told you about our night at the Port and the explosion on the salvage ship," Bob said.

"Yeah, he did. Sounds like the enviro girl blew herself up.

Messing with explosives is not for amateurs. Believe me, I know," Van replied with a wry smile.

"EF&J is still using the explosion to raise money," said Bob. "They continue to deny Amy's actions and imply instead that Guadalupe was somehow involved in her death, even though they have absolutely no evidence to support their claim."

"They don't need evidence, Bob. You know that. Whatever they say still gives EF&J name recognition, which results in more money. Too bad Amy gave her life for some fundraising," Luke said, shaking his head slowly.

"EF&J's lawyers are asking for a new deposition date," Bob said. "We should probably schedule them in the next two weeks. We might be able to do the depositions without having to travel. We'll see."

"Sounds good. Also, Debbie and I will work up a budget for the full-scale groundwater cleanup. We'll start with the feasibility study that Antoine is asking for," Luke said. "If we keep it high level at this time, it shouldn't cost too much."

"I've heard that before," Bob said, rolling his eyes. "See you soon. Nice to meet you, Van." Bob turned and walked quickly to the parking lot.

Van shook his head. "He's guilty of something, Luke. I can see it in his eyes, and that little twitch is a dead giveaway. Remember, I interrogated a lot of Iraqis and saw those human mannerisms many times."

***

Luke and Van drove into Madera's trailer park looking for Oscar Trujillo's single-wide mobile home. Oscar had told them it was number fifteen, and that there would be a German shepherd chained to the house in the front yard. "You can't miss it," he'd said.

He was right. The dog, living in the yard of dirt, weeds, and cactus that lined the chain-linked fence, began a non-stop bark as they neared the gate. In the street was a dilapidated 1979 Chevy pickup with a large Army decal in the back window.

Oscar stepped onto the front porch and yelled at the dog, "Gunny, shut the fuck up! These are my friends." Luke and Van stared at each other for a moment. "Don't worry, he won't bite."

"Yeah, that's what all dog owners say, until you get your hand chewed off," Van said.

"How the hell are you, Lieutenant Russo? Good to see you, man," Oscar yelled out, emphasizing the second syllable of Van's last name.

Oscar and Van gave each other a back-slapping emotional bear hug. "I'm so glad you came out here to see me, you son of a bitch. I sure miss our old platoon. And this must be your amigo." Oscar looked at Luke and thrust his hand forward.

Even though he had a wide, warm smile, Luke was intimidated by Oscar, just looking at him. Oscar had piercing dark brown eyes that conveyed a sinister personality, or maybe the discussion with Carl had shaped Luke's opinion. He couldn't be sure.

"I hope you all are ready for the best barbecue in the valley. I know just the place," Oscar said, with a wide grin.

Luke quickly offered to drive all three of them for fear of not being able to leave the bar until Oscar was ready. Luke had a feeling that Oscar could drink and talk until closing, especially since he hadn't seen Van in years, and they would have to relive their military stories.

The smell of barbecue wafted through the hot summer air as Luke pulled the car into the gravel parking lot. Smoke bellowed from the exhaust fan, and the sound of Tim McGraw flowed from the open front door. Peanut shells were scattered over the vinyl floor by customers encouraged to throw them there. The middle-aged waitress, who wore lavish blue eye shadow and bright red lipstick, sat them in a booth and asked for their drink order. Oscar made the decision easy for everyone.

"Make it a pitcher, Barb, and by the way, my friends have never been here before, so I told them you have the best barbecue in the valley."

"We won the county fair the last three years with the Hot and Sweet Rub. I guarantee you boys will love the rub," Barb said, winking at Oscar as she hustled away.

"Damn, she's good-looking," Oscar said. "She may be a few years older than me, but who gives a shit? I'd do some hot and sweet rubbing with her anytime."

"You haven't changed a bit, Oscar," Van said. "What's keeping you busy these days?"

"I joined my father's business as a mechanic and welder," said Oscar. "He owns a farm equipment repair shop that he started thirty years ago, and he wants me to take it over someday. He says I have to work harder before he will sell me the business. But I have to tell you guys—I can make more money in a weekend training wannabe warriors in small-arms tactics than I can in a week at the shop. It's amazing how much some people will pay to shoot a few hundred rounds up in the foothills. I have to admit, we have a lot of fun. I set up a shooting range with pictures of Islamic terrorists, and they shoot the shit out of them. You guys should come up for some refresher training."

"That's great, but I need to change the subject, Oscar," Van said. "My friend, Luke here, had a guy break into his hotel room a few weeks ago and put a 9mm in his face. I'll skip the details, but we now have the 9mm in our possession, and the person who did this lives in Fresno. For all I know, you may know him. He's all worried about DDT in the soils out here in farm country and blames Luke for it. Go figure."

"Now, this is getting interesting," said Oscar, with a smile and a squint. "I figured there was an ulterior motive on your part for coming to see me, Russo. Who is this bastard, and what do you need me to do? Do you want me to run him over with some farm equipment, or accidentally kill him at my shooting range?"

Van and Luke chuckled, but Oscar kept a straight face. Luke sat back in the booth and nervously looked around the table to see if anyone was listening.

Oscar was silent for another moment and then broke into laughter. "Had you guys there, didn't I? My days of killing bastards for fun are over, and I don't need to get in any trouble, or I'll never own my dad's business. I guess a little intimidation might put this guy in his place. Is he former military?"

"Everything we know about him says he is just a family guy with kids and a farm," Van said.

"He's the cousin of a good friend of mine," said Luke. "So, I'd rather not do anything over the top. I think we scared him enough, Russo. He'll forget us after a while."

"Luke, we're talking about a guy who could have blown your head off. That's attempted murder in most courts. He isn't going to say anything to anybody except his wife if we implement some military intimidation," Oscar said, with authority. "I'm thinking I'll pull up next to him on the street or in a coffee shop and say something like, 'Hey Carl, or Ross, whatever the fuck your name is, it sounds like I have some friends in common with you and your cousin. Maybe we could all get together sometime and have a beer; I'll give you a call.'"

"You know the other thing you can do, Oscar, that scares the shit out of people, is sit across the street from his house with your binoculars when he comes home with the wife and kids, and you make sure he sees you. It's kinda funny to watch people run into their houses and close the curtains," Van said. "You know Carl will never call the police after what he did to Luke."

Some of Luke's hesitancy must have shown on his face. "Lighten up, Luke. We're just gonna have a little fun with this bastard. It'll all be okay. C'mon, let's go shoot some pool. From what I hear, you flyboys are supposed to be good at this. Let's see how good you really are," Oscar said.

Luke hid a smile. His parents had bought a pool table and a ping-pong table when he was in junior high school so that he and the neighborhood kids could stay busy after school. Several years of playing both games had resulted in Luke holding his own throughout college and the Navy. He cleared the table many times in Eight Ball, without letting his opponents get a shot. Van, who had seen Luke play many times before, just grinned as Luke trounced them. Oscar, however, wore a perpetual frown. Without a doubt, the man had thought he'd be the one doing the trouncing.

They sat down, and Oscar ordered another pitcher of beer. Luke listened as Van and Oscar caught up on the last decade and slammed down several more beers each, just like old times in the military, when fear and relaxation were at extremes. Their conversation reinforced a realization he had come to in the Navy: College-educated officers and enlisted personnel could be very different people yet have a strong bond from military service. Combat made that bond even tighter.

***

Luke refrained from saying anything when Van wore his sunglasses in the Fresno airport the following morning.

"Rattler." Van paused to take a sip of his second cup of coffee. "Why did you let Oscar buy that last pitcher? You're older and wiser. You're supposed to look out for me."

"I'm not your dad, Russo, and I'm only three weeks older than you. You start hanging around Army enlisted guys, and you do stupid things. Now, if you were Navy…" Luke shrugged, while Van gingerly shook his head.

"By the way, I think they said something about a lot of turbulence on this flight today," Luke said, conforming to an uncomfortable airport chair, trying not to spill his coffee. He opened his laptop and pulled up the investigator's final report on the explosion. "This will clear your head. I have the investigator's report in my inbox, and I'm sending it to you right now. Let's start reading."

Van spoke first, while rubbing his temples. "You can tell by the way the report is written that the investigator went into his analysis with the presupposition that Amy planted the bomb. Just because they didn't find any prints, other than Amy's and Lenny's, doesn't mean that someone else wasn't in the room or planted the bomb. Most bad guys wear gloves so they don't leave prints behind. Also, the investigator didn't obtain security camera video from earlier that evening, before Amy was seen going to the pilot house. Someone else could have planted the bomb in the pilot house before Amy got there. The security video from earlier in the day was automatically overwritten, so we'll never know."

"But even if someone knew Amy was going to break in, how would they know what time she would be there and set the bomb to explode at that exact time? That just seems too coincidental to me," Luke said.

"Maybe." Van's voice was laced with doubt. "The bigger question for me is, why would Amy want to blow up the pilot house in the first place? I can see EF&J wanting to make sure certain salvage disposal documents never appear in discovery, but why destroy them in such a brutal fashion? It doesn't make sense to me," Van said.

He shut his computer and sat back, closing his eyes. Luke went for a walk down the terminal concourse and called Kara.

"Hi, honey, where are you?" Kara asked.

"We're in the Fresno airport, waiting for our flight. How do the kids like day camp?"

"They seem to be having a lot of fun, and they're making friends. Plus, they're worn out when they get home and go to bed early. It's nice having the house to myself for a few hours."

Luke let Kara's comment go. "I got a copy of the investigator's report this morning. We've been looking through it. It's disappointing because it reads like the police report. The chemical residue indicates the bomb was made of dynamite, but that's about it. There were no fingerprints or signs of another person involved in the explosion. The report concludes that it was Amy's inexperience with bomb-making that resulted in the explosion that took her life," Luke said.

"Hmmm. I'm gonna channel my inner Columbo for a second. Let me make sure I have this right. You and Bob found out about the explosion when you were in the bar and he got a call from Lenny, right?" Kara said.

"Yeah. He'd just flown in from Boston."

"How do you know he didn't fly into LAX on an earlier flight, set the bomb, and then lie to you about his arrival time? Did you ever see his itinerary?" Kara said. Her voice was rising, and she sounded more and more serious as she spoke.

"I suppose that's possible. Bob was wearing a sports coat and tie, as if he had just arrived. I never thought twice about it," said Luke. "I'll ask Van to look into his itinerary."

They chatted for another minute or two, then hung up. Luke returned to the gate.

Van opened his eyes and appeared slightly better than fifteen minutes before. Luke seized the moment. "Russo, you have a friend who works for the airlines, right?"

"Why do you ask?"

"I need you to check on Bob Burrows' itinerary for the afternoon of May 10."

28

Brooke Burr began most work days by parking at the Caltrain Station in Belmont and riding the train twenty-two miles to her office in downtown San Francisco. She often enjoyed dinner by herself on the return trip near her home, knowing she was far enough from her office that the possibility of running into a work acquaintance was very remote. It had been a long week, and she had a reservation at her favorite Italian restaurant.

She wore her favorite Friday jeans, a purple silk blouse, and a classic black leather jacket that hugged her figure. The hostess sat her in the familiar booth in the back corner, even though it was thirty minutes before her reservation. It was a quiet and secluded booth. Brooke pulled a draft lawsuit from her briefcase and began to read, sipping on her merlot. She couldn't ask for a better way to relax on a Friday night.

Bob Burrows' shadow fell across the table, and she smiled and stood. They wrapped arms around each other for as long as acceptable in a public restaurant. "It's so good to see you," Brooke said, whispering in his ear and pressing her body against his. "The public meeting in Torrance was a long time ago, too long." Memories of that night flooded her mind.

She'd first met Bob when they were legal interns in 1978.

Although Bob was almost ten years older than she was, and they'd both been in serious relationships, they developed a trusting and intimate bond. Upon graduation from law school, they went their separate ways, agreeing to have a guiltless affair whenever they could get together. They also agreed to never testify against the other, should the occasion arise. Now, they were both divorced, giving them a little more freedom to enjoy each other's company. But they kept their relationship quiet, given the obvious conflicts of interest between a chemical company attorney and an environmental activist.

They sat across from one another while the waiter took Bob's drink order.

"What would my donors say if they knew I'd been having a relationship with the attorney for the largest DDT manufacturing company in the world for the last twenty years?" Brooke said once the waiter had disappeared. It was a question she had asked herself more than once.

Bob shook his head. "Your donors will never know. Even if a TV reporter noticed us here, you could simply say that the purpose of our dinner was to get me drunk so that I would divulge highly confidential information about Guadalupe's nefarious activities and total disregard for the environment upon which we are all dependent. You could easily pull off that story. It's a testament to our scheming ways that we have gone on for so long, and no one has ever found us out."

"Knock on wood, Bob. Don't jinx us. I understand that you are going to be deposed next week. That should be fun for you. You've always liked the challenge of depositions. Our attorney is young and doesn't have much experience, so please, go easy on him?" she asked.

"I can probably teach him a lesson or two without going so

far as to make him wish he had never chosen law as a profession. You know this case will go nowhere, though. There isn't a shred of evidence that supports the claim that Guadalupe directed DDT waste to be dumped near the shore," Bob said.

"I know, but I can drag out the lawsuit for another year and then reach a settlement with Guadalupe. EF&J gets publicity and donations, and we raise awareness of the contamination off the Palos Verdes shelf. And Guadalupe gets to put a nail in this conspiracy theory for the final time," Brooke said.

Bob smiled. "Sounds like another win-win scenario. We're getting better at pulling these off all the time, Brooke. Too bad we can't tell anybody about what we've done over the years. It would make for a great book."

"I must admit that I am perplexed at the lack of public interest in the offshore contamination. It affects so much of the marine life in LA, and yet people don't seem interested," she said.

Brooke knew she had more passion about the environment than Bob, but how much more had always been in question. At times, Bob would appear to support her causes, but his support was often disingenuous. They both knew it. During their long relationship, she'd made a game out of getting him to reveal his occasional, genuine concern for the environment. She honestly didn't care how he felt about her environmental issues. She spent so much time during the day trying to convince others of her views, she didn't need to convince her friend and lover. Bob was her escape.

After a delicious dinner and drinks, she stopped by her house and fed her cat. She took her time, packed some casual clothes and lingerie in a small overnight bag, freshened up, and headed to room 435 at the Hilton.

***

Breakfast was delivered the next day to Bob's hotel room suite. Brooke stayed in the bathroom, waiting for Bob to settle up with the delivery staff, before emerging in a white bathrobe made from Egyptian silk. Bob poured coffee for both of them and sat back on the sofa, sampling the Hilton's best blend. Brooke sat on his lap while Bob opened her robe and began massaging her well-toned body, still damp from her recent shower.

"I received the investigator's report yesterday. It concludes that the cause of Amy's death was due to the accidental detonation of the bomb she had made. They found no evidence of involvement by others and consider the case closed," Bob said.

"Congratulations, you did a great job. I'm impressed you got the timing just right, so Amy was in the pilot house when the bomb went off."

"It helped that you told her to be there at exactly 9:45," Bob said.

"I told her the security guard made regular rounds, and she would go unnoticed from 9:45 until 10:15," Brooke reminded him. She rubbed Bob's hairy chest. "I have no regrets. She brought it on herself. It was time for her to go. She had been blackmailing me for months, asking for money to remain silent about my actions and threatening to talk to our large donors. I'd given her several raises and additional vacations, but it was never enough. When she started making flippant comments around the office, that was the final straw."

"You weren't taking money from the company kitty again, were you?" Bob said.

She sighed. "You know I like to fly first class, stay in five-star hotels, and have the company pay for club memberships and massages. I started EF&J, and I'll do what I want with the money I raise, as long as I continue to get good charity ratings. I'm not going to let some stupid twit take down my company after all of my hard work over the years."

Bob pulled her in closer and slipped the robe off her shoulders. "Lenny's records were destroyed in the fire, so there won't be much to look at when the case moves into document discovery. We were lucky that Lenny kept a few gallons of gasoline under his desk."

"Where did you get the dynamite? If you don't mind me asking."

"My contractor buddy sold me a few sticks last year when I was blasting rock from under my cabin foundation in Vermont. I had two sticks left over and took them to Torrance that afternoon."

Brooke started to loosen the belt on Bob's robe. "Does that mean you put the dynamite in your baggage on the airplane?" She raised an eyebrow.

"I thought about doing that. The dynamite would be safe in my luggage; it won't explode, but airport security seems to be getting tougher, and bags are being randomly searched these days. Getting caught with dynamite in my luggage would not be a good thing. Actually, I shipped it by UPS Ground last week to our chemical distribution center near Fullerton. Told them to hold the package for me, specifically. I picked it up after we landed and assembled the bomb in the car. It's a bit of a drive to Fullerton, but I had the time. I put on my dark running sweats at the hotel, parked a few hundred yards away from Lenny's boat after dark, picked the lock on the pilot house, and set the bomb for 9:55. Then I went to the hotel bar and had a drink with Luke."

"You sound like a trained assassin, Bob, not a lawyer. This talk is getting me excited," said Brooke. "I've heard enough. Let's enjoy ourselves while you still have time."

29

uke awoke to a quiet Saturday morning, with Kara beside him, and Columbo sleeping at the foot of the bed. It took him a moment to remember that Nathan and Kaylie were at their grandparent's house for the weekend. He tried to go back to sleep on this rare occasion, but it was already an hour later than his usual time to wake, and his mind was moving ahead. Columbo jumped to the floor, and Luke quietly left the bedroom while Kara slept. He checked messages on his phone while Columbo surveyed the backyard and coffee brewed.

"The subject arrived at 12:30 p.m. on 10 May, the day of the explosion. The flight was on time," Van's message said.

Luke stepped outside with a cup of black coffee and sat on a plastic deck chair. Columbo jumped into his lap, and Luke listened to the message again. Bob had overtly lied to him about his arrival time at LAX. Why? Had that happened before? Bob was a master at answering a question without answering the question, but it never seemed to be a flat-out lie. Luke went back inside, poured another cup of coffee for himself and one for Kara with cream and sugar, then headed upstairs to the bedroom.

He placed the steaming coffee on Kara's nightstand, and she instantly awoke to the aroma. She smiled, and the impish look in her eyes told him she remembered the kids were with Shawna and Frank. She sat up in his favorite nightgown and looked at him.

"You look like you have something on your mind," she said with another smile.

"I received a message from Van last night. You were right. Bob lied to me about when he got into LAX last month. He got in about nine hours earlier than he said he did. I don't know where he was during all that time. Maybe he had another meeting, or maybe he has a girlfriend I don't know about, but one thing's for sure, Bob didn't want me to know he had been there all day and lied to me in a very nonchalant way," Luke said.

"I still think he had something to do with the explosion. Who else would want to blow up Lenny's boat, pilot house, whatever you call it? Why would Amy blow it up? She wants the files, especially the day before a deposition. I suppose Lenny could have done it to get rid of evidence, or collect on insurance," Kara said.

"Lenny was so distraught by it all. If he was the bomber and acted the way he did that night, he deserves an Academy Award," Luke said.

"Bob is the only real suspect then," Kara said, taking a sip of coffee.

"Why would he want to kill Amy, though?" Luke asked.

"My guess is he didn't plan to kill her, unless he wanted to bring EF&J into the spotlight and make them look like the bad guys. He wasn't even at the scene when the bomb went off, so how would he know she was there? It could have been simply bad timing that she was in the pilot house after him. I know it sounds like quite a coincidence, but it's still possible, given that everyone would be giving depositions the next day," Kara said.

"Maybe I should go back to the investigator, tell him what we think, and ask him to investigate Bob," Luke said.

"Honey, you need more evidence than just saying 'My client lied to me about his schedule.' Plus, if Bob finds out you sicced the investigator on him, you'll be looking for a new job while we're cutting coupons. You need to find out where Bob got the dynamite and where he went that afternoon. He either got the dynamite in LA that afternoon, or he got it in Boston and brought it out on the plane. Ugh, that's not a comforting thought. Maybe he shipped it," said Kara.

"Now that you mention it, I remember when we were being interviewed on the boat dock, Bob mentioned he had demolition experience," Luke said. "He knew the place had been dynamited. Maybe there is another side to Bob that I don't know about."

"There have to be transaction records of purchases or shipments somewhere. You should also find out how many miles he put on the rental car. Then you'll have an idea where to start looking."

"Hmm. You should have been a detective, Ms. Columbo. Sounds like I need to talk to Van," Luke said.

"Now, are we going to take advantage of the kids' being at Mom and Dad's?" Kara asked.

***

"You're asking me to get into corporate databases that I may have a hard time justifying to my management," Van said.

"Russo, I know you can dream up a legitimate reason to investigate someone's actions. That's what you guys do for a living. I need to know if my client committed a murder. How can I work for someone who may have intentionally killed a young woman? We're not talking about an enemy combatant here; we're talking about an innocent person," Luke said, his voice rising.

"All right, all right. You should lay off the caffeine for three hours. I'll make up a bullshit story for my boss and get the records you need," Van said. "Now, what will you do for me since I am risking my career for you?"

Luke paused for a moment. Van always wanted something in return for his favors. "Russo, you should be thanking me. I'm providing you with the opportunity to be instrumental in the arrest of a dangerous threat to society and helping save our country," he said.

"That's a lot of patriotic bullshit, and you know it. You sound like an Army recruiter. Why don't you try: 'I need your help because you are such a great guy, plus I like your cat, and I'll buy you a beer'?"

"Okay, everything you just said. Can you get it to me in twenty-four hours?"

***

Luke sat in the kitchen with Kara on Sunday morning, drinking coffee and reading *The Denver Post,* which was scattered all over the granite kitchen island. Columbo was asleep in his bed. The TV was off. It was so quiet that Luke's phone startled Kara.

"It's Van."

Luke put the call on speakerphone.

"Bob shipped a package weighing 1.1 pounds to Guadalupe's Fullerton Distribution Center. The package was delivered on the afternoon of 7 May. That's about the weight of two sticks of dynamite, by the way. Bob also put 102.6 miles on his rental car when he was in LA on 10 May and 11 May. That's enough miles to go from LAX, to Fullerton, to the Port of Long Beach, and back to LAX. He caught a direct flight to Boston at 0812 hours on 11 May," Van said, in his security consultant voice.

Luke and Kara stared at each other.

"Are you there?" Van asked.

"Yeah, yeah, we're here. We're just thinking about what you said. If we only knew what was in the package," Luke said.

"I can't help you there, Luke. I don't know how you figure that out. Let me know if you need something else, and don't tell anyone where you got this information."

"What if someone at the distribution center opened the box and saw… I don't know. Sticks of dynamite?" Kara said. "If we could prove that dynamite was delivered to the distribution center for Bob Burrows, from Bob Burrows, it would be case closing evidence."

"It's a long shot, but I have an idea," Van said. "One of you could call the distribution center and pretend to be Bob's assistant. Ask them for a shipment receipt for his expense statement. It won't sound surprising that he isn't calling himself. Lawyers never step down to this level of minutiae. See if you can reach the person who received the package and delivered it to Bob. You watch a lot of *Columbo,* Kara. You'd be better than me making that call. Just be your charming self and see what you can discover."

Luke choked on his coffee and looked at Kara for a reaction. She smiled and leaned in to speak directly to Luke's phone on the kitchen island. "What's the worst that could happen? They call Bob and say that his assistant just called. So what? Bob may wonder who's asking questions, but he would probably suspect EF&J, right?" Kara said.

"I like the way you think," Van replied.

"Wait. I need to think about this," Luke said, looking down at Columbo for advice. "What if Bob's innocent and finds out I'm involved? I would lose my job in an instant."

"So what, honey? With your skills, you can always get another job. Your job isn't that great anyway," Kara said, with obvious enthusiasm. "You're gone all the time and you work a lot of hours you don't get paid for."

"Weren't you the one telling me *not* to lose my job? Which is it?"

"I don't have time for domestic disputes," Van said. "Let's keep thinking."

"Bob will never know it was me who made the call, Luke, and if I get some incriminating evidence, he'll be gone soon enough," Kara said, leaning away from the phone and returning to the newspaper again.

***

Kara stepped into the privacy room at her company's office at noon, Monday, and called Luke on the conference phone. "It's me," she said when Luke answered.

"Hey babe, you ready? I'll be on mute while you call the distribution center. Just pretend I'm not here and act like Columbo. You'll do great," Luke said.

She dialed the number, and it was answered on the second ring. "Hi, this is Tammy from the corporate office. My boss, Bob Burrows, Senior Legal Counsel, had a package delivered to your office on May 7. He picked it up a few days later. I'm hoping you still have a receipt so I can complete his expense statement. May I please talk with the person who signs for deliveries?" Kara asked, just as she'd rehearsed.

"Let me see if I can find who was at the front desk that day. What was your name again?" the receptionist asked.

"Tammy Smith. My boss is Bob Burrows, with corporate."

Smooth jazz muzak came onto the line. Kara took a few deep breaths, closed her eyes, and waited for what seemed like an eternity. *How does Columbo always make this look so effortless?*

"Hi, this is Mack. Is this Tammy?"

Kara thought Mack sounded about sixteen years old. "Yes, this is Tammy. How are you doing today, Mack? Did they tell you I'm looking for a receipt? I'm telling you, honey, the paperwork in this company never stops."

"I hear you, Ms. Smith. That's why they need us paper pushers," Mack said, laughing loudly at his comment. "Yeah. I remember Mr. Burrows came into the office, and I just handed him his package. But, I think he said thanks and left. I didn't get a receipt or nothing."

"Hmm, I was hoping Bob may have opened the box and pulled a receipt out."

"No, ma'am," Mack replied.

"Mack, you can call me Tammy, okay? Hey, just one more thing before I let you go back to pushing paper," she said, with a slight chuckle at her own spin on Columbo's routine. "Bob told me the box looked like it had been opened and then resealed. Did it look like that to you?"

There was a painfully long pause. For a moment, Kara wondered if Mack had hung up.

"Tammy, I have to admit that I opened the box by accident when it arrived. I wasn't paying attention and thought it was for the office manager. I usually open packages for her when stuff comes in, so I wasn't expecting a box for someone else. I'm sorry."

"That's okay, Mack, it happens all the time. I do it too," said Kara. "I know what was in the box. I hope you weren't alarmed by it. Actually, I was the person who packed the box, if that makes you feel better. Bob's building a cabin up by Big Bear, and he's always blasting away some rock under the foundation or something like that," Kara said, crossing her fingers under the desk.

Mack's voice became even quieter. "I didn't expect to see dynamite, but then again, we handle some nasty stuff around here, so I didn't get too freaked out. Don't worry, I won't tell anyone," Mack said.

"Well, thank you. I was hoping you would understand. We'll keep that a secret between us, so nobody gets in trouble," Kara said, her heart pounding.

"I understand what you're saying. I like this job and need the paycheck," Mack said.

"I guess I'll have to try to get a shipping receipt from the shipper. That call will probably take an hour. Oh boy, I hope they have good muzak," Kara said.

"It was fun talking to you, Tammy. If you ever get out here, make sure you stop by and say 'hello.' I'd love to meet you in person," Mack said, and he hung up.

"I can't believe what Mack just confirmed," Luke said, with excitement in his voice.

"He's our first and only witness, but he's a good one. Let's call Van. I'll add him in," Kara said.

Van picked up on the second ring. "What's up, Kara?" he asked, with his own obvious excitement.

"I talked to a young guy named Mack at the Guadalupe Distribution Center in Fullerton, and you'll never guess what he said." She then continued to tell Van the details of her conversation with Mack.

"Congratulations, Kara. If I could give you a promotion, I would," Van said.

"Wow, Kara, I promise not to give you a hard time for watching *Columbo* reruns anymore. Now, what do we do?" Luke asked.

Van jumped in, having clearly thought through the scenario. "First off, neither of you talk to anyone about this, not even your kids. You don't want anyone to know you are involved in Bob's investigation. Understood?" Van said.

Van continued. "Luke, you need to call the investigator and methodically lay out the new evidence against Bob, including the rental car mileage, lying to you about his travel times, and the dynamite delivered to the distribution center. Don't tell him where you got the information I gave you, no matter how much he presses you for it, okay? He can do his own investigation; he has the authority and needs to obtain the info legally."

"I thought I should let Nancy know what's going on, since I work for her, and it's her company," Luke said.

"Absolutely not. First, Nancy doesn't need to know; she's better off if she doesn't. Second, she may know Bob better than you think and tip him off. You don't know. Only share information on a need-to-know basis, and then, only with people you completely trust, which is almost nobody," Van said. "Take a few hours and get your thoughts together, then call the investigator, and then both of you forget about it until something happens. You hear me? I gotta go." Van said and dropped off the conference call.

Luke and Kara were silent for a moment. "I guess we have our orders," Kara said.

"What if nothing ever comes of this, and I have to continue working with Bob, knowing what I now know?"

"Let's just take it one day at a time, honey. You'll have a better understanding after you talk to the investigator, but you're right for now. We'll have to act like we never figured this out and keep our little secret."

30

A month later, Nancy called Luke to her office and shut the door behind him. Nancy had an open-door policy, so he knew it was serious when she closed the door behind him.

"I received a call from Caroline Woodson this morning, which is somewhat unusual because I typically have to call her. She is a bit standoffish, as you know. She wanted me to share this with you and no one else, so please keep this on the q.t. She told me that Bob Burrows was found dead in his house in Boston this morning, in an apparent burglary. He had been shot several times, but there was blood from another person that Bob had evidently shot. I know you and Bob have become friends, and I'm sorry to have to deliver this news. It's a real tragedy. I'm sure we'll discover more details as time passes."

"Wow. I wasn't expecting this news today. He was murdered? This seems surreal," Luke said, genuinely in shock. "I should probably give Caroline a call today or tomorrow. She's probably really upset. They got along so well."

However, Luke couldn't wait to tell Kara. He decided to wait until dinner, not knowing how she would react. His emotions were mixed, relief and sadness at the same time. He went to his office and dialed Van. "Russo, I've got some Secret Squirrel stuff for you," Luke said.

"You're making my day, Rattler."

"I was just told that Bob Burrows was murdered last night, in an apparent robbery that went bad. He was shot several times in his home."

"Do the police have any leads?" Van asked.

"Nancy didn't have any more information on his death. That would really suck, to wake up in the middle of the night and be shot in your own home by some low-life burglar," Luke said.

Van paused for a moment and then replied slowly, "Don't be so naive. I'll bet you my next paycheck, there's a lot more to this 'robbery' than you think. This isn't the end of the story, not by a long shot. You and I will be following it closely."

EPILOGUE

July in Denver was meeting its expectations, with temperatures nearing 100 degrees and the office air conditioning struggling to keep up. Many of Webber's employees were on vacation, and clients were also absent. It was a slow time; a time to catch up. Luke and Kara had a week off and took the kids to Los Alamos to visit Luke's parents. Spirits were higher amongst the Guadalupe project team since they had been authorized funding for the groundwater remediation study, although Bob's death was constantly on everyone's mind. Rudy took it the hardest.

Luke sat in his new office, much closer to the Coffee Nook, but facing east, toward the plains of Kansas. Nancy needed to make room for a new operations manager, so he'd had to relocate. She'd tried to sweeten the deal by telling Luke he would be closer to his project team and coffee. Luke accepted it without complaint, as he had often done in the military. *Nancy probably moved me instead of someone else because she knew I wouldn't complain and suck it up. Maybe I need to practice being more of a pain in the ass. Kara wouldn't settle for this.*

"Hey, Simone. How's your summer going?" Luke said into his phone.

"Alison and I are having a lot of fun, but it's hot in Fresno. I think we might move back to Concord next week, and Mark misses us. I haven't had any more death threats, and it really doesn't bother me anymore, so it would be good to get back to normal."

"I haven't heard any rumblings about Jimmy Mendoza," Luke said. "Earl hasn't run into him or heard anything about him. He's probably still pissed off at us and holds a grudge, but I don't care. I can live with that."

"Mark and I have concluded he was involved in all these threats, in some way or another," Simone said.

Luke wanted to focus on Ross Jennings. "It was nice to meet your cousin, Carl. I hope his jaw is getting better. You know that when we had dinner, and you left to take a call, he seemed to get really fired up about the possibility of DDT in the farm soil. Does he ever talk to you about DDT?"

"There were times over the years when we would talk about pesticides and DDT in the soil, and what I did for the EPA. He's a little bit of an anti-government guy, so we usually get in an argument if we talk about my job. The topic comes up once in a while, but we try to avoid it. He hasn't said anything about DDT since you and Van were here."

Luke smiled to himself and pressed on. "I haven't heard anything else about Lenny's boat exploding and Amy's death, have you?"

"EPA told us that she blew herself up planting a bomb on the boat. I should probably ask about EF&J and see what the agency knows about them. Whatever happened to that lawsuit about the offshore dumping?" Simone asked.

"You know, we never did have the deposition on the EF&J lawsuit. We were supposed to have it the day after the explosion, but now that Bob is gone, I don't know when or if it will ever happen," Luke said crossing his fingers in the air above his head.

"How are you all progressing on the groundwater remediation study? Are we going to see that anytime soon?" Simone said, with sarcasm in her voice.

"Well, I'm glad you asked. We have completed the draft, and we'll be sending it to Guadalupe soon for their review. We should get it to you and Antoine in August, like we promised," Luke said, with a huff.

THE END

CONTINUE THE INVESTIGATION

The deeper you dig… the more there is to uncover.

Step further into *Contaminant of Concern*
with exclusive access to:

- The official crossword puzzle based on the investigation
- Additional insights into the science behind the story
- Early updates on future releases

Scan the code below or visit:
www.joelsjohnson.com/uncover
Some truths are too important to stay buried.

ABOUT THE AUTHOR

Joel S. Johnson works by day as a small business executive in the environmental and energy profession and by night as a creator of historical and modern mystery/suspense novels.

Contaminant of Concern is his first book in a series and is an attempt to share the often complex and divisive realities of the environmental industry. Interesting stories emanate from the numerous stakeholders with changing and opposing views including regulators subject to political winds, corporate interests, lawyers, activists, scientists, and consultants.

www.ingramcontent.com/pod-product-compliance
Lightning Source LLC
Chambersburg PA
CBHW031139160726
47991CB00004B/1481